ravens

GEORGE DAWES GREEN

sphere

SPHERE

First published in the United States by Grand Central Publishing,
a division of Hachette Book Group, Inc.
First published in Great Britain in 2009 by Sphere
This paperback edition published in 2010 by Sphere

A CIP catalogue record for this book
is available from the British Library.

ISBN 978-0-7515-4250-9

Printed and bound in Great Britain by
Clays Ltd, St Ives plc

Papers used by Sphere are natural renewable and
recyclable products sourced from well-managed forests and certified
in accordance with the rules of the Forest Stewardship Council.

Mixed Sources
Product group from well-managed
forests and other controlled sources
www.fsc.org Cert no. SGS-COC-004081
© 1996 Forest Stewardship Council

Sphere
An imprint of
Little, Brown Book Group
100 Victoria Embankment
London EC4Y 0DY

An Hachette UK Company
www.hachette.co.uk

www.littlebrown.co.uk

George Dawes Green is a highly acclaimed novelist and poet, and the founder of the groundbreaking storytelling organisation, The Moth. He currently divides his time between Georgia and New York.

Also by this author

The Caveman's Valentine (aka *The Caveman*)
The Juror

Crashing wildly around your light,
Skye,
always

WEDNESDAY

Romeo was driving down from the Blue Ridge Mountains in the baffling twilight, going too fast, when a raccoon or possum ran in front of the car. The impact was disturbingly gentle. No thud—just a soft *unzipping*, beneath the chassis. Still, it tore at Romeo's heart. He braked and pulled over.

Shaw awoke. "What's wrong?"

"Hit something," said Romeo, and he got out and started walking back up I-77, hunting for the carcass. Shaw followed him. A tractor-trailer bore down on them with a shudder and the long plunging chord of its passing. Then the night got quiet. They could hear their own footsteps. Cicadas, and a sliver of far-off honkytonk music. "God," said Shaw. "This is it. We're really in the *South*."

But they found no trace of the animal.

They walked quite a ways. They waited for headlights so they could scan up and down the highway. They backtracked and searched along the shoulder. Nothing—not

3

so much as a bloodstain. Finally Romeo just stood there, watching the fireflies rise and fall.

"Hey," said Shaw, "I bet your friend got lucky."

"Uh-uh. I hit it."

"Well maybe it was like a sacrifice." Playfulness in Shaw's tone. "Maybe it just wanted us to have a propitious journey."

When they got back to the Tercel Shaw said he was wide awake and could he drive? That was fine with Romeo. He got in on the passenger side, and they descended into the North Carolina piedmont. His ears popped; the air grew humid. He tilted his seat all the way back and looked up at the moon as it shredded in the pines. Somewhere after Elkin, NC, he let his eyes slip shut for just a second—and then the highway started to curve beneath him, and he felt himself spiraling slowly downward, into a bottomless slumber.

Tara kept away from the house on Wednesday nights.

Wednesday nights were jackpot nights. Mom would start drinking early. Pour herself a g&t in a lowball glass; then fan out all her lottery tickets on the coffee table and gaze lovingly at them, and touch them one by one and wonder which was going to be *the* one. The TV would be on but Mom would disregard it. All her thoughts on the good life to come. Yachts, spas in Arizona, blazing white villages in Greece, the unquenchable envy of her friends. She'd finish her first drink and fix herself another. Her boy Jase—Tara's little brother—would put his head in her lap while he played with his Micro. She'd tousle his hair. She'd swirl the ice in her drink. At some point the colors of the dying day, and the TV colors, and all the colors of her life, would begin to seem extra-vivid, even gorgeous, and she'd tell herself she was the blessedest woman in the world, and pick up her cell phone and text her daughter:

```
I know we win tonite!!
```

Or:

```
I need u!! Tara baby!! My good luck
charm!! Where are u? Come home!!
```

They were siren calls though, Tara knew. She had to be deaf to them. Study late at the library, catch a movie, hang out with Clio at the mall—just keep clear of the house till the jackpot was done and Dad would come home to take the brunt of Mom's drunken post-drawing tirade. By midnight Mom would have worn herself out with rage and grief, and she'd have passed out, and the coast would be clear.

But on this particular Wednesday, Tara had made a blunder. She'd left her botany textbook, with all the handouts, in her bedroom. She'd done this in the morning but she didn't realize it till 7:00 p.m., after her organic chemistry class, when she checked her locker and saw that the book wasn't there.

She had a quiz tomorrow. She hadn't even *looked* at that stuff.

She thought of calling Dad. Maybe he could sneak the book out to her. But no, it was too late. He'd be on his way to church by now, his Lions of Judah meeting. Maybe Jase? No, Jase would tip Mom off; Jase was in Mom's pocket.

No. What I have to do, Tara thought, is just go back there and be really docile and *don't* let Mom draw me into a fight, whatever she says don't fight back—and first chance I get I'll slip away to my room before the drawing, before she blows up.

Tara went to the parking lot and got in her battered Geo, and left the campus of the Coastal Georgia Community

College. Fourth Street to Robin Road to Redwood Road: streets she despised. She hated their dull names and their blank lawns and their rows of squat brick ranch houses. Hers was the squattest and brickest of all, on a street called Oriole Road. When she got there, she slowed the car to a crawl, and looked in through the living room window. Mom, the TV. The painting of Don Quixote tilting at windmills. The wooden shelf of Dad's # 3 Chevy models, and Mom's Hummels. Jase's feet stuck out at the end of the couch. Everything that Tara despised about her home was glowing and warm-looking like an advertisement for low mortgage rates or pest control, and such a depressing show she had to call Clio and tell her about it.

"I'm spying on my own house."

Said Clio, "*That's* kind of perverted."

"It's a really ugly house."

"I know."

"I can see my brother's little marinated pigs' feet."

"OK."

"But I have to see how drunk Mom is."

"How drunk is she?"

"That's the problem, I can't tell. I can't see her hands. I have to see how she's holding her glass. If she's swirling her glass with her pinky out, then I'm already in deep shit."

"Are you going in there?"

"I have to."

"But isn't this your Mom's freak-out night?"

"Uh-huh."

"So what are you *doing* there? Come over to Headquarters. You know who's coming? That Kings of Unsnap guy. Jonah. The one who wants to do you."

"You told me that, Clio."

"So come let him do you."

"I got a botany quiz in the morning."

"Oh God. You're such a boring geek."

"Why don't *you* do him?"

"OK," said Clio. "You talked me into it."

"You're such a whoring slut."

"I know. Hey I gotta go. If your Mom does something interesting, like touching your little brother's weewee or something, let me know."

"I'll send you the pics," said Tara. "You can post them." She hung up, and sighed, and pulled into the carport.

As soon as she stepped into the living room, Mom was at her: "Where were *you*?" Tara consulted the lowball glass and saw that the swirling was quick and syncopated, with the pinky fully extended, which presaged a grim night.

"I was in class."

8

"You should call me when you're gonna be this late."

Not late, Tara thought, but drop it.

Mom kept pressing. "Which class was it?"

"Um. Organic chemistry."

"Why you taking *that*?"

Leave it alone. The only goal is freedom. "I don't know, I guess it's some kind of a requirement."

"But if you're only gonna be a goddamn *whatever*— why do they make you take organic chemistry?"

Tara shrugged.

Said Mom, "They want all our money and what they teach you is worthless."

Hard to let that pass. Inasmuch as Mom contributed not a cent to her tuition—inasmuch as every penny came from Tara's job at the bank plus help from her grandmother Nell plus a small scholarship, and all she got from her parents was room and board for which she paid $450 a month so that wasn't a gift either—it was a struggle not to snap back at her. But what good would that do? Remember, all you want is to get to your room. Remember, this woman is the same birdnecked alien you were just watching through the living room window a moment ago. Pretend there's no family connection, that you're invisible and you can slip away unnoticed at any time—

"Wait. Sit for a minute. The drawing's coming up."

"Got a quiz tomorrow, Mom. So I should probably—"

"You know what it's worth this time?"

Tara shook her head.

"You're kidding me," said Mom. "You really don't know?"

"I really don't."

"Three hundred and eighteen million dollars."

"Wow."

The sum touched Tara's life in no meaningful way, but she thought if she showed sufficient awe maybe Mom would release her.

"Though if you take the lump sum," said Mom, "then after you pay your taxes, you'd only have a hundred some million."

"Oh."

"Like a hundred twenty-odd. Hardly worth bothering, right? You mind freshening this for me? So I won't disturb the Little Prince here?"

Mom swirled her glass.

On the TV was *Nip/Tuck*, which wasn't appropriate for ten-year-old Jase but then he wasn't watching it anyway. He was playing *Revenant* on his Micro. Oblivious as ever—and Tara was happy to ignore him back. She carried Mom's glass to the kitchen, filled it with ice and Bombay and tonic, cut a thin half-wheel of lime and placed it festively. Be solicitous, servile. Try to soften her. Don't resist in any way.

But when she returned, Mom was holding up a thin windowed envelope, a bill from some credit card company, and demanding: "Know how I got this? Came right to the office. *Angela* gave it to me. I didn't even know this bill existed. It's for seven hundred dollars. Your father never *mentioned* it."

What would be the least resistant reply possible? Tara tried, "That's awful, Mom."

"Awful? It's the most humiliating thing that can ever happen to *anyone*. *Anyone*. *Ever*. Of course your father isn't worried. Your father thinks we'll be fine."

"Well, won't we?"

Oh, that was dumb. That was way too cheerful. Mom pounced. "You don't get it *at all*, do you? They're gonna *foreclose*. They're gonna take our *house*. They're gonna take it out from under our feet and take the damn Liberty with it. You're gonna have to leave school. I'm sorry, cupcake. You're gonna have to start producing some *income*."

"Mom, I'm a little tired. Would you mind if I—"

"Do you think I'm *not* tired? I am so *damn* tired of being this poor and your father in total denial and you kids thinking this is some kind of bad dream we're gonna wake up from! We're gonna lose *everything*, do you not get it? This boat is *sinking*. Nobody's gonna bail *us* out. The boat is going down! I mean, baby, sugar-cake, you're gonna have to start *swimming*. You're gonna—"

But then came a fanfare on the TV, and instantly Mom left off. She gave Jase a little swat and he hustled out of her way, and she leaned forward to check her flotilla of tickets.

"And now," said a somber announcer, "here's tonight's drawing for the Max-a-Million jackpot. Tonight's jackpot is worth . . . three hundred and eighteen *milly-on* dollars."

No one onscreen. Just the voice of that undertaker. And a hopper in the shape of a funeral urn, full of lightly waltzing plastic balls. One of them flew up suddenly on a puff of air and rolled down a serpentine ramp and posed itself before the camera.

"The first number is . . . tuh-*wenty*-seven."

Mom murmured, "Uh-huh. Got that here." Trying for indifference. But her eyes were full of eagerness.

Tara quietly cheated a few steps toward the hall.

"The next number is forty-two."

"Well I do have *that*," said Mom.

And Tara made her move. Melted silkily away while Mom was too dazzled by the numbers to notice.

In her room, Tara shut the door and sat at the laptop on her desk. Clio had just posted:

u still "studying" bitch? do u think jonah wrights sperm has beneficial properties of healing? wil it help u lose pounds from hips waist and thighs? he wasn't at headquarters tho just creepy seth from jax. I h8 the wick. die if I dont getout of the wick.

Tara wrote back:

Havent started yet. Caught by Mom. She's watching the drawing. In 20 seconds she'l lose and go skitzo.

And right on time: Mom's hell-on-the-loose shriek from the living room. Worse even than usual. Then: "TARA! TA-*RA*!"

Tara typed brb and opened the door. "Yes?"

"*TARA!*"

Particularly anguished tonight. Tara returned to the living room to find her on her knees before the TV, with Jase cowering in the corner. Mom had utterly lost it. Her mouth was open and she was holding up one of her tickets and tears were pouring down her cheeks, and this wasn't just another drunken display of self-pity: there was true fear. "GRACE OF GOD!" she cried. As though she were beholding His face at that very moment. She clutched the ticket in her fist and rocked back and forth. "GRACE OF GOD! GRACE OF GOD! GRACE OF GOD!"

THURSDAY

Shaw was roasting to death. So feeble the a.c. in this '91 Tercel that he had to leave the windows open or die. Though the air that came in was as hot as jet exhaust, so he was dying anyway. For a while he crowded up to a big rig in the next lane, for the shade. But the truck turned off at a weigh station and left him in the oven again, and he hadn't slept for more than twenty-four hours and he'd been behind the wheel all night with only the one nap at that rest stop near Charlotte, and he was jacked to the gills on Red Bull, coffee, and Dextrostat. And the Georgia landscape was nothing but slash pine and ribbon-of-highway, forever. Also Romeo's sleeping was getting on his nerves. Romeo had been sleeping ferociously since the mountains: sweating, shivering, sometimes grinding his teeth, which annoyed the hell out of Shaw. It was high time to wake him up.

But not yet. Less than an hour to Florida. He could deal with the heat. It had been another cold miserable

17

Ohio spring and now Florida by his calculations was fifty-six minutes away. If he endured the heat and the boredom, and stayed at eighty-one miles an hour, they could be in Florida in fifty-five minutes and . . . forty seconds—more or less, and stop for breakfast in *Florida*.

Then he noticed the pull. There was a slight shimmy in the wheel, coaxing him to the left. He thought he knew what it was. The left front tire had a slow leak, which Romeo was supposed to have checked before the trip, but he must have forgotten. Shaw took the next exit. There were four gas stations, but all he wanted was air, so it didn't matter: he chose one at random. He drove up to the air hose at the side of the lot.

After he cut the engine, it still seemed that the world was hurtling along.

He got out and picked up the air hose, and found that the pressure gauge was busted. He knew Romeo wouldn't have one. He went into the store. It called itself "Chummy's Gourmet Shoppe", but it was just standard convenience-store junk. Chips and salsa, banks of candy, a great wall of electrified soda. The air was sweetly cool though. And the counter girl had nice upstanding breasts under her T-shirt.

"Hi," she said, and it had a Southern flip at the end. His first Southern girl. He'd met girls from the South before but this was the first girl he'd met *in* the South. Her nametag said Cheryl. He ran his tongue over his teeth to clean them, and wished he had something clever to say back. But he couldn't think of anything.

"You got like a tire gauge?" he asked. "I have to check my tires."

She placed a much-worn gauge on the counter. "Don't drive off with it."

"I won't."

She gave him a warm smile.

He went out to the Tercel and squatted beside the left front tire and tried not to touch the hubcap. He read the pressure at 28 psi, which seemed not too low considering. He gave it a few jolts of air, then went and read the rear tires, which were right at 30 so they were fine.

Romeo's door swung open, and his voice came out: "Sup?"

"Car's sort of pulling."

"Where we at?"

"Georgia."

"They weren't shitting about the heat, were they?"

If it wasn't the tires, Shaw thought, it was probably the alignment. Or even the bearing. It had better not be the bearing. He'd agreed to split costs on this trip, but he wasn't paying half on a new fucking bearing when it was

Romeo's car. Maybe they could ignore it. Just nurse it as far as Key West and then sell it (the plan was to hire out on fishing boats and work their way to Trinidad and never return to their zombie jobs at Dayton Tech-world).

He went up to check the right front. He thought about the clerk again. At least this would give him an opening with her. He could go back in and say, "The tires were OK. I guess my car was just pulling me—it wanted me to come in here." Should he leave it like that? Subtle, mysterious? Or should he explain how there were lines of power running under the Earth, called ley lines, and vortices where they crossed, and how these vortices could act as huge magnets? Well. That might strike her as too weird.

Maybe he should just say, "My car likes blondes."

God. *Yes*. He was a thousand miles from Piqua, Ohio, and nobody was here to judge him except Romeo, and his judgment didn't count. Why not say whatever comes to mind?

As he was going back into the store, a truck pulled up: one of those TV satellite trucks. WSAV from Savannah. It wasn't coming for gas. It pulled off quietly to the side, and Shaw watched for a moment as the driver got out, and then this smartly dressed dude who was probably the reporter, then some other guy. They conferred amongst themselves. Shaw felt stupid just standing there watching, so he went in.

Cheryl wasn't at the counter anymore. Some Asian guy now. On his cell phone, talking animatedly in Chinese or Korean or whatever. Shaw handed over the tire gauge and the guy took it without a glance and went back to chirping into the phone.

Then Shaw noticed Cheryl standing by the front window, looking out at the TV truck. She had her back to him. He approached her, thinking he could still say the thing about blondes. But she was also on the phone, and she seemed excited about something. Saying, "He's like friends with my brother? They're both in third grade? And he's bragging how it's *his* family that won."

A little pause. Then she said, "Yeah, but Ashley, nobody even knew this was the store! It hasn't been announced yet! And they buy tickets here all the time."

Another pause. Then she said, "No, he owns that copier place. They're like, I know them, they go to Renewal. Oh shit. Well, you'll hear about it tomorrow!" She laughed.

She became aware of Shaw. "Hold on," she told her friend. She asked Shaw, "Help you?"

"I brought your gauge back."

"What?"

"I mean, it wasn't the tires. It was the, just, it was, you know, pulling."

"Pulling?"

"Like my car was pulling me *here*."

"Oh."

She had no idea what he was talking about, and didn't care. She was checking out another TV truck pulling into the lot. She told the phone, "Oh my god, there's another one! From Jax! Ashley, I gotta go." Calling out, "Mr. Hu! Here's another TV station!"

The Asian guy said, "Call Courtney, tell her come in! And find Wes!"

When she turned away from the window, she was surprised to find Shaw still standing there. "You all set?" she said.

He asked her, "How come those trucks are out there?"

"Um. 'Cause we sold the ticket outta this store."

"What ticket?"

"For the jackpot."

"Out of *this* store?"

"Uh-huh."

"How much?"

She gestured to a sign, by the lottery display. THIS WEEK'S MAX-A-MILLION JACKPOT IS

WORTH . . . Under which someone had written, in magic marker: "$318,000,000.00."

The reach of it, the vastness, caught him in the gut.

"That's. *Millions?*"

She nodded. Already dialing another friend.

He tried to steady his breath. "And you know the winners?"

She shook her head. "No. Nobody does. They have to come forward. Could be weeks." Her call went through and she left him, telling the phone, "Hey, Rosemary. Guess what?"

Why had she lied to him? Telling him nobody knew who won, when he'd just heard her gossiping about the winners. She'd probably seen him checking the tires on the Tercel, which looked like an old beat-up filing cabinet on wheels—and had zero respect for him, and thought he wasn't worth sharing this secret with.

And did he give a shit? The girl was a clerk in a palace of crap in the middle of nowhere, she was empty-headed and kind of unpretty, and did he give a damn what she thought about his car?

But he did, he realized. He was all worked up. A shaft of anger had opened inside him.

He walked down the aisle that led to the ATM. Planning to withdraw some cash, but then he couldn't bear to. He couldn't face his paltry balance. He stopped beside the Party Time ice chest, which looked like a pirate's chest, with loose pieces of ice glittering and smoldering, and he considered that while he had all of nine hundred fifty dollars to spend on this whole vacation, someone else had just won *three hundred eighteen million*. Out of the blue! Thrown away on a family of South Georgia nothings! And would they even have a clue how to use it? No. In fact it was bound to destroy whatever meager happiness they had. Leave them feeling unloved, untrusting, miserable. Prey to any scavenger who got a whiff of their feast. He heard Cheryl laugh into her phone, and the sound came to him like fingernails scraping down a blackboard, and he walked out into the sunlight just as the TV crews were coming in, and he thought, goddamn this shitshack to hell.

Romeo was awake by now but still sleep-paralyzed. It seemed like a good idea to get out of this frypan and go take a leak. But that would have required unfolding his legs, raising up the seat, brushing the crumbs off his shirt. So he stayed where he was. He lay there and looked out idly at the TV trucks and wondered what all the commotion was about. He was still turning this over when Shaw opened the door.

"What's with the TV trucks?"

"It's 'cause you're such a star, Romeo. They're stalking you." Shaw snapped off the music and started the engine. To deal with the scorching steering wheel, he grabbed a T-shirt from the backseat and made it into an oven pad. He drove out of the lot.

He was in one of his moods. The kind of mood he got into only when some girl had snubbed him.

Said Romeo, "I gotta take a leak."

"Should have thought of that sooner." Shaw pulled out into the four-lane—but *away* from the interstate. A sign said DOWNTOWN BRUNSWICK.

Said Romeo, "I was asleep. Could we go back there for a second?"

"No."

"Why not?"

"Place is full of shit."

"She was that fuckable?"

"Who, the clerk? Who cares about the clerk?"

So he *had* been dissed. The clerk must have flirted with him on account of his charming skewed smile—but then he'd come on a little too odd, or too needy, and she'd shut him down. Happened all the time. And these rejections always got him going. But this time his pique seemed to be mixed with a kind of ebullience. His lips were moving; he glistened with sweat. He said, "You know what I do care about? Here's this universe filled with power, right? These energies, all around us, in every molecule. And you and me, we're smart, we're capable, we're clever. You know? But we might as well be ghosts. We can't seem to get hold of a fucking thing. You notice that? Everything just passes right through us and gets pissed away. Everything goes to someone else. It's amazing."

"Yeah," said Romeo. "I hear that." But really he only half-heard it. Mostly he just wanted to piss and for Shaw to let go of whatever was burning him up.

Tara was at her desk at the bank, closing out her accounts, when she looked up and saw Mrs. Potro approaching. Oh this is great, she thought. Last day here, last *hour*—and what do I get for my parting gift but the meanest and lyingest of all the mean lying bitches who've made working here such hell.

"Hello, Mrs. Potro. What can I do for you?"

The woman had a long blue vein in her neck that throbbed when she got upset. Which was every frikkin time she came in. She slapped a letter on Tara's desk: *Notice of Insufficient Funds.* She really did *slap* it down, and said, "Twenty-five dollars? You're charging *me* twenty-five dollars? For what, for the privilege of having you steal from me? No no no. This time you will *not* get my money."

Tara tried to remember what life had been like when anything Mrs. Potro said had mattered. But she couldn't. Already the world before the jackpot was beginning to seem remote. Just don't laugh in her face, she thought, just let's get through this one final demon and I'll be done with this moronic job forever. Then I'll let it fall away and never think of it again.

She checked her computer and said softly, "Well, ma'am, um, it shows here that the funds in your account on June 11 were not—"

"I made a deposit on the eleventh! You don't see that?"

"I see one for June 13—"

"Right! Because, on the eleventh, my sister had a diabetic attack. Do you have any idea of how debilitating that can be? *Any* idea?"

"Sounds horrible."

"I wasn't making deposits on the eleventh because I

27

was at the *hos*-pital. You think I like going to the hospi-tal? So I made a deposit first thing on the twelfth—"

"Or the thirteenth."

"Young lady! I've been a customer of this bank since before you were *born*. I used to think I was a *valued* customer. I used to *imagine* . . ."

But Tara was thinking of the flowing blue skies of the jackpot. The jackpot which overruled and eclipsed everything, including Mrs. Potro, and which held the silver keys to the future. And in less than an hour she'd be telling Nell about it! Should I just lay it on the table, or should I tease her first? Make it a guessing game? So every time Nell guesses wrong I can say, "No, bigger. Think bigger," and then should I—

"Are you *ignoring* me?" said Mrs. Potro.

"What."

"You're? Ignoring? *Me?*"

"Well yeah. I was sort of in my own thoughts there."

The neck-cobra pulsed. "Let me speak to Mr. Allen this instant."

"Why? You gonna get me fired?"

"I want to speak to Mr. Allen!"

"Mr. Allen's gone home. You can come see him tomorrow. But you can't get me fired, 'cause I don't work here anymore. This is my last day. Actually, this is my last minute in this dump. So. What is it you were whining about again?"

Right before her eyes the woman was turning into an open-mouthed gargoyle. A pleasure to witness.

"So what was it again?" Tara asked her. "Twenty-five?" She reached into her own purse and counted out a twenty and five ones, and set these down before the wounded duchess. "Here. Little farewell gift," she said. Then added two quarters and a nickel. "With interest."

She turned away, went back to her monitor, her accounts. After a while she heard Mrs. Potro sniff significantly and totter away.

But only after scooping up the money. This is the crowning touch, thought Tara. This makes this day *perfect*.

She finished her paperwork and said goodnight to the tellers like it was any other day, and took off. On the way back to Brunswick she played Santogold as loud as she could. "Break it break it you can't stop me in this race!" The sky over the marshes had no end, the whole world was in her grasp, and it seemed as though she was lifting off above herself; tooling along in her Geo and at the same time lifting into the sky, and so filled with excitement and freedom that she had to open her mouth and *scream*.

Then her phone beeped. Message from Clio.

```
Headquarters. Code Blu.
```

Code Blu meant a full-on panic attack—usually brought on by some bass guitarist messing with Clio's head.

Tara wrote back:

```
Cant.
```

A moment later she got:

```
Code INSANELY frikkin Blu!
```

Tara gave up then. What else could she do? She went to Headquarters, which was the name they'd given to Skeet and Bobbie's condo. It was out on Altama Avenue, in the gloomy whitetrash hive called Spanish Gardens (nothing Spanish about it except a crude Moorish archway on the sign, and no gardens either). Bobbie let her in. Everyone was smoking weed and watching Sarah Silverman on TV. Tara went looking for Clio. She found her in the kitchen heating a frozen pizza. The guy Jonah from Kings of Unsnap was with her. He was trying to look languorous and slouchy and world-weary, but his big quivering Adam's apple spoiled the effect. He wasn't uncute though, and his band was not unbearable, and yesterday Tara had even been considering him a little. But now the jackpot had swept him off the planet. Now, when he drawled "Heyyy, Taraaa," she found she had *no* interest. She scarcely nodded. She looked to Clio, who gestured toward the sliding back door.

Jonah said, "Where you going? You doing lesbo stuff? Hey, I'm a dyke too." They ignored him. They went out to the yard (weeds, beer kegs in the weeds, a rusted weedwhacker) and slid the door shut.

Tara said, "Sup?"

Clio said, "Sup with *you*? Sup with all this *I'm too busy, I'm too busy* shit? 'Cause what you're doing is like, I'm not your bitch anymore?"

"Well no, I really have been busy—"

"Rat, don't lie to me. Just tell me. You guys win the lottery?"

Meteor crashing. Try to keep your wits. Try to look bewildered. "What?"

"Do *not* lie to me. You're a terrible liar."

"I just don't understand what you're asking."

"Laurie Massey told me you guys won the Max-a-Million jackpot."

31

"The what?"

Enough variations on *what*. Fight back or you're finished. "Is she, like, joking? Is she nuts?"

Said Clio, "Apparently your brother told some kid
y'all had won it."

Clio was a big girl, striking, with tattoos up and down
her arms and a silver serpent that looped through her
cheek. Her stare was demanding. Tara loved her, and
hated to lie to her. But she'd made a solemn pact with her
family: we won't tell *anyone*. If Jase had broken this vow,
that was Jase's business, but Tara wasn't going to let her
family down. She met Clio's gaze and said, "My little
brother is *delusional*. As well you know."

"Well, *somebody* won the thing."

"Yeah? Not us."

"But here you've gone into hiding and all—"

"Hiding? For shit's sake, dude, I'm just *busy*. I just got
out of the bank. You think I'd go work at that bank if I'd
just won like all the money in the world?"

Clio took a long thoughtful pull on her cigarette. She
said, "It's just, if you *had* won, I'd be so happy for you I'd
be peeing my pants. But if you're like, hiding this from
me? And if it's like I'm *losing* you or something—then I
don't know what I'd do. I'd kill myself. I mean it. I
would."

32

"Oh shut up. You're not gonna lose me. Who's my bitch?"

She put her hand on Clio's neck.

Said Clio, "Let go of me *now*, degenerate."

Tara said, "You'd love it."

Said Clio, "Hey, guess who got his snake milked last night?"

"Oh God. Not that FLETCY guy? Oh god. That's too gross."

"You have no frikkin *idea*."

I just have to keep this safe for another day or two. Then we'll let the truth out and I'll take her to New York first and then Paris, and it'll be the sweetest trip of a lifetime and she'll forgive me, she has to; she loves me. And anyway winning the jackpot means you get *everything*; love, riches, dreams, forgiveness, sky, ocean, shoes, power over the Mrs. Potros, everything, nothing denied: this is how I intend to proceed.

Shaw surfed. The motel room had a back door which he left wide open, and the outside came pouring in—the heat, pollen, salt air, and some heartbreaking vineflower that was blooming just outside the door. All this was mixing with the cinderblock-mold smell of the motel itself; also there were the shouts and sudden splays of music from unsavory folk trawling past on Rt. 17. It was paradise. He took deep guzzles from his Wendy's ice tea, and searched the web.

Cheryl at that convenience store had said that he, whoever *he* was, had a copier store. Shaw went to Yellowbook and found there were only two independent copier businesses in Brunswick, Georgia: Murray Copiers and Boatwright Office Supply and Copiers.

He clicked on Murray's, which was painfully slow to load, and when it did there was a notice from '06:

Dear Customer. Due to rising costs and
foreign competition . . .

Belly-up. Gone.

He went back and clicked the link for Boatwright Office Supply and Copiers, and got a pic of Mitch Boatwright, CEO. Studio halo. But with slightly bulging eyes that made him too bulldoggish, too eager looking. And that shadow in your ear, Mitch—is that *earhair*? In your business photo? Are you a simpleton?

More important: are you my quarry?

mitch boatwright brunswick ga brought him oceans of useless stuff. For example he discovered, in the 1870 City Directory for Scranton, Pennsylvania, that Henry Boatwright had been an ironworker, and that Greta Schuleit, laundress, hailed from Brunswick, Germany. He wondered if they had ever met. Were they lovers? Did she come to his room above the ironworks?

I better focus here.

Look at this: "Joseph Boatwright deceased 1892 survived by his wife Kathleen, two sons, Abner and Edgar, also by his daughter Louise who is married to Dr. Mitchell Vermillion of Brunswick, Georgia."

Vermillion: now there's a name. Should I change my name to Shaw Vermillion?

He kept floating. Boatwright after Boatwright, but most of them were in the ground: in the graveyards of Brunswick, Georgia, Brunswick, Maine, and New Brunswick, New Jersey. And the few that were living were uselessly faraway. He placed half a dexie on his tongue and let it dissolve. It tasted like a Sweet Tart but drier, more businesslike. He drank from his Wendy's giant cup of tea.

Behind him, Romeo, sound asleep again, started grinding his teeth.

That bitch Cheryl had said, "They go to Renewal."

What would Renewal be? Some kind of church? Or gym, or club or something? He typed in renewal brunswick ga and found he was right the first time: the first two hundred entries were for the Faith Renewal Church on Altama Avenue. He typed faith renewal mitch boatwright brunswick—and was granted a vision:

A girl, on stage. Tara, age 12. Daughter of Mitch and Patsy Boatwright. She was wearing donkey ears. It was Christmas 1999, at the Faith Renewal Church of Brunswick, Georgia. The girl was kind of skinny but what intense eyes!

Tara. He loved the Deep-South cheesiness of the name.

She'd be twenty-one or twenty-two now.

tara boatwright facebook

But Facebook's Tara Boatwright was an old crone from Perth, Australia.

Maybe, because this was a small town in Georgia, *his* Tara hadn't gotten around to Facebook yet?

tara brunswick ga myspace

And that was it.

She was now twenty-one. Her handle was johnny's girl—the page was backdropped with a sprawling Johnny Depp. He went right away to her pics. Those eyes again. Oh my god. Curious, large, innocent.

36

Though not *too* innocent. In one beach pic she was turning to look back at the camera and you saw that not only did she have a devastating ass; she also knew what you were looking at. Another shot had her wearing smudged mascara and a black choker and black bangs. Severity in her jawline. She was representing danger. God. Will you fight me, Tara? He grinned. I imagine you will.

Shot of a rock concert with some goth girlfriend: Drive Fast & Shut Your Eyes. in Savannah. With Clio! Favorite band evvvuh!

Another shot, also with Clio and some other girls: CRUNK POSSE!

Shot of her little brother Jase.

Various boys. James, a dull boy, and Wynn, equally dull. No, maybe Wynn was one degree cooler, shaggier. James was posing woodenly in front of a church bus.

Various shots of other relatives and friends.

Two somewhat strained poses with her father, Mitch. Only one with her mom.

But more than a dozen pics of her with her grandmother Nell.

The two of them laughing, waltzing arm in arm: Me and Nell in New Orleans. Then they were in Tunica, Miss, before a row of one-arm bandits. Looked like Tara was only fourteen or so—had Nell sneaked her into a gambling joint?

I LOVE:
John Christopher Depp, Jr.
Nell
Biking to the beach
Our Lord!
Mom and Dad and Jase
Clio
BarbeQue shrimp at Southern Soul
Golden retrievers
Frida Kahlo
Cousin Alfred
Being scared
MOVIES: Anything with JCD, Jr!
Also Donnie Darko, Kill Bill 1 & 2, The Passion of the
    Christ, Ghost World.
Hot hot summer days

Had she really written *Being scared*?

Everything I need, thought Shaw, is right here. All that the girl cares about, all she prizes. Into the basilica of Tara comes the beast. The pillager, the barbarian.

He looked down and saw that his hand was shaking.

He pressed his palm into the corner of his desk, to steady it. But it kept shaking.

Why? Because I'm terrified? Probably. Yes. But so what? I can't live the way I've been living, not another hour. Not as a gonking field mouse for Dayton Techworld. Not another *second*.

BOOKS: The Bell Jar. The Wind in the Willows. The Monkey's Paw, by W. W. Jacobs.

Being scared.

GOAL IN LIFE: Get out of the Wick.

The Wick? What could the Wick be? And why be so intent on escaping it?

Could "the Wick" represent time going up in smoke? The grindingness, the ephemerality, of day-to-day life?

Oh. Wait. Of course. Bruns-*wick*.

The tea was sweet and dilute; it slapped against his gullet and was about the best thing he'd ever tasted. The feeling in his limbs was cool, stony. He brushed his fingers against his thigh and his own touch was distant to him. I believe if she crosses me I'll be *happy* to let her feel some of what I'm capable of.

39

In her JOURNAL, in an entry from a week ago, she'd written:

Worrying last night and once I start worrying I can't stop and cant sleep. is everything in the world about money? But Nell never had money &she's so happy. I want to marry edward scissorhands. I want to BE edward scissorhands.

She also wrote, and this came as a shock to him:

Do not mess with the people I love because I will CUT you and no one will ever fix you again, I'm serious.

He consulted 411.com. There was a Nell Boatwright on Egmont Street, and a Mitchell Boatwright at 38 Oriole Road.

On Birdseye, there were aerial views of Brunswick that seemed to have been made on a day as sepulchral as this one. Scattering of cars on Rt. 341, and on Gloucester Street, but most of the streets were completely empty, lifeless, not a soul in sight.

38 oriole road.

Birdseye took him in a great arc over Brunswick, the chemical plant, the railroad tracks, the hospital, and then softly downward. Descending as though on spidersilk into a neighborhood of middling prosperity. Till he was dangling just above the Boatwrights' home. A brick ranch house, no more or less soulless than the houses to either side. The oval blob in back might be a kiddie pool. One spindly tree out front. Looked like a hedge on one side; on the other a wooden fence.

He was so juiced he had to get up and walk around.

He came back to the laptop. Look at that, he thought. That house—his workshop. Jesus. Could he really do this? He had to. He had to live. He couldn't not-live any longer. He knew that if there were any resistance, it would have to be crushed mercilessly. If they challenged him, he'd have to kill their loved ones while they watched. And how would he withstand their looks of horror? By tapping into a vein of steadfastness and wisdom. By knowing what he needed. What he needed was beauty. A life of pure beauty, nothing less. He'd pay any price for it.

OK.

I'm ready then.

But Romeo? What about Romeo?

He turned and looked at Romeo asleep on the bed. Whimpering in his dreams like a wounded dog.

Tara, the moment she shut her car door, heard a whoop from inside the bungalow and cats meowing in concert, and then Nell came out to the front porch to greet her. "Well hello, *ba*-by!" Her voice was hoarse, crackerish, high. She had a powerful embrace. She held Tara and they rocked back and forth. Tara always thought her grandmother's hair smelled like popcorn.

Nell dragged her into the kitchen to show off her new toy: a singing buck's head. It had a six-point rack and it sang "Killing Me Softly with His Song." It kept rolling its eyes toward a trophy fish on the opposite wall—which sang back, "Hook, Line and Sinker." Nell cackled wildly.

Then she and Tara sat at the kitchen table and ate crabcakes and drank Yellowtail shiraz. The cats writhed at their feet. Tara thought of the jackpot, and waves of bliss washed over her.

She asked Nell how school had gone today. Nell was sixty-two and semi-retired, but she still taught a summer school program called Great Expectations, for kids who had no expectations at all. Nell said, "Well, Jeremiah tells me he's been suspended. I say, 'Why, Jeremiah?' He says, ''Cause I *rose up* against Mr. Briggs.' I mean, he's but thirteen years old, but he's about as big as Mr. Briggs already. Twice my size. I taught his father. I taught his *grandfather*. Both of 'em hooligans, and Jeremiah's a hooligan too. I say, 'Jeremiah, you better not rise up against *me*.' He says, 'I ain't never gonna rise up against *you*, Miz Boatwright. I'm *scared* a you.'"

She howled with pleasure.

They finished their crabcakes and cleaned the table; and then played pot-limit seven stud—their custom on Thursday afternoons.

They each had private sacks filled with coins and currency of various countries. The Romanian ten-*bani* coin was worth a quarter. That old Chinese coin with the hole in the middle was valued at fifty cents. An ersatz Confederate dollar was worth a dime. But the game wasn't all whimsy: if Nell wanted to bully you, she'd throw down legal tender—a five or a ten or even a twenty—and you'd better stand up to her. You were permitted to fold from prudence but never timorousness. If she caught you shrinking from a fight, she'd turn surly, withering; she'd send you home early.

But so long as you fought back you couldn't lose. Even if Tara dropped sixty or a hundred dollars in a single evening, it would all be returned to her. When she opened her next tuition bill, she'd find it magically marked PAID; and next time she came to Nell's she'd find her sack was brimful again, with new and ever odder coins.

This afternoon, Grandmother had a rampage of good fortune. Tara was dealt a straight, but Nell topped it with a full house. Tara picked up a set, but Nell beat it with another boat. Just one of those days. Nell was giddy. She tsked, "Poor poor unlucky child."

When she dealt, the cards flew from her fingers.

The cat called Horace Jackal jumped up on the table, and she swept him off with an outstretched arm, without looking. She shouted at Tara. "Bet! It's your turn! Bet or get out!"

In one hand, all four of Nell's up-cards were hearts. After she took the pot, she showed her hole cards: *all* hearts. Seven of them. "Blood everywhere!" She was already tipsy. "Reminds me of my prom night."

"What happened on your prom night, Grandmother dear?"

Nell shuffled and said, "Oh, well, my date and I, we went to his car to make out? And I was so drunk, and it was so dark in his backseat, I didn't realize my period had started."

"Oh my God."

"Oh my God is right. We open the door and the light comes on, and it was like the Manson family had been in there. It was like helter-skelter in there. It was the single most mortifying moment of my life."

She shuffled again and again. She held her tongue between her teeth, like a child.

Tara asked, "Who was your date? Was that Grandpa Bill?"

"Nah, I hadn't even met Bill then. Just some local yokel." She dealt. But she was still lost in that memory. "Actually, you know the guy. You know who it was?— it was Burris Jones."

Said Tara, "The old cop? The one who goes to our church?"

"Believe I'm gonna bet on this girlie here," said Nell, drawing attention to the queen she'd dealt herself. "I'll start this massa-cree at only fifty cents, to be kind."

"You *dated* Deppity Dawg?"

"I did."

"What was *that* like?"

"Oh, Lord. *Boring?*"

"Did the blood gross him out?"

"Not really. He was always crazy about me. You in?"

Tara called the fifty cents. More cards fell, and the pot grew, and soon Tara was showing the King, Queen, Jack, ten. In truth she had no straight, since her hole cards were trash. But the hand *looked* pretty, and the shiraz and the jackpot and Nell's stories were making her light-headed, and she decided to make a charge.

She bet the full value of the pot: twelve dollars.

She was not a bluffer. Against Nell, bluffing was suicide. But she thought, who knows, I pulled it off with
Clio. Maybe the ability to bluff is just another gift of the
jackpot.

Nell said, "Look at me, child."

Meet her gaze. That was all she needed to do. Same as
with Clio. Well no, *much* harder than with Clio but still,
she could do it. Just hold her gaze without wavering and
remember: the jackpot makes everything possible.

But her grandmother's gaze was too searching.

Nell could be foolish; she could be petulant, sullen.
Her taste was all over the place: she loved equally the
Texaco Saturday opera and her singing fish from the
Dollar store. She'd had affairs during her marriages; she
drank too much; her house was unkempt. She could be
cool to the people she loved, sometimes even to Tara.
But Tara thought her divine, and believed her to possess
supernatural powers of wit and clairvoyance. And
now it was impossible to endure her gaze. Tara let her
eyes flicker away for an instant, and though she swung
them right back, she knew it was too late. Nell was
already calling her bet. Tara quietly folded. Nell raked
in the pot. "I'll catch you every time; don't you know
that?"

Tara laughed. "I momentarily forgot."

"Like right now I can tell you've got some good news you're not telling me. I feel it coming off you. Why aren't you telling your grandmother your news?"

"I'm that easy to read?"

Nell nodded. "You are when you're sittin there grinnin like a jack-o'-lantern. You in love?"

"Uh-uh."

"Something about school?"

"No."

"Well, what then?"

Tara smiled shyly. "You want to guess?"

"No I don't," said Nell. "There's no profit in guessin'. If I guess right, you'll be disappointed 'cause you didn't get to tell me your secret. And suppose I guess wrong, but my guess is better than the truth? That'll make us both feel rotten."

"Your guess won't be better than the truth."

"Child. Tell me."

"Really? Just like that?"

Tara couldn't recollect a more pleasurable moment in her life, and she hated to surrender it. But Nell was losing patience. "OK," said Tara. "But don't ask me if I'm kidding. I'm not kidding. Don't ask if there's been a mistake. There's no mistake."

47

"Wow. This is a really big thing?"

"Yes it is."

"Well then get to it."

"OK. Soon."

She laughed, and picked up her glass, and walked out of the kitchen. She went to Nell's back porch. She lay down on the swinging bed, at an angle, relaxing into the old pillows. The porch was screened in, and a vine of Lady Banks' yellow roses was climbing up the pilasters. Tara called, "Come on, Grandmother, come out here and I'll tell you."

"I'm sick of fooling with you!"

"I promise I'll tell you!"

She'd been waiting for this all day. Not just to be here at Nell's—but to be on this back porch, on this bed, at this particular angle, with the mound of fancy cushions rising behind her, with the toes of one foot just touching the floor, so that now and then she could push off and keep the bed rocking, while she looked out at Nell's garden, the crepe myrtle tree and the chili peppers and the clawfoot bathtub, the mock-banana fragrantly in bloom, the roses clinging to the screen. She took a sip of shiraz. She called again, "I *promise*!"

Nell came shuffling in. Took the rocker without a word.

Outside, a breeze silvered the leaves on the crepe myrtle.

Tara said, "OK." She drew a breath. "We won the jackpot."

"The jackpot?"

"The Max-a-Million. I mean Dad won it."

"You kidding?"

"You promised you wouldn't ask that."

"There's been some mistake?"

"Grandmother."

"How much did you win? A lot?"

"Yes."

"A hundred dollars?"

"More."

"A thousand dollars?"

"Little more."

"A *hundred* thousand?"

"Even a little bit more."

"Stop it," said Nell. "You can't lie to me."

"I know I can't."

"You're telling the truth?"

"*Yes.*"

Nell essayed, in a small birdlike voice, "You won a million dollars?"

"Higher."

"Sweet baby Jesus."

"Yeah."

"*Tell* me, child!"

"OK. Ready?"

"Yes."

"We won three hundred and eighteen million dollars."

"Good. God."

"And on the way over here? They announced it on the radio. I mean, not about us, but that the ticket was sold out of Brunswick. And they said there's only gonna be one winner. So it's not even split. It's all ours. But I mean we're going to take the lump sum, so I guess it'll be less. And then taxes, you know. What we'll wind up with is only like a hundred and twenty-something million."

"A hundred and twenty something. *Million.*"

"Uh-huh."

"You're really trying to tell me y'all are gonna *take home* a hundred and twenty million dollars?"

"Or so."

"Mitch don't have to cart toner all over the county no more?"

Tara shook her head.

"And you can get your degree?"

"If I want. Maybe I'll just buy my own college."

"And I can just strut around like I'm Queen Marie of Romania?"

"You do that anyway, Grandmother dear."

They laughed so hard that Nell sprayed her wine, and Horace Jackal disappeared.

Nell noticed that her own wine glass was empty.

"Damn, we got to toast this. I'll get some more."

Said Tara, "I can't drink any more. I got to drive home."

"No, you'll drink a toast with old Nell. I'll call Willie; he'll drive you home. Wait."

She weaved back to the kitchen.

Tara lay there and her heart was weak from too much joy. Too much! Everything was hers! Of course it wasn't really her money and if it were up to Mom she wouldn't see a nickel—but she knew Dad would make sure she had anything she wanted. Travel. New York for wild nights with Clio. The Galapagos for a summer trip with Nell. And she could go to some great school, maybe Duke. And clothes. Maybe one or two dresses. Like those Marc Jacobs' in *Marie Claire*. And she didn't care about shoes but she wouldn't mind owning one pair of great heels. *Stop*, she thought. But if she *was* going to Duke she'd absolutely need a car to get around in. Not a falling-apart Geo. Maybe a convertible BMW though it didn't need to be brand new. Though really, why *not* brand new? And a nice apartment of her own. And a garden. With a clawfooted bathtub!

As she lay there the tumbling of all these things through her thoughts—along with the swinging of the bed, and the heat and the wine, became dizzying. When Nell came back with a new bottle, she must have sensed something was wrong because she squinted and said, "Honey, you OK?"

"Oh. Uh-huh."

"You sure?"

"I'm great. I'm just, maybe a little . . . I don't know."

Nell refilled Tara's glass, then her own. And asked, "You're not scared, are you?"

"Scared of what?"

"All that money."

"Oh. Maybe I should be?"

"Well everybody says how it ruins your life, getting rich all of a sudden."

"Are *you* scared, Nell?"

"No, ma'am."

"Well, then I guess I'm not either."

"Uh-huh. We must be in *denial*."

"I guess so," said Tara, laughing.

Said Nell, "I think it's *great* to be Queen Marie of

Romania! Let's drink to denial. Let's drink to Romania. Let's *buy* Romania. Holy crap!"

Romeo awoke in the motel room. Shaw was still at the little desk, his back bathed in sweat, leaning in toward the screen. Romeo could see he was looking at pictures of some girl. It wasn't porn though. The girl wasn't even naked—but he was looking at her like she was.

Romeo got up and stumbled into the bathroom.

Said Shaw, without turning, "You up?"

"Uh-uh."

Romeo was still stuffed with his dreams. He elected to sit while peeing.

Shaw said, "It scares me how much you sleep."

On the frosted shower glass was the biggest cockroach Romeo had ever seen. It didn't even try to run. It just crouched there, twirling its mustaches.

Romeo came back into the room and said, "It's a furnace in here. You mind if I turn on the air-conditioning?"

"Too much racket. Wait till I'm done."

"Done with what?"

"Changing our lives."

Romeo put on his jeans and sneakers. He went out to the Tercel and opened the trunk and dug in his duffel for a T-shirt. He put it on there in the parking lot, in the stunning heat. There was some kind of death smell hanging in the air. He hoped they would soon get the hell out of there.

He went looking for the soda machine, which he found under a concrete stairwell. He was shoving in quarters when a girl showed up, looking for ice. She had a big bony brow, and a T-shirt with Jesus on the cross. She gave him a quick smile and filled her bucket. He was surprised to find he wasn't afraid of her.

He said, "Hey, you smell that?"

She sniffed. "Uh-huh. It's what they call Confederate jasmine."

"No, I mean the other smell. It's like, I don't know, like something rotting?"

"Oh." She sniffed again. "Maybe the pulp mill?"

"I thought there was like a mass grave or something."

She said, "I don't really smell it. I guess I've been here too long."

"How long you been here?"

"Four months."

"What's that say under your cross?"

"The Church of Jesus Triumphant."

"That's your church? You go there?"

"It's not like a church you go to. It's a missionary church. From Missouri. I'm a missionary."

"You should mission to me."

"You mean, *witness* to you?"

"Yeah, but good luck."

She didn't try, though. They talked, but not about Jesus. They talked about the heat. Romeo said how could it be so hot when it was still May? The girl said it got hot early down here. Romeo asked her if it got this hot in Missouri. She said sometimes, and then she told him how boring Missouri was. He told her how boring Piqua, Ohio, was. She told him Brunswick was boring too, but not *so* boring because there were beaches nearby, although she didn't go to them much.

She was leaning up against the ice machine and chewing a piece of ice, which he thought sexy. Her name was Tess. She invited him up to her room to meet her roommate.

He took her up on it. He met her roommate Megan and the three of them hung out and watched a *Gilmore Girls* rerun.

The girls had a boxful of leaflets telling how the world

was on its last legs. He took one and tried to read it, but it was instantly, stingingly depressing, and he was afraid it might get them started. So he put it in his pocket, to read later. Then he said, "I guess you girls don't drink, do you?"

Said Tess, "We can when we're not witnessing."

"Well, let's witness me some other time then," said Romeo, and the girls laughed. He asked them if they had boyfriends. They looked at each other and laughed some more.

Megan said, "Tess had a boyfriend. But he was a total asshole."

Tess asked him, "You know Arroyo?"

He shrugged. "You mean like from around here? I don't know anybody."

"Oh, right."

Megan said, "You know what he does? He does body suspensions. He's got that old auto-paint shop up on 17, and there's like this crane thing behind it, where he puts hooks in you and hangs you up in the air."

"He puts hooks in you?"

"Yeah."

"In your flesh?"

"Yeah."

"People *let* him do that?"

Megan shrugged. "Don't ask me why."

But then Tess spoke up, with a flicker of pride: "*I* let him do it."

"Really?" said Romeo. "What was it like?"

"It's hard to explain," said Tess. She had a faraway look.

Romeo asked, "Did it make you feel close to God?"

"No, it made me feel like I *was* God. When He was on the Cross. And then after it was over? *Oh*. Like so good. Like *nothing* sucks."

"Yeah, but then he dumped you," Megan reminded her. "Because he's a total asshole."

Romeo liked listening to them. He'd never met missionaries before. He invited them down to his room for Jack-and-Cokes, and on the way, he walked behind them, trying to decide which girl was prettier, so he could offer that one to Shaw. But there was no prettier one. Tess had the disturbing forehead and Megan was squat like a traffic cone, and they were equally unappealing, unless you were in a generous mood. Shaw was in a weird mood. He was still flying around on the web when they got to the room, still working on that mysterious project. He seemed unhinged. He nodded when Romeo made introductions but didn't speak and didn't shake hands, and the look he cast Romeo was on the order of *What's with the bitches?*

This hurt Romeo because he had brought these girls as gifts. "They're missionaries," he said. "From Missouri."

Shaw said, "Missionaries to what?"

Tess said, "We go door to door."

"Here?"

"Uh-huh."

Shaw stared at them. "You're on a mission to Brunswick, Georgia?"

"Uh-huh."

"You're evangelizing the *Bible Belt*?"

He smiled and the girls smiled too. Whenever Shaw got one of his insights into the true heart of things, his lips would curl up on one side and he could be charming and off-kilter and really funny if he didn't go overboard.

Romeo fixed drinks for everyone. Liberal measures of Jack. It was turning into a party; he was excited. But then Shaw turned away without a word and went back to his laptop, *clickety-click*. It got kind of awkward, just listening to that, so after a minute Romeo and the girls decided go back upstairs.

However, as they were all leaving, Shaw said, "Wait. Romeo, hang around a second. I want to ask you something."

Romeo told the girls to go on ahead.

It was clear that something was coming. He had a feeling. The best course would be to say no right away, even before Shaw launched. Not even wait to hear Shaw's proposal. Just clear out, go get trashed with the girls. But he didn't do that. He sat on one of the motel beds while Shaw sat on the other, facing him, and when Shaw said, "OK, listen, I need you," Romeo nodded meekly.

"For what?"

"Something I couldn't trust anyone else in the world with. I mean you and me, we're the only ones alive who can do this. Because we've got this trust between us. But it's going to be scary as hell and at any moment we could get ourselves killed and if you're not up for it you just say so right away and I'll understand. OK? You go back home and do tech support. But I'm going to do this. And if you want to do this with me, I mean if you want to *live*, well I mean, we *will* change the world."

Romeo said, "What do you need?" Because he was terrified, it came out as a croak—but he said it.

"I don't mean just change our lives," said Shaw. "I mean change the whole fucking world."

"What do you need, Shaw?"

"I need you to play kind of a role. Like what you'd call *angel of vengeance*. You ready for that?"

Tara found the whole thing amusing. The way Dad had to work so hard to maintain his air of righteous outrage. The way Jase had to pretend he was really chastened: tucking into infancy, burrowing his head between Mom's shoulder and the couch. "Caleb *swore* he wouldn't tell. I made him *swear*, Dad."

Said Dad, "But you promised us, Jase. You gave us your word you'd keep your trap shut. Remember? You weren't gonna tell anyone about the jackpot. Anyone."

"So I'm *sorry*."

Serene in his brattiness because he knew he was in the clear. He wouldn't be punished *tonight*. Dad's lecture came out sounding formal and half-hearted. "Well now I'm sure it's all over town. I hope you learned something. This is a tough world, and it's going to get a lot tougher. Get this into your head now—trust your family and your faith and nothing else. You hear me?"

"I said I was *sorry*."

"You better pray no reporter gets hold of this."

"Dad?"

"What."

"If we buy a mansion on the beach? Can I get a Jet Ski?"

Tara had to smile. Poor Dad, compelled to wind himself up again: "ARE YOU HEARING A WORD I'M SAYING?"

Naturally Jase started snuffling again—but Mom smoothed his head and murmured, "Oh, of course you can have a Jet Ski."

"What are you *telling* him?"

"For God's sake, Mitch. We're gonna be trillionaires. It won't kill him to have a Jet Ski."

Tara laughed. "Then can *I* get a Jet Ski? Can I get a Jet Ski made of pure gold?"

"Just stop it," said Dad.

Jase said, "I don't care if mine's made of gold or not. I just want a fast one."

Tara said, "Yeah, I also want fast. But I mostly want gold. And amphibious. I think it's only fair—"

Jase took the bait. "If *she* gets an amphibious Jet Ski, I should get—"

"NOBODY'S GETTING A JET SKI!" Dad thundered.

Then he shook his head slowly and sighed. "Or, I don't know. What the heck. Let's *all* get Jet Skis."

It was an astonishing thing for Tara, to see her whole family laughing at once. She couldn't remember the last time this had happened. More of this jackpot magic—more of these waves of bliss and wide-open freedom.

Mom went into the kitchen to make herself a little drink, and Dad started telling them about this financial guy he'd met today—some big muckety from Sea Island, and also some big lawyer from Atlanta; and the jackpot ticket was in the safety deposit box so that was taken care of; and tomorrow he'd arrange with some security firm about bodyguards because they'd probably need them, at least for the first few weeks—

The doorbell rang.

Dad said, "Oh Lord. Already? If that's a reporter. I swear, Jase, if that's a reporter *already*—"

Tara answered the door. A young man: late twenties, kind of pallid, ungainly, and his corduroy jacket didn't fit him well. But he had a nice smile. And he knew her name. "Hello, Tara."

"Who are you?"

"Bill Rooney," he said. He flashed his ID. "Georgia Lottery Commission. Your folks around?"

Dad was already at her shoulder. "What can I do for you?"

"My name's Bill Rooney." The ID said, *William B. Rooney. Agent. Georgia State Lottery Commission.* "May I come in for a moment?"

Dad was nervous. "I thought we were supposed to come to you. Anyway how do you—why would you think *we're* the winners—"

Rooney laughed. "None of my business, Mr.

Boatwright. I'm just here to share a little advice in case you *should* win something. OK? Could we talk a moment?"

Dad was still wary. "You mind if I call my lawyer first?"

"Well, that would make it an *official* visit. Which would limit what I could tell you. All I want is to run your family through a few hypotheticals. Take less than ten minutes."

Mom said from her sofa, "Oh, let him *in*, Mitch. Don't be rude."

Finally Dad shrugged. "All right."

He stepped aside and the visitor came in. Mom was bustling about, straightening the room. "Mrs. Boatwright? My name is Bill Rooney and it's a pleasure to meet you."

"What can I get you?" Mom asked. "Scotch, gin and tonic? What do you like?"

"I'm good, thank you. I'd just like to talk with you all."

"All of us?"

Rooney nodded. To Jase he said, "Hi fella. You should hear this too."

They all sat. Rooney took Dad's big easy chair. He unlatched his briefcase and drew from it what looked

63

like a case file. His every move seemed studied, deliberate.

"Well, I guess what I want to tell you," he said, "boils down to this. Be ready. Because, because everything in your lives is about to change. And this change could be a source of great joy or it could be terribly destructive."

Softspoken but fervent. Not like any bureaucrat Tara had ever seen. *Terribly destructive?* Was he stoned? Well, why not? If he was smart, and he seemed to be, this job had to suck ass, and maybe getting baked was the only way to deal with it. The thought made her smile. Rooney saw this, and gave her a little smile back.

And he reminded her a little—though maybe just at the corners of the jaw—of JCD Jr.

"Mr. Boatwright," he said, "may I ask you something? What are your plans? I mean suppose you did win the jackpot. Would you give up your business?"

"No sir. Not at all. I'd like to *expand* my business."

Rooney kept smiling. "Yeah? Well. I know you think you would. But you won't. I'm sorry. I'm not calling you a liar; I'm just telling you, one night pretty soon you're going to party too much, and the next morning you'll think, what the hell, might as well sleep in a little. Just this once. And next day you *will* go back to work, but you won't be able to concentrate. Because you'll be thinking, well maybe, since I've already got all the money in the world, maybe keeping up a marginal copier business in East Jesus, Georgia, is absolutely pointless."

Dad gathered himself to protest: "Actually, I'm not sure, that it's, um, appropriate for you to—"

Rooney raised a hand to silence him. "Sooner or later you'll tank it and get yourself an estate in Hawaii. Then you can all get some sun, which'll be great except you'll get too much and you'll start looking like iguanas. And you'll try to make friends but who can you trust, right? So you won't know anybody and you'll stay home and watch TV and you'll be lonely as hell and bored out of your goddamn *skulls*—"

"Sir!" said Dad. "Watch your language—"

"And gorge yourself on disappointment, and bitterness, and welcome to the wonderful world of winning the jackpot. And what I'm here to tell you, all of you, is there's only *one* way to save yourselves from that living death. And that's to use these riches you've been given for something good. You follow me? Bring kindness into the world. Show love. Alleviate suffering. And to hell with the house in Hawaii. To hell with the fancy toys and the—"

"Now hold on!" said Dad. His voice finally with some heft. "I won't have this foul language in my house!"

Rooney didn't even look at him. He said, "Calm down, Mitch. I'll tell you a story. About this guy I know. This guy, he's doing tech support? Little old ladies, their bridge programs won't load, he talks them through it. 'Go to All Programs, click on that.' 'Go to Add or Remove Programs, click on that.' Kind of a dumb job, a grueling job, but in all those years, it never breaks the guy. He never stops dreaming. Because he knows there are powers he can tap into. Whenever he looks at the world, he thinks, this can be a world full of beauty, this can be a *rapturous* world. He thinks, somehow I will find the power to bring rapture and beauty into this world.

"So one day he's on vacation. Going south—for the first time in his life. He's on I-95, he's maybe a little jacked up on dexies. He stops at a convenience store. He goes in and discovers that in this very store a jackpot ticket has just been sold. *The* ticket. And he's thinking: now here I am, I have this great dream. I have all this love; I want to bring kindness and truth and virtue to the world. But I've never had the tools before, and here a tool is set down before me—"

Dad suddenly rose up. His hands clenched. "Get out of my house."

"What, now?"

"I'm calling the police. Get out."

"Mitch, I'm talking about our future—"

Dad drew his cell phone from his pocket and flipped it open.

But Rooney dipped his hand into his briefcase and brought out a gun.

And said, "Put the phone down."

Mom cried out.

Rooney placed the muzzle of the gun against her temple. "PUT THE FUCKING PHONE DOWN!"

Dad let the phone slip through his fingers. It clattered on the floor.

Jase was crying, "MOM! MOM!" But Rooney grabbed him with one hand and pulled him close and said, "One more word and I'll *kill* your mommy, little boy. Right in front of you. So shut up."

Jase heaved with sobs but managed to stop screaming. Rooney pushed him away again, and Tara took him into her arms.

"OK," said Rooney. "Do I have everyone's attention?"

Looking from face to face.

Then he lowered the pistol. Took a breath and slowly exhaled.

"OK then. Everything in the open. My real name is

67

Shaw McBride. What I want is half your winnings. When I get that, I go. If you cooperate and don't fuss, then I'll leave and you'll be safe, and happy, and still rich beyond your wildest dreams." He was looking right at Tara. As though it were she and not her parents who made the decisions in this household. He said, "You understand me?"

She kept her eyes lowered. "Yes."

"You'll do what I ask?"

"Yes."

But he cocked his head skeptically. "No, you're already scheming. I can see it. You're thinking, how can we get word to the cops? How do we make a sign to the cops so they'll come rescue us and cut this weasel down? Right? Are you scheming against me?"

She kept her eyes down. "No."

"You want to know why your scheme won't work?"

She didn't know what to say. Finally she whispered, "All right."

He commanded, "Jase. Turn out all the lights."

Jase didn't move.

"TURN OUT THE FUCKING LIGHTS!"

Jase, in tears, got up and flipped the wall switch, then the lamp switch. All that remained was a trickle of feeble streetlight from the window.

Shaw McBride said, "Look out there. You see him?"

A shadow, a trace. Beneath the hickory tree.

Mom moaned in fear.

Said Shaw, "I want you to go out there, Tara."

"Out there?"

"Yes."

"Why?"

"*Why?* Never fucking say 'why' to me again. Just go."

"I'll go with you," said Dad.

Again Shaw set the pistol's muzzle against Mom's ear. "Sit down, Mitch. This is just for Tara."

Dad considered resisting, thought better of it. Sank back down. Shaw told Tara, "Go now."

She got up and went to the door and opened it. And stepped out into the front yard. The figure beneath the tree said, "Come here."

Her breathing was no longer under control. She thought she might lose consciousness. She tried to pray, but every prayer flew from her head.

Again the man summoned her. "Come here."

Then she was with him beneath the tree. Close enough to see his face in the dark. Childish. Big soft eyes, an overbite.

She wasn't sure, but she thought he might be trembling.

He said, "Listen. If you oppose us in any way, I'll kill the people you love."

He was silent a moment. Then he said, "You believe me?"

"Yes."

"I will, I really will. Your friend Clio? I'll kill her. You hear me?"

"Yes."

"I'll kill your grandmother. That's just . . . Fuck it. And your cousin Alfred. And your cousin Vanessa, and your uncle Shelby and his whole family. Everybody. When Shaw sends me the signal. Or if I call to check in, and he doesn't answer? I go. In whatever order I choose. You won't be able to stop me. You think I'm scared? I *am* scared. All I want is to get the hell out of here, go home. But so what. I'll do what I have to."

She nodded.

He said, "For my friend. Not for the money. For him. I hate this whole deal, but I won't fail him."

Silence.

He said, "You don't care about the money either, do you, Tara?"

"No."

"So then. It's up to us. You and me. Not Shaw, not your parents, just us. You hear what I'm saying?"

"Yes."

Then a plaintive tone—almost begging: "So let him have what he wants."

Romeo, two hours later, was driving through the dark to Nell Boatwright's bungalow—guided by the map that Shaw had made for him. 'Points of Interest' had been marked with stars, and Nell's house was the southernmost of these. It was in an old, leafy part of town. When he got there, he pulled over across the street and cut the engine. She was in her bedroom. He saw the TV glowing, the footboard of her bed, her slippered feet. He waited.

Presently she rose (first carefully relocating the cat she'd been holding), waddled past another window, and showed up in what he guessed was her bathroom. He couldn't see her face, but he liked how she walked. A directness, despite her stooped carriage. There was another cat on the bathroom sill, and Nell gave it a brisk knuckle rub. Then she vanished and Romeo didn't see her till she went back to the bedroom, regathered the first cat into her arms, and lay down again.

71

If Shaw were to text him: Go, it would mean the Boatwrights were in open rebellion, and Romeo would have to step into her house and kill her without hesitation.

He wondered, could I do that?

I told Shaw I could. Why did I tell him that?

He stayed there watching till the old woman shut off the TV and turned out the light.

Then he drove out to Rt. 17, the main north-south drag. He went to the neighborhood called Belle Point, where Tara's Uncle Shelby and Aunt Miriam had a rangy house and a basketball hoop and a badminton net, and a big backyard that unrolled right to the edge of the marsh. According to Shaw, Shelby and Miriam had two children. In an emergency, Romeo would be expected to execute the whole family.

He headed south on 17. He put Cradle of Filth in the CD player and let the music batter his cerebrum. That crematory stink was in the air. It was so heavy he could almost taste it.

At Island View he turned off and drove to Clio's house, which bordered an empty, jungly lot. He pulled over, got out and clicked the door closed, and ventured into the palmettos. It was heavy going, and with everything so dry and brittle he couldn't help but make a racket. But all over the neighborhood air-conditioners were blasting away. He doubted he'd be heard, and even if he were, he was making pretty much the same noises that a deer or a dog would make, so who would give a shit?

He broke through to Clio's lawn, finding himself at the back of the house. White vineflowers, and deep grass, and one lighted window. He moved till he was below this, till he could look up and see Clio in her bedroom. At her desk, her laptop. She was tall and loose-limbed. Tattoos all over her arms and that silver serpent coiling through her cheek. Shaw had shown Romeo her pics on MySpace. It was as if Shaw had been goading him, trying to get him hot and bothered, knowing this girl was the kind he favored. And now here she was in the flesh, wearing only a T-shirt and panties, her right leg tucked beneath her. She seemed to feel safe. The night pressed snugly against her window. She had posters of rock bands on the wall behind her: Arcade Fire, TV on the Radio, and some band called Drive Fast & Shut Your Eyes. She wore headphones. For a moment, while she considered what next to write, she hugged herself, and this brought out the shape of her breasts, and Romeo felt anxious just looking at her.

You made *her* a 'Point of Interest'? Shaw, were you kidding? How am I going to hurt *her*?

At last the mosquitoes and no-see-ums drove him away. He pushed through the jungle again, with the bugs all over him. This was too much. This heat, this assignment, these no-see-ums flying around his head; and Clio flying around, and that other girl flying around: Tara. Tara who had stood there in the dark while he'd delivered his threats, saying yes yes yes to him but not yielding an inch. If she's not scared of me, then we're fucked. When he got back to the car the prevailing stink assailed his nostrils again, and the car was filled with dancing gnats, and every fucking thing was flying around his head.

He got back onto Rt. 17 but didn't get far before he had to stop. He pulled into the parking lot of the Rent-All store, which was illumined by one of those old snappish mercury-vapor lamps. He opened his door and leaned out over the pavement. His dinner came tumbling out, blue as laundry. He stayed doubled up a while, breathing in the reek, thinking he might hurl again, but he didn't. After a while he wiped his mouth and drove on. He found a gas station called Happy Times, and in the men's room he gargled and brushed his teeth. Then he went back on patrol. No time off. Have to keep working. According to Shaw's great plan I have to keep moving at all times.

Shaw awoke from a thousand-eyed nightmare. House full of enemies, enemies everywhere. His heart swinging wildly in its cage.

He groped on the bed beside him till he found his Walther .32 autoloader, and let his fingers close around the handle. He sat up. Peering into the gloom. Where am I? Somebody's in here with me. Somebody's breathing. I see him. A malicious presence, glowing. Should I shoot? Kill him before he kills me?

Finally it came to him: the kid.

Jase. This was Jase's room, and Shaw was in Jase's bed while the kid himself slept on a cot. The Boatwrights, the jackpot: it all rushed back.

Except for the kid's breathing, everything was silent.

But he knew they were awake. They were just waiting for their chance.

Ah God.

What was the matter with him? How did he think he could survive this? This lunacy? Now there was no way out. Only way out was prison or death. No retreat, no running away. *I even gave them our real fucking names.*

He looked at the clock on his phone. Twelve till two. Romeo should make his check-in in twelve minutes. But oh Christ, he was depending on Romeo? Romeo was his dark servant? If the cops ever touched him, he'd buckle. How had he gotten into this? Because of that MySpace page, because of Tara. Tara and her whole family coming off so naïve and big-eyed and pliant and spineless: she had sucked him into this; it was her fault. He had been minding his own business and their 'innocence' had roped him into this. Oh, you fuckers.

The heat built up inside his skull till all his fear was gone and there was nothing but fury.

He drew a deep breath. He reached up and turned the light on, and instantly the room was filled with toy warplanes and a glow-in-the-dark Iron Man doll, and behind the warplanes, a ceramic statue of Jesus. Shaw sat there gathering himself. Holding the gun. Jase was in the other bed pretending to sleep. Though he knew the kid was awake; of course he was awake: like everyone in this house he was scared out of his mind. All of them were awake. And that was OK with Shaw. *You all lie there and be afraid now; you think about Romeo and Romeo's sickness and Romeo's bloodlust while I tap into the power and get the ground settled under me. You think about fighting back, all of you. Go ahead. I'm ready for blood whenever you want.*

Mitch kept rehearsing in his mind what he'd do if he heard any sound from his daughter's room. Supposing Shaw tried to sneak in there? Mitch didn't have his pistol anymore—Shaw McBride had confiscated it—but he could still jump out of bed, grab the letter opener off the rolltop desk, and rush into her room and with luck get in there before he could take aim. Go in low. Swing underhand, with *all* my strength, and twist as I pull out. Grab his gun arm with my left hand, and with my right stab and twist, stab and *twist.*

Or should I wait?

Till when? Till he's *in the act of raping my daughter?*

Maybe. Because he'll be more vulnerable then.

But the *price.*

And what if he makes her go on top, uses her as a shield, keeps his gun in his hand and his eye on the door while he forces her to whatever. Oh my Lord Jesus.

Maybe should I wait till he's done? Till he's sleepy after his business?

Oh my Lord. How can I *wait*?

Help me, my Lord. Guide me.

Maybe he's asleep by now? The bastard had looked exhausted when he lay down. Must be asleep. Kill him in his sleep?

The rush, the terror in McBride's eyes, me stabbing the knife and be sure to twist it so the blood will *fly* out of him and remember to clench tightly so my hand won't slip even with his blood all over me, and keep *plunging* it and *plunging* it, and the blood *flying,* my Lord.

But then there's that other guy. The guy out on the road, the madman.

My God, my God, why hast thou forsaken me? Why art thou so far from helping me, and from the words of my roaring?

Next to him, Patsy slept. Amazing to him that she could sleep. But she was pretty drunk. The fumes curled from her nostrils when she breathed out. While Mitch just kept rehearsing the rush, over and over, a thousand times: the stabbing, the blood, the making ribbons out of that son of a bitch. Killing him all night long.

Shaw got up and went into the bathroom and pissed. He left the door slightly ajar, and when he was done he stopped to listen for a moment. Stillness came pouring through that door. It struck him as an aggressive stillness—rebellious. He flushed, and went out and stood before the door to Mitch and Patsy's room.

"Mitch?" he said quietly.

Naturally there was no answer.

"Mitch, I know you're awake. Say something before I get annoyed."

That earned a soft croak: "Yes."

"I just want you to know, Mitch, I'm not going to rape your daughter or anything, unless you're planning to fuss with me. You're not planning to fuss with me, are you?"

"No."

"Good. If you do I'll rape her and cut her tongue out so she'll never be able to tell you how much she blames you, but you'll see it in her face every day for the rest of your long shitty life. But if you cooperate with me, I'll treat her like a princess, and no harm will befall her. Or you, or anyone else you love. All right?"

A long wait. "Yes."

"OK. Get some sleep."

Shaw went through the house and out the back door,

into the panting night. He stood on the wooden deck and waited, and at exactly 2:00 a.m., Romeo called.

"Hey, Romeo."

"How'd I do?

"With Tara? I think you did well. She's scared."

A silence, then Romeo said, "I feel like I fucked up."

"You got to seem like you're batshit. Like you've got the killings all planned out in your head. Like you're ready to blow, like you're just waiting for the spark."

"Yeah."

"Where are you now?"

"Riding around Brunswick."

"You finding everybody's house OK? You find the grandmother?"

"Yes."

"Clio's? Uncle Shelby's?"

"I found 'em. But I still don't know what I'm supposed to do."

"Keep moving. What I said: if I send you a mayday, you go kill whoever you're closest to."

"Right."

"But keep moving, so they'll never know where you are."

"OK."

"And if I don't answer a check-in call, that means I'm

probably dead. You keep trying me for twenty minutes—then you start killing."

"Starting with which one?"

"Doesn't matter. So long as *you* know which one."

"Start with Nell?"

"Whatever you want. Just make a plan, get it in your head. Make it concrete. You've got to believe it so they'll believe it."

"OK."

"You understand?"

"I think."

"If it's true for you, it'll be true for them."

"Right," said Romeo.

Romeo, after that call, felt a dead ache in his stomach. It wasn't hunger but still he thought he better eat something. He went over to I-95 and found a Huddle House. The bounteous light was repellent to him, but nothing else was open, so he went in and took a booth. The menu was so shiny he could hardly bear to look at it. He felt conspicuous and awkward. The waitress hovered. Though he knew perfectly well what grits were, he thought she was expecting to be asked, so he said, "Could you tell me something about grits?"

The waitress shrugged. "They're white."

He approved of this opacity: he thought it fitting. The hour, this job, this hash joint half-full of drunks, toads, and marginal grifters: why in the world should she open up to anyone? He ordered the grits plus scrambled eggs and bacon, and she went away. Then the woman in the next booth turned, and sized him up, and said, "Grits is nothing. It's what you put your butter on. You makin a big thing about grits, you *must* be a Yankee."

He said, "I am."

"Knew it."

She turned to the gnarled cracker who shared her booth. She gave him a look like, *what did I tell you*, and he conceded, "You called it, Wynetta."

She turned back to Romeo. "I'm Wynetta. This is Lonnie."

"OK. I'm Romeo."

Naturally Lonnie thought that was funny. His laugh was petty, jagged. Wynetta killed it with a sharp look, and asked Romeo what he thought about the trial of Miss Glynn County. Was that a travesty or what? Romeo said he didn't know anything about the trial of Miss Glynn County. Wynetta showed him the picture in the

Brunswick News and laid the whole thing out for him: the cheating, the recriminations, the secret baby, the missing bullet.

Presently Lonnie got tired of being ignored. He paid for his coffee and took off, and Wynetta came to sit in Romeo's booth.

She was large. She had thinning hair and a mail slot for a mouth, and there was nothing sexy about her unless you weren't looking, and even then you smelled her breath which was a bouquet of onions, slim jims and gin. When Romeo's breakfast arrived, he couldn't begin to eat it. But he probably wouldn't have eaten it anyway, and he was glad for the company, glad that Wynetta was talking a blue streak. It distracted him from his obligations.

After a few minutes the waitress came by again and noticed his untouched plate. "You don't like the grits?"

"Oh, no, they're fine, I just can't eat right now. Could you maybe just bring me the check?"

She muttered, "You don't pay if you don't eat," and swept the plate away. She was vexed, but there was nothing he could see to do about this.

Wynetta had lost the thread of her chatter. For a moment she and Romeo were quiet, looking into each other's eyes. Then it occurred to her to ask, "So what're you doing down here?"

That was a tough one. Shaw had told him something to say to this but he couldn't remember. He tried, "Well. I'm with my buddy."

"Yeah?"

She waited.

"And, um, we're in business. My buddy and me."

"What business?"

"Well, like insurance."

She said, "I used to sell insurance. Who you work for?"

"It's not like regular insurance."

She waited.

"It's hard to explain," he offered. "It's like, I don't know. Like *secondary* insurance."

"What's that?"

"Oh. Well, it's like if all the people you loved went out to a field in a thunderstorm? I mean, we could tell you the odds they'd get hit by lightning, and how much money you'd get if they did. But that's secondary because we can't give you anyone's life *back*. You know?"

"I need a drink," she said. "Buy me a drink?"

"OK."

She checked the time. "Everything's closed, but we

could go to Pigeon's out in Sterling. They'll let us in. That's where we should go."

However, they wound up not going there.

When they stepped out to the Huddle House parking lot, there was all that heat again, and next door were the remains of a pickup truck immersed in kudzu, and out of the night came a deep-throated train whistle. It was sort of like the South as Romeo had imagined it, except for the Huddle House itself, which looked to him like any box-shaped interstate diner anywhere.

Wynetta asked him, "Where you staying?"

"Blackbeard's Motel."

"That's a real shithole, isn't it?"

"I guess."

"But all of Brunswick is a shithole, to tell you the truth. I got a trailer out on Balm-of-Gilead, if you want to stay there. Really it's my dad's trailer, but he's in the hospital."

"What's he there for?"

"Congestive heart failure."

"Whoa."

"Yeah."

Romeo supposed that this trailer would turn out to be some kind of redneck nightmare, with cockroaches as big as owls. Still, it'd be a lot more private than

Blackbeard's Motel, and it wouldn't hurt to take a look at it. So he got in the Tercel and followed her. She drove fast and made a lot of turns, and it was a challenge to keep up—but also sort of relaxing, like a low-level video game. He let her lead him along, this way and that, no questions. He wouldn't have minded if she'd led him clear out of Georgia.

He wondered why he'd ever said yes to Shaw.

What's the matter with me? Shaw says I need you— I say, OK, at your service. Why don't I tell him I can't do this?

Wynetta led him through a neighborhood where everything was built out of cinder-block. All the houses looked like outbuildings at a sewage-treatment plant. The churches also. He kept following Wynetta as best he could, and he remembered the first time Shaw had ever said to him, "I need your help."

They had been twelve years old. Shaw had come to Romeo's house—a visit that Romeo thought miraculous. And they were up in Romeo's room, and when Shaw said, "I need your help," he said it in a voice as throaty and resonant as an adult's, and that little lopsided smile went crawling up his face, and Romeo had been dazzled, in awe, and had no chance.

OK, he thought. But now I should tell him: "I'm not

good at this. I love you but get someone else." Why not say that? What is the *matter* with me?

Wynetta took another turn. The street sign said Balm-of-Gilead Road. Romeo turned after her, and in a few minutes they came to the trailer. He pulled up behind her. They went in together. To his surprise, the place turned out to be clean and shipshape. Wooden models of shrimp boats, and on the walls were neatly framed photos of little Wynetta and her mother. Romeo said, "So that's your mom?"

"Yeah."

"Where is she now?"

"Dead."

She gave him a Pabst Blue Ribbon; she turned on the TV and ate a can of Vienna sausages while they watched one of those famous Christy Brinkley infomercials. Then she came on to him. It wasn't so bad. At least she was brisk and matter-of-fact about it, and although drunk, not sloppy. Once, with her weight splayed out over him and his face wedged between her great white breasts, he imagined himself stuck between the *Titanic* and the Iceberg, and this almost made him forget where he was.

FRIDAY

Tara scrambled eggs for the bastard, since that's what he said he wanted. She cracked the shells and whisked the yolks. In her slippers she shuffled to the fridge, and as she got out the bacon, and milk and butter, she wondered what she might poison him with. There was a can of Drano under the sink. But he'd smell that, wouldn't he? Also some kind of roach thing: Combat— wasn't that like a nerve poison? Wouldn't it be odorless and tasteless? She conjured an image of little scorched-earth glittering crystals. How much would it take? How much, you bastard, to tie your spine into knots? Maybe I could mask the taste with cayenne sauce? Or maybe not. She had no idea. And anyway, even if he did eat it, would it really kill him? Maybe it'd just make him sick and rabid and more dangerous than he already was.

And suppose he died—would that even help us? His friend Romeo would still be out there.

And Romeo would kill Nell. And after that . . .

But who cares about after that?

I can't afford, she told herself, this anger. Keep my head clear. Scramble his eggs and pour the OJ and watch every move he makes, every gesture. Find out who he is. Maybe I can figure out how to trap him. Also keep an eye on Mom, that she's not sneaking shots; also make sure Dad's not boiling over where he sits. Keep everyone calm and floating on an even keel.

The sunrise shoved in through the big sliding glass door. She went and shut the blinds.

The family ate without a word. When they were done, Shaw wiped his lips carefully, cleared his throat and said, "OK. It's time to work on our story."

They looked at him.

"Here's my idea. Flat tire. I was on the road and got a flat tire. And then, Mitch, you came along and helped me out. Like a good Samaritan, OK? We took the tire to that convenience store to fill it with air. And then on the way back you remembered you were supposed to buy lottery tickets for your wife. And I said, hey, would you buy some for me?"

He looked for their reaction. No reaction. He sipped his coffee and pondered. Then he shook his head. "No. You're right. It feels phony."

He thought some more.

"Mitch, you go to bars?"

"I don't drink," said Dad. "Patsy does, sometimes."

Tara kept her gaze on Shaw. He was biting his lower lip, and his gray eyes had a stormy light to them. He said, "It might work better if we'd met before. You ever been to Ohio?"

Dad shrugged. "Through it. Once. On my way to Chicago."

"When was that?"

"Um—'85?"

"Way too long ago. Where else you been?"

"Well. I went to Columbus when I was in the Guard. I mean Columbus, Georgia. That was, well, like '91?"

"Anything more recent?"

"They had me up to Greenville once for training."

"Where's Greenville?"

"South Carolina."

"Training for what?"

"Service Mita copiers."

"How long were you there?"

"Don't know. Two months?"

"This was when?"

"Few years ago. '03."

"No bars?"

"No sir."

"Well then," Shaw pressed, "how could I have met you? Say, if I was just passing through Greenville, South Carolina?"

Dad shrugged. "I stayed at the motel when I wasn't training. That's about it. Except church."

"What church?"

"Faith Renewal. Same as my church here."

"So I might have gone to that church and met you there?"

"Might have."

"Would you say that church is welcoming to strangers?"

"Oh, yeah. We had a crisis center there. You know, for anyone in trouble. I volunteered there. I guess I could have met you through that—"

"What's a crisis center?"

"Um. If you're suicidal? Or, you know, you just need someone to talk to, you're depressed, or if it's drugs or whatever. Or any kind of trouble and you need to talk?"

"You just walk in?"

"Mostly people call."

"But you *could* just walk in?"

"You could."

"And how many people would work there at a time?"

"Well, just one, mostly. Or they had it rigged so a call would come in and get switched to your own phone. But I didn't have a phone, 'cause I was staying at the motel. So I went in. Sundays and Mondays."

Shaw's eyes were incandescent.

He held out his cup and Tara filled it. He sat there holding the cup close to his lips but not drinking. He'd forgotten to drink. He was lost in thought and had a little smile working. She could guess the story that was unspooling before his mind's eye: the meeting of two strangers, a lost lamb and a kindly shepherd. He started laughing, and Dad must have thought he was laughing at the idea of a Christian crisis line, because he said, "No, we really helped some folks, we really did."

Shaw said, "Oh, God, I *know* you did. I know you saved souls. You saved mine."

Burris, the old city cop, was at Trudy's Café on Newcastle Street, waiting in line for the cashier. Rose Whittle was right behind him; they fell to talking and she asked him what he thought about the jackpot news. He said he didn't know what she meant.

She was astonished. "You really don't know? The Boatwrights won the Max-a-Million jackpot."

Long awkward moment. Finally he asked her, "Which Boatwrights we talking about here?"

"Mitch and Patsy."

"Is this a prank?"

"No, sir."

"How much was in the jackpot?"

"Huge. Like three hundred million. More."

"Rose. Tell me the truth."

"That is the truth. Well, I guess it's only a rumor. But I believe it."

Rose had a demonic streak of white in her hair, and voodoo fingernails an inch and a half long, and knew everything about everybody—not through voodoo but because she worked Dispatch at the Brunswick police. If Rose was crediting a rumor, it was probably solid.

Stupidly then, insufficiently, Burris responded, "Wow."

Then he attempted a little smile.

Then he exhaled slowly and said, "Well that's just great."

He paid, fumbling the change, and went out to the blinding street where everything was white, erased, and the fumes that came off the asphalt were so hot he felt they might carry the hat off his head. On the way to his cruiser, he passed the Chief of Police, who was headed into Trudy's with a couple of city commissioners. The Chief was a young guy. He had an abundance of hair. He gave Burris the slightest of nods, then murmured something to the commissioners. Whatever he said amused them. Burris hadn't heard it, but it was probably, "Well, here comes Deppity Dawg," or "Well, if it ain't Deppity Dawg," or something like that. Why did the Chief call Burris Deppity Dawg? Burris wasn't sure. It had been his tag for years. Maybe owing to his years of faithful police service. Or his jowliness, or because he was such an entertaining idiot.

He nodded back at the Chief.

Keeping his shoulders at the proper angle of hunchment. Limping to his cruiser and getting in and driving away. Give 'em a show of debasement and get the hell out of here. He drove to his favorite hiding place on Rt. 17, near the Spur, behind a mess of oleanders, and raised dutifully his radar gun. But today was a lucky day for speeders in Brunswick, Georgia, because he wasn't even looking at the numbers. All his thoughts were on Nell Boatwright. Now she'll be lost to me forever. Her son Mitch will buy her a mansion in the south of France, and she'll have tea with duchesses and play seven-card stud with Bea Arthur who will adore her drawl and her crazy piercing laugh, and she's lost to me. It's finished now. I'm done and I just ought to own up to that fact.

Tara had to drive Shaw over to Nell's. She begged him not to make her do this. She said, "I can't lie to Nell. She'll know something's wrong. Please."

But he wouldn't listen. "I'll have to meet her sooner or later. Why not now?" He tucked his pistol into the holster that fit against the small of his back, and put his dull corduroy jacket on over it, and they went off together, in Tara's Geo. They went by way of Norwich Street, which seemed to fascinate him. He told her to slow down so he could look at things: the down-at-heels bodegas and money order stores and old men sitting under oak trees playing dominos. Then they left the Mexican neighborhood and came to the black neighborhood: custom-wheels shops and Marvin's Grocery, and one storefront church after another. Shaw read aloud their names: "Fisher of Men Ministries." "Healing & Deliverance Bible Institute." "Christ's Church for the End Times."

"Jesus," he said. Laughing. "What a great town."

She drove and kept silent.

"Tara," he said, "are you worried?"

"Yes."

"Don't be."

"I know I'll give it away."

"No. I'd kill you in front of her. Wouldn't be that hard on you, but for her it'd be better if she'd never existed. Like her whole life was just the build-up to this suffering, and she'll regret every minute of it, everything she ever did because it all leads up to watching you die. I'm sorry to say it so bluntly. But you have to fool her. You *have* to. So you will."

Shaw looked at her for a while. Then he turned away and watched the city go by and thought: what *I* have to do is keep this fire going. This furnace of black flames. Be unafraid to have it inside me. Be willing to create every horror. Fear becomes discipline becomes profoundest love, and if I don't hold these people to the highest standards, everyone's life will turn into shit. If I'm timid, or irresolute, it all goes to shit. For all parties involved. Everything rests on my shoulders here.

Romeo awoke to the sound of a car outside Wynetta's trailer. Christ, what's this, a boyfriend? He went to the window. In the drive was some kind of official van, from which a black man in white uniform was emerging. He didn't look to be a boyfriend. He looked like he had business here.

Romeo gave Wynetta a shake. "Someone's here."

She growled in her throat and turned away.

He pulled his jeans on. Through the window he saw the black man lower a ramp from the side of the van, then roll out a wheelchair. In the chair was a child, all bundled up: the oddest-looking child Romeo had ever seen. Frail and hairless, Victorian, consumptive-looking.

Romeo shook Wynetta again.

She opened one eye. "What the *fuck*?"

"Hello?" called the black man from outside the door. "Hello? I have Mr. Santos here."

That finally roused her. "What? Oh my God. Wait!"

She grabbed her bra from the floor. It was a full harness, an iron maiden, and it took her a while to get it all fastened. Then she struggled to get her shorts on, and her T-shirt, and opened the door.

The black man was standing there, with the child cradled in his arms.

"Daddy!" she cried. "What are you doing here?"

The child rasped, "I'm not. Dying. In that place."

Close up, Romeo could see it wasn't a child at all, but a withered old man. The black man—evidently his nurse—carried him to the bed and laid him down.

Said Wynetta, "He checked out of the hospital?"

"Marcus? What do they. Call it?"

"AMA," said the black man. "Against medical advice."

"That's," said the old man, "me."

Wynetta said, "You gotta go back, Daddy. I'm supposed to go to Tifton today. With Jesse."

"Well. Good."

"But I can't just leave you."

"You can."

"You're too sick!"

"I'm fit. As. A fiddle. Except for the. Dying." He gave Romeo a wink. "Son. What's your name?"

"Romeo."

"Mine's. Claude. Santos. Pleased. To meet you."

Lifting his hand from the bed. Romeo held it a moment, then stepped away when the nurse came back in with his IV setup. The man had a deft touch. He coasted his thumb along Claude's wrist till he found a tender spot, then slid home the catheter tip. Claude never winced but was stoic throughout. Nor did he rebuke his daughter for her whining.

She said, "Dad, what are we gonna *do*?"

He replied mildly, "How about. Tennis?"

"Come on, Daddy. Be *responsible*."

"OK. I'll chop. Firewood. I'll clean. The gutters."

His grin was toothless but went from ear to ear.

He asked Romeo, "Is that really. Your name?"

The sudden fixity of his gaze made Romeo blush. "Well, my mama knew what a lover I'd be."

"Ha! You're Italian?"

"Half. I'm Polish on my dad's side."

Said Claude, "I'm Portuguese."

Romeo smiled.

Claude said, "My grandfather. Came here. For the fishing. First to Darien. Then Brunswick. He had. Shrimp boats. Him and my uncles."

"Did you work on the boats?"

"Oh yes. My grandfather. Would stand. On the dock. And say, '*Galo pequeno. Quem o ama? O pescador. Idoso. Ama-o!*'"

"What does that mean?"

"It means. 'Little Rooster! Who loves you? The old. Fisherman loves you!'"

Wynetta whined, "Daddy, I gotta take you back to the hospital."

"He carried. A netting needle. Made from bone. In his pocket."

"Could you say it again?" said Romeo.

"Say what?"

"What he told you."

"Oh." Claude tucked his chin down and cocked his elbows. "*Galo pequeno! Quem o ama? O pescador. Idoso. Ama-o!*" He was a childlike wraith posing as an old fisherman posing as a roosterish kid. This pierced Romeo.

"Could you say it again?"

But Wynetta had had enough. "I'm taking you back, Daddy."

Said Claude, "No, no."

"I *got* to."

"This. Is where I'm. Dying. Right here."

Romeo saw that it was time to go. He had no business here. "Well I guess I got things to do. Nice to meet you though. Both of you."

He went out into the blazing day, got in the Tercel and drove off—and then the Brunswick stench hit him. Gone, instantly, was 'The old fisherman loves you.' He shifted forward in his seat and set his face grimly and drove back into the city of Brunswick without seeing anything.

Tara poured the Madeira while Nell showed Shaw her toys: the singing buck, the trophy fish, the sunflower who dipped coquettishly toward the windowlight and sang, "On the Sunny Side of the Street."

Shaw laughed. "At last! Technology produces something useful! Where'd you get these, Nell?"

"Well, the buck I got at Wal-Mart's. I went to Dollar but they don't have 'em yet. You play poker, young man?"

"Sure."

"You play pot-limit seven stud? Or just that TV crap?"

He grinned. "I guess I play pot-limit seven stud."

She said, "We don't cotton to Tedious Hold'em around here. Where you go all-in on a pair of nines and cross your fingers and pray? There's more skill in Bingo. But if you're up for *poker* let's get to it."

Tara downed her Madeira right away, while she was still standing by the sink. Then she refilled her glass and set her face. Remember how much you love her. Think of nothing else.

She brought the glasses to the table. Shaw toasted Nell's cats. Nell told him all their names, and he toasted them again. Then he looked at Tara, and Tara told her first lie: "Shaw's an old friend of Daddy's."

"What, dear?" Nell was hauling the coin sacks off their shelf in the china closet, lugging them to the table.

"I said Shaw's an old friend of Dad's. He was just passing through and he called Dad, and the two of them went in on the jackpot tickets together."

Nell poured out a mound of coins, and started counting it. She told Shaw, "We like the feel of *money*. Chips are for sissies. Sell you twenty dollars' worth, that good?"

"Grandmother," said Tara, "you're not listening."

"I'm not?" She kept counting. "I'm sorry. What were you saying?"

"I'm saying Shaw paid for half of our jackpot tickets. The day we won."

"Oh. Well then, how come he doesn't get half the jackpot?"

"He does. That's what I'm trying to tell you. Are you listening?"

Finally Nell looked up. "You're saying what?"

Do not lower your eyes. "Shaw gets half of everything."

Nell's gaze narrowed. "Why didn't you tell me that before?"

"Because Dad didn't tell *us*. He was afraid Mom'd be mad."

"I *bet* she's mad. I bet she's screaming her head off."

"Well. She is. But fair is fair."

If it's to save her life, it's not really a lie.

"Well," said Nell, "if your mom ain't mad, I am. You're telling me we're only *half*-gazillionaires?" She turned to Shaw. "*You* get the rest?"

He said, "I'm sorry."

"You little punk. I already had that half-gazillion *spent*. I was gonna buy Brunswick—turn the whole town into my private putt-putt course. You like putt-putt golf? Wait, you gotta see my polar bear."

The bear was on top of her refrigerator. When Nell switched it on, it swung a golf club and sang, "It Don't Mean a Thing If It Ain't Got That Swing." Shaw chuckled. Nell exploded with laughter. Then she shuffled the cards and dealt out a hand.

"I'm winning it back right now," she announced. "All of it. Every penny you stole from us. How much was that again?"

Shaw coughed and murmured, "Um. Pre-tax? Something like. A hundred fifty-nine million?"

"Well, get ready to lose it."

She bluffed right out of the gate. Tara had an ace showing and another ace in the hole, so she stayed with Nell's bets for two more rounds, and even drew a third ace. But when Nell threw forty dollars into the pot, Tara figured her for a straight, and folded. Nell raked in. Shooting Tara a sharp critical look. Tara knew she was in trouble. She was playing too timidly. Was she playing so timidly that Nell would guess something was wrong?

Shaw said, "You ladies mind if *I* play a little bit here?"

Said Nell, "Not at all. I'm waiting for you. Every last penny." She slapped the deck down. "Your deal."

As he dealt, he started talking. He called the hands as they developed. "Jack, possible straight. Eights a pair. Oh, look, I got three diamonds showing. My flush is in plain view. Well, I might as well bet it big and hope you'll think I'm bluffing."

He threw in five dollars, and Nell folded and Tara did too, and he laughed and tried to bully the next hand as well. Nell caught him that time, and burned him. But he didn't back off. As the hands went by, he kept coming. Tara could see what he was up to. He was covering for her. While she regained her balance, he was distracting Nell, drawing her away from the truth—the way a bird draws predators from the nest. He kept guffawing and gesturing and holding forth: "Doesn't anybody notice I have two cowboys *showing*? I got a posse over here! You don't hear the thundering hooves?"

He lost twenty on that hand.

Nell dealt the next one. He complained, "Gimme

some *cards,* will you? Deal me something for once that isn't crap? Pardon my French."

Nell, on her third Madeira by now, said: "You take what you get! You get the three of spades!"

The two of them barking, baiting each other, laughing. Tara tried her best to laugh with them—which got a little easier as the Madeira flowed. She started to relax a little.

Then Shaw leaned toward her, pretending to look at her cards, and she snapped, "You cheater!"—and this came out sounding playful.

She noticed that Nell was eyeing her and Shaw. Checking out the chemistry.

As though there might be some kind of romance brewing.

And Tara realized she had found the perfect mask. If she were sweet on Shaw it would explain everything. Her nerves, her stilted laughter, the mousiness of her game. Everything could be chalked up to a new and sticky-sweet infatuation. So on the very next hand, when Shaw was about to bet, Tara tapped his wrist and warned: "Go easy on yourself, cowboy," and made it look like an excuse to touch him—and Nell caught this. And grinned.

A few hands later, Nell went off to the back porch to

feed the cats, and Shaw said softly, "Tara. You're astonishing. You're perfect. You're going to save them all."

His little slant smile.

A sentiment flared up inside her then, which had the shape of a pillar. If it wasn't pride, she didn't know what it was. In an instant it was gone, vaporized by self-revulsion. But it had been there.

Nell came back in and sat and said, "Deal! Let's go!"

And now Tara raised the stakes. She bet thirty dollars on a hand that looked like a bust. Shaw cried, "You got nothun!" and raised her back, but with a kind of manic confidence Tara brought her face close to his and said, "I have an army of scorpions." And reraised—a hundred dollars.

Shaw folded. Nell hollered with delight. Shaw proposed a toast to Tara's *cojones,* and they all drank deep.

Romeo was parked up Egmont Street from Nell's house. His seat was tilted back so he could barely see over the dashboard, but still he had a clear view into the kitchen. The three of them so festive in there. Playing cards and drinking and throwing back their heads and laughing wildly. Meanwhile, in the Tercel, he sat there silently baking. For two hours, not moving except to brush flies away, to wipe the sweat off his face. At last the alarm in his phone went off. Time to check in. He pressed the number 7. He saw Shaw excuse himself from the kitchen table and come out onto Nell's little portico and lift the phone to his ear.

"You're being watched," said Romeo. And he could see, even from this far, how much this annoyed Shaw.

Shaw scanned the street till he spotted the Tercel. "What are you doing here? It's dangerous when you're this close to me! Why aren't you patrolling?"

"I can't."

"Why not?"

"The smell of this city is making me sick."

"What smell?"

"They say it's the pulp mill. But to me it's like everyone's dead. I think all these ranch houses and condos are filled with dead people. If they're not dead, how come the streets are so empty? How come Brunswick stinks so much?"

"Smells OK to me," said Shaw.

"Maybe you're just too drunk to smell it."

"I'm not drunk at all."

"Oh shit," said Romeo. "I been *watching* you get

drunk. What, are you trying to seduce them? That's what it looks like. All that drinking and joking and flirting."

"I'm trying to put them at ease."

"OK. Good plan. You be the charmer; I'll be the ghoul."

Romeo didn't know where that had come from. Lack of sleep probably. But Shaw cast him a long troubled stare. Forty yards between them, but still it felt Shaw was searching right into his eyes. Finally Shaw said softly, "Listen, Romeo, I know how hard this is. What you're doing is a lonely thing and I'm amazed how well you're doing it. But just, you got to know, I'm *with* you. You know? I'm with you every second. All we got to do is get to the end of this deal; then we put our money into the bank and retire and all the rest is play, OK? You know what I want to do? I want to go to Trinidad like we were planning on, and when we get there, we'll open a hospital for the poor. OK? Or an orphanage or something. I mean it. Just spread the fucking love wherever we go. And drink cuba libres and have a big swimming pool and bang all the pretty nurses and have a constant blast but one thing I promise you is I'll never forget your courage here this week. You know?"

"I guess."

"I told you I needed you, and you were there. And everything that's happened since comes from your courage. I'm not ever going to forget that. OK?"

"Sure. I mean you don't have to say this."

"You OK then?"

"Yeah."

"We just have to make it to the end of this."

After Shaw went inside, Romeo did another counter-clockwise turn around the city. Rt. 17 to Clio's. Up to Belle Point, where Shelby and Miriam lived with their kids. Then west on Chapel Crossing to Altama Avenue, to Poinsettia Circle, Vanessa and Henry's.

I told you I needed you and you were there.

In fifth grade, in Ohio, Romeo had heard about these kids who had gone under the Vandemark Bridge and with a Swiss Army knife had carved the letter D on their chests and rubbed gunpowder into the bloody wounds so the mark would never fade. No one knew what the D stood for. Romeo wasn't acquainted with any of these kids. He just knew he wanted to join that club.

All through the school year, he obsessed over it. Having that mark. Having blood brothers who would die for him, as he would happily die for them. Then one day he was on Hardy Street, walking home from school, and he saw the club's leader, alone, coming toward him. Romeo summoned up the courage to stop him. "Shaw?"

The guy squinted at him. "Yeah?" He had no idea who Romeo was. "What?"

This took place in front of Wendy's (at that time there had still been a Wendy's at the corner of Hardy and Pine). It was in October, and the wind was kicking up yellow and maroon leaves.

Say it, Romeo thought. But he couldn't. "Nothing."

Shaw started to walk away.

"Wait. I want to join. Can I join your club?"

Shaw turned. "What club? Who are you?"

"Your club. I'd be a good member."

"There's no club," said Shaw. "And if there was a club why would we want you?"

Romeo didn't have an answer. Nothing was in his head but the prayer that he wouldn't start crying while Shaw McBride was glaring at him.

Shaw walked away.

But a week or so later Romeo was walking up Adams Street after school and Shaw was waiting for him.

"So suppose there *was* a club. What would you be willing to do to get in?"

"Anything."

"*Anything*? Why?"

"I don't know," said Romeo.

"That's like, fucked," said Shaw, and again he walked away.

The next day, when Romeo came up Adams Street, Shaw and some other guys were there in a kind of huddle. They called Romeo over to them. He was scared but he went. They said, "Come with us."

They took him down below the Vandemark Bridge, for his initiation.

The initiation was this: you had to take a dump on a piece of cardboard and then rub it on your face like warpaint. Then go to the river and jump in, and stay under for thirty seconds. Then you'd be in the club.

Romeo did those things. He rubbed his own shit all over his face, and jumped in the icy water and stayed under for half a minute and came up choking. The boys were gone. His clothes had been cast into the water. He swam out for them, rescued them from the current, and dragged them ashore. He wrung them out and put them on. He was freezing and hyperventilating. But he knew the boys were hiding nearby, spying on him, and he kept himself from bawling as he climbed up to the bridge.

Next day in school was the first time that nobody called him 'Wherefore art Thou'. Instead everyone called him Shitface. Everyone except Shaw—Shaw didn't call him Shitface. Shaw didn't recognize his existence in any way.

Romeo spent the next few months thinking up ways to kill himself. But he never did cry in public, and never complained and never ratted anyone out, and endured his new name and the interminable passing of time until one day in December Mom came to Romeo's room and said, "A friend is here for you." And there was Shaw.

Mom made a fuss over him, offering cookies and lemonade and all, and Romeo was mortified. But finally she went away, and Shaw told him, "Hey, I'm sorry I was such an asshole back under the bridge. All that shit we did—it wasn't my idea."

Romeo shrugged. "It's OK."

"'Cause you were like a good soldier about it."

Romeo tried not to show any emotion.

Then Shaw said, "I need your help. Will you help me?"

There had been some kind of palace coup in the club. Shaw had been deposed. Romeo said he'd help in any way he could, and he accompanied Shaw to Hollow Park and they hid in the forsythia bushes waiting for the ringleader of the mutineers to come by. Shaw was perfectly still and patient. He didn't move for hours. Romeo was freezing. Once he tried to whisper something, but Shaw just raised his hand. They waited. Finally when it was nearly dark, the ringleader came by, and Shaw made a sign to Romeo and leaped out and started fighting the guy. Calling, "Romeo, help me!" But Romeo was scared, and he couldn't move.

But then the guy got Shaw into a headlock and Shaw howled with pain—and something changed in Romeo then. He just lit into the kid, his fists whirling: he was ferocious; he was a cyclone. It felt like he had left his body: that he was watching himself from afar. And then Shaw was holding the guy so Romeo could keep hitting him and kicking him, and the guy was bleeding and begging for mercy but Romeo wouldn't stop till Shaw dragged him off.

"Jesus!" said Shaw. "What're you, fuckin insane?"

But Shaw was laughing as he said this. He told the poor kid, "OK, kneel and beg my forgiveness or my guy will kill you right here."

The kid did what he was told. That was the end of the coup. Shaw got his power back. The gang came under his sway again.

And Romeo was granted full membership in the club. This time the rites were for real. In the presence of all the members—including the poor bruised-up mutineer—

Romeo incised a D into his own chest. The club's secret name was The Devourers, Shaw told him, reminding him that he'd be killed if he ever revealed that fact. After the cutting, Romeo's chest streamed with blood, and he had to rub gunpowder into the wound, which burned like a branding iron. The pain was annihilating, but still—this was far and away the best hour of his life.

Patsy was overwhelmed.

Her daughter was still out with that fiend. *The Real Housewives of Orange County* was on TV, a lot of squawking she couldn't follow. Her husband was at the little fake 'empire' desk in the corner, studying Scripture, studying so hard that drops of sweat were falling from his brow onto the Holy Book. Meanwhile Jase kept up that blaze of vengeance on his Micro, shriek after shriek, and when Patsy couldn't bear any of this for another moment she got up and went back to the bedroom and shut the door, and climbed into bed with her laptop.

For a while she tried to play internet *Tetris*. But she couldn't follow that either.

Outside it was getting dark, quick. Thunderstorm

GEORGE DAWES GREEN

coming. Where was Tara? Why weren't they back yet?
My little girl.

With that demon, my little girl!

If she could just find some way to get her mind off all
this.

She went to Google. Into the oblong box she typed:

mansions

She thought a moment. Then she added

malibu

It was wrong to be doing this, she knew. Here they all
were in peril of their lives—not just she and Mitch and
the kids, but her brother Shelby too, and her mother-in-
law, and others: who knew which of her family and
friends that monster had singled out? And Tara was out
with one of them right that minute! What was the
matter with her, that at a time like this she could be
thinking of California real estate?

But these *were* lovely cottages. And this browsing was
only to help her endure the terror. Letting her think
about the good times to come. When all of this would be
over. With property values in the toilet there were bound

to be genuine bargains out there. She could swoop in like a bird of prey and snatch a jewel.

She skated lightly through the listings.

What she found though, was dismaying. Everything was so unbelievably expensive.

For example, here was a nice 5-bedroom with a 2-car garage and "beach access just steps away." Modern, high ceilings, lots of glass. But the list was $18,000,000.00.

Eighteen million?

Wasn't the market supposed to have *tanked*? How could they be asking eighteen million and it's not even on the water? Eighteen million and she had to *hike to the damn beach*? Along some tourist path? Trudging with Mitch and his purple flipflops, and Whoopi and Barbara and Sting looking down on her and laughing, ha ha, look at those stinkbugs crawling in the sand!

No chance, Patsy thought. I won't be Whoopi's clown. Washed-up C-lister who's never funny anymore, giving *me* crap?

Well. She searched some more, and finally found a property right on the beach. Just above the pounding surf, and it had 4 bedrooms which at least was one more than she had now, so fine—they could have a guest now and then. And the place had been designed by some fancy architect. But it looked like a lean-to. Like a glorified concession stand. Look at it! Squeezed in between the neighbors on either side, and the asking price was $22,500,000.

-Twenty-two point five *million*? For a 4-bedroom hot dog shack?

Were they kidding?

Or here—an empty two-acre lot. Right on the beach, but with the Pacific Coast Highway running right behind it, and what was that warehouse-looking building across the highway? A discount furniture store? And they want $19 million? For two acres of sand?

It was beginning to dawn on her that she didn't have all the money in the world.

She wished she hadn't started with this.

She wondered how much wealth she really did have. Starting with that lump-sum-vs.-annuity scam, which meant that her so-called $318-million jackpot was baloney to begin with. Then subtract taxes, then subtract Shaw's 50% cut, what was she left with? Less than $65 million. And she was supposed to spend half of that on a pathetic snack bar on the beach?

Of course, she didn't *have* to live in Malibu. If she didn't mind living away from the beach, up in the hills somewhere, maybe she could find herself something really swank for twenty million. If she didn't mind having dentists and tax attorneys for pals. Instead of Mel and Goldie and Matthew McConaughey.

OK, fine then; I'll go live in the sticks.

But of course, whatever she got, she'd have to refurbish and redecorate. That, she knew, would run her another five million or so, minimum. So now she was down to thirty million odd, the interest on which would bring in . . . two million a year? Million and a half after taxes? She could already feel the squeeze here. Because what about the housekeeper? And a chef and gardeners and maids and security? All that would run a couple of million per year at least. And she didn't require the fanciest yacht in the world but if she wanted to entertain on the ocean at all, that meant at least a half-million-dollar boat, and God only knew how much to staff it. And couture wasn't cheap. And private schools and club memberships and spas and a nanny . . .

She got up and went to the kitchen to fix herself a g&t. Going easy on the gin because it was early. Though she did allow herself one little dollop because all this was so incredibly sad. For one moment she had been truly rich. For an instant. Before that bastard had come into their lives. If it hadn't been for him she'd have twice as much now. A hundred and twenty million, and then yes, she could have afforded a decent spread. A nice place, forty million or so, in a friendly seaside neighborhood, where she could've had Nancy Reagan over for tea and had some silver to serve it on. And she could have thrown a few bucks at one of Nancy's charities, to make her smile. "Oh, sweetie, I almost forgot. Little something for the stem cells." Nancy saying: "Oh! I *wish* Ronnie were here right now." Then a quick hug—very gentle of course—and the poor old widow weeping softly in Patsy's arms.

She could have had a horse in the Derby! And a fun little jet to fly her out to Lexington, to watch it run. Would've been all right. And yesterday, she had had all that! That had been her life!

Her fury running away with her. She polished off the gin in a single swallow, and got up to fix herself another. Goddamn the bastards! May they burn in hell! And they would, she thought. Because if they ever tried to leave Brunswick, to enjoy their loot, she'd bring the FBI down on them like a hive of hornets. The FBI would put so many holes in them, their own mothers wouldn't want what was left.

Romeo was starting to feel a little better. He even thought he might be able to hold something down, so he drove to the Burger King drive-thru on Altama. But then when he looked up at the big sparkling menu board, he realized he wasn't feeling *that* much better. Not a single item he wouldn't have instantly upchucked. So he drove away—sailing past the pickup window, with the counter girl scowling at him as if driving thru without making a purchase was some heinous crime against humanity. He took a left, and took Habersham to Poinsettia Circle, to Vanessa and Henry's house.

Vanessa was Nell's niece. She was an artist who painted pastel seascapes—this Romeo knew from her web page, where there was also a picture of her wearing some kind of fancy South American blouse. Her husband Henry was black and debonair, and worked for Glynn County—something about delinquent youths. Romeo parked across from their sweet little house, and waited, and after a while Henry came out in a seersucker jacket and got into his car and drove away.

Romeo went the other way. Headed downtown.

OK. Here's how I could do it. Knock at the kitchen door. Vanessa answers, I say I'm from PETA. She'll be all sympathetic, and as she opens the door I raise the pistol and shoot her in the face. Right? Though she probably won't die right away but she'll scream and blood will come hurling out of her head, and I can't.

He looped past Alfred's house, and then Nell's, and came back to Gloucester Street. He took a right. The speed limit was 25 mph. He did not exceed it. He wanted to go even slower; to trawl along at bicycle or milkwagon speed. But that would have drawn too much attention. So he went at exactly the limit, and the sepulchral city opened up slowly on either side of him. When he crossed Lee Street and saw a shop that advertised Antique Maps, Firearms, and Swords, he pulled in.

As a coldblooded killer, as an angel of vengeance or dark servant or whatever, he should have been turned on by a place like this.

The store's proprietor had a face like a battered satellite dish. He seemed to be receiving signals this very moment. He let Romeo alone to wander amidst the merchandise, to run his gaze along the edges of the knives, to ponder the rows and rows of dull-witted bullets. It all seemed cold, harsh, repellent. But there was one item that did catch his eye: a broken cavalry saber up on the wall. He liked it *because* it was broken. It had an air of fallen nobility. He studied it from afar, until the proprietor surfaced from his deep-space communion and said, "Revolutionary War. French-made, Solingen steel, but it's got the American double eagle. I guess Lafayette might have brought it over here, or one of his men. You wanna see it?"

"Please."

The proprietor brought it down and let him handle it.

"How much?" said Romeo.

"Well, if it weren't broken, ten thousand. At least. But as it is, thirty-eight hundred. Which would include the scabbard."

Would it be easier to kill with this than with the .22? Oh, much. A touch of rakish glamor, he thought—that might give him some confidence. Also, knowing that the moment of truth wouldn't be so distant and hollow. That might help. So if he hadn't yet maxed out his MasterCard . . .

The card went through.

Romeo took the saber out to the Tercel and built a nest for it, from newspapers and T-shirts, in the trunk.

Then he drove on. But this time the stench returned quickly, bullyingly, and he realized: it was here. In this car. Not in the city; not in the air; but *in this car.* There had been no foul odor in that antique shop. It was either in the car or in his brain. He crossed Rt. 17 and pulled into a little park on the marsh. He was the only one there. He got out and walked away from the Tercel. He followed a wood plank walkway into the marsh. It ended at the bank of a creek, and he stood there, looking at seagulls. A small hot breeze was in his face. He took a deep breath.

Nothing really stank here. There was a mud smell, a vague brininess. That was all.

But when he went back to the Tercel, the stench walloped him again.

He opened the door, got down on his haunches and felt under the seats. Old coffee cups, toll receipts, Subway wrappers. A years-old road map for *Cincinnati Including Southwestern Ohio*. But nothing to generate this kind of odor.

He squatted there, trying to puzzle this out.

Then he got up and slowly circled the car. Sniffing as he went. He bent low and sniffed again.

He lay down on the ground. Now he was shaded from the swollen sun by the Tercel's bumper, but the asphalt was as hot as an oven rack.

He squirmed under the chassis, on his back.

Directly above him, staring down at him, was an animal, wedged into the wheel well. No telling what species it was. The gases of decomposition had swollen its eyes halfway out of their sockets, which gave it a look of fury, of a bottled-up avenging hatred looking for release. It held up its bony forelimbs: the claws were out, ready to kill. Oh Jesus, and Shaw thought it had come to bring us *luck*. But all this time, it had been riding along down there, radiating resentment and foulness and putrefaction. Who knows how it managed to get stuck up there? Must have jumped at the wrong moment, or the wheel had kicked it up and it had snagged on something. And probably had lived for a while. Maybe survived the whole journey, all the way down here to Georgia, watching the highway passing underneath, the broken white line, the merciless unraveling of everything it had ever fucking cared about.

He tried to keep meeting the animal's eyes, but the odor was asphyxiating him. Maggots were seething up there, and bits of loose gravel dug into his back. He'd had enough. He slithered out and lay there in the sun, gasping for breath.

He drove to a self-service car wash just off the Altama Connector. He used the long nozzle of the soap squirter to dig the creature out of the wheel well. The bulk of the carcass fell to the concrete in one piece, with a soft thud. One side of the animal was concave and perfectly smooth—maybe at some point it had been pushing up against the wheel? He coaxed it into a black plastic trash bag which he tied shut, then used the hose to blast away the vestiges, and then, since he was there anyway, he decided to clean the rest of the Tercel—clean it thoroughly, inside and out. With soap and hot wax and finally the vacuum. At the end of his labors, the car still looked like an old beat-up lunchbox, but now it was a shiny old beat-up lunchbox.

He went to Ace and bought a collapsible spade, and took a lap around his patrol route, hunting for a good spot to bury this poor soul, some place with a clear view of marshes and stars and the moon.

Burris, the old cop, finally gave in. He'd been fighting the desire all day, but at last he surrendered and drove past Nell's bungalow, just to get a glimpse of her.

He looked through her kitchen window and there she was, feeding her cats. She seemed so at home that it occurred to him maybe she wouldn't leave Brunswick after all. Despite the windfall. Really, you think about it, why should she? Her whole life is here. She's not going to just uproot herself and go dancing off to France, that wouldn't be like her at all.

Which led him to a surprising and happy thought. Maybe the jackpot would even work in his favor.

Because after the phonies and the scavengers start to cluster around, wouldn't she come to appreciate the one guy who had always cared for her? The one guy she could trust? And then, the money that he had made or hadn't made, or his rank in the police department, or whether he was slow-witted or not, or bald and jowly or not: all that wouldn't matter so much, would it?

If Nell could just hear what her heart was telling her.

At Rt. 17 he turned north. Pursuing his usual counter-clockwise patrol route around the city. The sunlight faltered, and he glanced up and saw a bank of black storm-cloud coming from the west. Its shadow rolling over the marsh. He thought, well, we could use some rain here. He took a right onto Riverside Road, which was a long cause-way that wound through the marsh toward an enclave of wealthy houses. Some of the city commissioners lived out here, so no amount of patrolling was too much.

A brown Toyota Tercel was parked on the shoulder, in the grass—'91 or '92. The tag said Ohio. The driver, a white male, was taking a black garbage bag from the trunk.

Burris pulled up behind. The driver had a slight build, dark hair. He was somewhat meek of posture. But he had a friendly face.

Burris told the radio, "43, dispatch?"

Rose, sounding bored as usual, probably painting her nails, said, "Go ahead, 43."

"Out on Riverside past the first curve. Gimme a 29 on a '91 or '92 Tercel, Ohio tag JBX-681?"

The driver was waiting patiently, holding that bag. Burris didn't feel he needed the tag run, so he got out of the cruiser and approached the man and said, "Good afternoon."

"Good afternoon."

"Can I ask what you got there?"

"Animal I found."

"A live animal?"

"Uh-uh. I found it up in my wheel well. I want to bury it."

"Sir, may I see your license and proof of insurance?"

The driver took out his wallet and handed over the license. Funny name. Burris puzzled over it while the guy went to the glove compartment and fished for his insurance card. When he came back, Burris asked "Sir, how do you pronounce your last name?"

"Zuh-DER-ko."

"First name Romeo?"

"Mama knew what a lover I'd be."

Sounded like a joke, though Burris didn't get it. "And your current address is Piqua, Ohio?"

"Yes."

"And what brings you here to Brunswick?"

"Um. Vacation."

Burris took the documents back to the cruiser and called Rose again, who told him the Tercel was registered in Zderko's name. He had her run a 27 on the OLN. Came back clean. No warrants. Everything good. He returned the papers to Zderko, and said, "Sir, may I see the animal?"

"Sure. But it'll be, well, when I open this bag, the smell will be powerful, OK? Just warning you."

"I'll try to be ready."

"All right then."

Zderko undid the tie.

Burris looked in and saw a lump of fur and cartilage and bones. The smell slapped him across the face, and brought tears to his eyes. "Whoa."

"Yeah."

"That's *ripe*."

"That's what I been living with."

"You can close it now."

Zderko retied the bag.

Burris asked, "How long's it been dead?"

"About forty-eight hours. What's today, Friday? Well, Wednesday night, I was coming down through North

Carolina? And I hit this thing and it must have been thrown up into the wheel well somehow, but I didn't even know it till a little while ago."

"I see."

"But I smelled it, you know? I mean, God. It happens quick, doesn't it?"

"Sir?"

"I mean the way things rot."

"Yes sir."

"But I didn't know what I was smelling till I looked up in there."

"You're planning to bury it, sir?"

"Uh-huh."

"Where?"

"Just, I don't know. Here, I guess."

"Not a good idea."

"Is it illegal?"

"Unless you got permission from the owner."

"Who's the owner?"

"Hercules, Incorporated. That big chemical plant down the way?"

"Oh. OK. So what can I do with this thing?"

"Well."

It was a good question.

Zderko pressed. "I mean, you're saying I could just

throw it away, that'd be OK, but it's against the law to treat it with any kind of dignity?"

Burris mulled this. "No sir, I'm not saying you can't treat it with dignity. You could treat it with all the dignity you want and that'd be fine, but you can't trespass here, because this land belongs to Hercules, Incorporated."

A flock of grackles went by, racing for cover from the storm.

Said Zderko, "I can't afford to buy a cemetery plot."

"I understand."

"I was just trying to do right by this animal."

"I see that."

"It sucks that it got carried all the way down here where it's a complete stranger, far away from its home, and now I just toss it in a dumpster or something. You know?"

Then Burris surprised himself. He said, "Sir, you see that little stick with the strip of yellow tape? Everything beyond that stick belongs to the city of Brunswick. I'm not saying you're allowed to bury anything out there. I *am* saying, whatever you do, don't leave no plastic bag behind." He glanced up at the sky. "And you better hurry. You hear me?"

"Yes sir. Thank you sir."

"All right."

It was like nothing Burris had ever done before. It was: I really give not a damn what you do with that sack of rotted meat, provided you do it when I'm not around.

He got back into the cruiser and drove away. Glad that he hadn't been too by-the-book there. If what's called for is a little tolerance, a little understanding, why not give that? It made him wonder, have I finally found the secret to being a successful cop? Mercy, maybe I have. Forty years too late though.

Mitch was reading the Psalms:

Mine eye is consumed because of grief; it waxeth old because of all mine enemies. Why standest thou afar off, O LORD? why hidest thou thyself in times of trouble?

He heard Patsy weeping in the kitchen. He thought of going to comfort her, but the rhythm of her sobs told him she was drunk, and what could he say to her anyway? Hell had come into their lives.

Consider mine enemies; for they are many; and they hate me with cruel hatred.

He thought, we have to stand up to him. Now. Now's the time to call the police. Is the bastard so arrogant and cocksure and self-deluded that he thinks I'll just sit here while he goes off to a poker party with my daughter and my own mother, while he threatens the lives of my family, while he steals half my fortune? Oh Lord. It'd be so easy to nab him. One phone call. Call that old cop Burris Jones who goes to our church. Or maybe Burris isn't the best choice since he seems kind of slow and dreamy and sad— but *any* cop. Just lay out the whole story. Tell them to grab Shaw right after he takes one of those check-in calls. Then they'll have plenty of time to look for that 'Romeo' guy. Probably his car's got Ohio plates, so they'll find him easy—but even if they don't, we can round up all my family and friends and put them under 24-hour protection and then what could the guy do to us?

O my God, make them like a wheel; as the stubble before the wind. As the fire burneth a wood, and as the flame setteth the mountains on fire; So persecute them with thy tempest, and make them afraid with thy storm.

Not that they'd really carry through on those threats anyway. It was all a bluff. This whole deal was just two smartass kids thinking they'd found themselves a pot of gold, except they weren't professionals and they didn't know what they were in for. When Mitch stood up to them, the wind would be at his back.

Let them be as chaff before the wind: and let the angel of the LORD chase them. Let their way be dark and slippery: and let the angel of the LORD persecute them.

He heard the sound of a car pulling up outside. A moment later, Shaw and Tara came in, loudly. They were drunk. Shaw declaring, "We took a taxi. Nobody in no condition to drive. God. Mitch, your mother fleeced us. Didn't she, Tara?"

"She fleeced *you*," said Tara—and Mitch thought he detected coquettishness in her tone. Ah, God. My daughter is *flirting* with him? Son of a bitch.

Break their teeth, O God, in their mouth: break out the great teeth of the young lions, O LORD.

Tara went into the kitchen to find her mother. While Shaw came over to the desk. "What you up to there, Mitch?"

"Nothing."

"Reading Scripture? I'm impressed. Hey, did the lottery folks call? Have they scheduled the press conference yet?"

"Tomorrow. Eleven o'clock."

"God. Great. That should be a blast."

The bastard kept standing there, while Mitch read:

Consume them in wrath! Consume them, that they may not be! And let them know that God ruleth in Jacob unto the ends of the earth!

Tara came back from the kitchen. "Mom wants to know, you want red or white wine with your supper?"

Shaw laughed. "Tell your mother she's not getting me drunk. That's the classic mistake of two-bit crooks."

"Seems like one you've already made."

"Oh, well then, if the horse is out of the barn, I'll take red." He grinned. And asked Mitch, "Hey, did I tell you your mother took us to the *cleaners*?"

Mitch nodded.

"That's the King James, right? You prefer the King James?"

Mitch shrugged. "I guess."

"How come?"

"Just the one I've always used."

"I know what you mean," said Shaw. "Same with me, I like the old ways best. All the beauty is in the old ways."

Be not thou far from me, O LORD. O my strength! Haste thee to help me!

Romeo only had time to kick some oyster shells and mud over the carcass before it started to rain. Fat teary drops that chased him back to the Tercel. He got behind the driver's seat just as a storm began to unpack itself all around him. Lightning on all sides. He turned up Worms of Wisdom, which boomed around in the car while the thunder clattered outside. The wipers worked like oars, and he seemed to be floating. He took the Rt. 25 spur to Cap'n D's. He pulled into the parking lot, and there he stopped and changed his shirt. Then rolled down the window, made a cup of his hand, and caught rainwater, which he slapped all over his face. He got his razor from his duffel and shaved. There was no soap, and the only light was the grisly light of the thunderstorm, but when he checked his work in the rearview mirror, he thought he'd done OK.

As soon as the storm abated a little, he made a dash for the restaurant door. He had a dinner of stuffed flounder and fried oysters, which was delicious. As he ate he thought, if Shaw says the scheme is in good shape, maybe it is. He *is* a visionary. He seems to have these folks all figured out. It's true that sheer audacity often wins the day. Maybe I won't have to murder anyone.

After his meal, he drove over to the mall and bought a T-shirt for his mother. She had wanted a Florida T-shirt, but now it seemed unlikely he'd ever get to Florida, so he bought one that said *The Golden Isles of Georgia*. It had a palm tree, a sand dollar, and a pirate. Next he went to Hermann's Candle Shoppe and bought a gift for Claude. Then he went to Camelot Music and got an album by the band Drive Fast & Shut Your Eyes—just to find out what kind of music Clio liked. It turned out to be all sparkly harmonic syrup. He played it as he made another circuit of the city. He couldn't stand it, but he played it through dutifully, while he visited, one by one, the stations of his patrol.

I should *try* to appreciate this gooey shit.

Shaw would love it.

After the rain, the air was full of earth-smells. The

light came down a thin, unstable gold, and somebody's straw hat was lying in the road. He decided to go by Blackbeard's Motel and see if the missionary girls wanted to come out. He could take them drinking on St. Simon's Island. Maybe I can even spring for dinner, he thought. Since now I'm such a wealthy tycoon.

Just then, by an odd stroke of fortune, he passed Clio's little Miata coming the other way. He saw her sitting behind the wheel, with that last bit of sunlight in her hair: the loveliest thing he'd ever seen.

Clio went up Norwich Street to Shambol's Tattoo, but Shambol had another customer so Clio had to wait in the front room. She sat there staring at the bongs and hookahs and CleanTest Powdered-Urine Kits, and she thought about Tara's betrayal. Clio had left Tara three voice messages and two text messages and a couple of emails, but only silence had come in return. Tara had made her choice. Tara's choice was goodbye. Her choice was to forsake her former best friend who could *disappear* for all Tara cared. Go off and die, just crawl to any corner of the frikkin Wick and die.

But would she really just drop me? *Tara?* She can't. She's not ignoring me. She's just busy, for God's sake. She loves me and I just have to be patient, not be so frikkin paranoid and crazy . . .

Then a strange guy came into the shop.

Shambol came out and told him he'd have to wait, and the guy said that'd be fine. He sat. He had large eyes like some kind of nocturnal animal. He sat there checking everything out, everything but Clio—he avoided looking at her. Finally though, she heard him suck in some air and then:

"Hi."

Oh God. Please don't frikkin try to talk to me.

Again, "Hi."

All nervous and enthused. Don't give him the least flicker of attention.

"You getting a tattoo?" he asked her.

What a stupid-ass question.

He said, "I'm getting one too. What tattoo you gonna get?"

"You know what, I'm really not in the mood for conversation."

"Oh. OK."

But ten seconds later he started in again: "Mine's going right here. Right above my ankle. It's gonna say, What's the damage?"

It took a moment for that to hit home.

She turned. "Did you say, What's the damage?"

"Uh-huh."

"You mean from the song?"

"Yeah," he said. "You know it?"

"The Drive Fast & Shut Your Eyes song?"

He grinned, and recited: "What's the damage? What's the cost?"

She said back, "Is there anything I haven't lost?"

He laughed. "You know our music!"

"*Our* music?"

"I'm their road manager."

"You're the road manager for Drive Fast & Shut Your Eyes?"

"Uh-huh. Though Truck's been such an asshole lately I probably can't do it much longer."

"You know *Truck*?"

He shrugged. "Well, I mean, we're not *that* big."

"You're *huge*. I went to your concert in Savannah!"

"Really?"

"Dude! It was so fucking awesome!"

"Cool," he said.

But then he got up and went to the counter and started leafing through *Prick* magazine, looking at the tattoos. Like he was completely done with her. She worried she'd come on too strong about her love for the band. Had she scared him away? When he'd said "Cool," was he mocking her somehow? This guy was friends with Truck Martin, and she'd weirded him out! What a loser she was!

But then he came back. "Hey, you know where that line comes from? 'What's the damage?'"

She shook her head.

"From when we were in Tallahassee and we were in this, like, diner or something, and we started throwing glasses and plates and breaking shit, oh my god, and the waitress comes in, and she's like, oh shit! Like, it looked like a bomb had gone off in there. And Truck was like: 'So what's the damage?'"

Clio beamed. "You were there?"

"Like if you're alive at all, there's *gonna* be damages."

"True that," she said.

They sat quietly.

Then she asked him, "What's your name?"

"Romeo."

She smiled.

He said, "Mama knew what a lover I'd be." But rolled his eyes to show he knew what a cheesy line that was. She thought, no guy in Brunswick would *ever* be named Romeo.

He said, "So will you tell me now?"

"Tell you what?"

"What tattoo you're getting?"

"Oh," she said. "The number thirty."

"Why thirty?"

"'Cause my best friend is selling me out for like thirty pieces of silver."

He was staring at her again. But now she didn't mind. Now she allowed herself to look back at him, and saw that his eyes were compassionate and forgiving. And so what if he does see me crying? And so what if I pour out my shame and my secrets to a total stranger, why not? Got to talk to somebody.

Romeo listened passionately and Clio told him the whole story: how Tara had abandoned her now that she was so rich, how she wouldn't even return Clio's phone calls, how the bottom had fallen out of Clio's life. It tore him up. He wanted to say something reassuring. But since he and Shaw were the root cause of her torment, reassuring her would be kind of sick, wouldn't it? He wound up saying nothing, just listening.

Then some big ox came in, biker dude with braided beard and no shirt, and across his chest a mural of tattoos depicting the Saga of Lynyrd Skynyrd. On his left shoulder, the badass eponymous gym teacher; all around his right nipple, the fiery plane crash. It turned out this dude knew Clio, from when she'd been a waitress at Southern Soul Barbeque on the island. He started telling her about something called Bike Week—going on and on about his misadventures, and Romeo thinking why don't you shut up, can't you see what she's going through? Why don't you shut up and go put a fucking shirt on? But he kept rumbling on till finally she arose and pleaded, "I gotta go. I guess I don't want that tattoo after all." Struggling not to cry. She said to Romeo, "Hey call me, OK?" and wrote down her number for him, and went out to her car.

The Lynyrd Skynyrd dude watched her go, and whistled softly and said, "Mm-*mm*. Look at the shitter on that critter."

Then he asked Romeo, "Yaw gettin a tattoo?"

What a lame-ass question, thought Romeo. Abruptly he got up and went out after Clio, but she'd already driven off.

He had her number though, and he might have called her right then. But he thought, no, too soon. Might look creepy. Would *be* creepy. My calling her. Ever. While I'm doing this to her best friend's family? No.

He got back in the Tercel, but didn't know where to go. The notion of patrolling seemed too crushing right now. So he went by Blackbeard's Motel, looking for the missionary girls. But the beady-eyed old buzzard at the desk said they'd checked out. So then he just drove around till he found a bar: the Oleander Inn near the mall. Bland as death. The décor of an airport lounge. Three big flatscreen TVs, with the sound killed on all of them. The customers looked like stranded travelers but were, in fact, locals. When one of them got up to stagger out, the others said, "See ya, Lloyd," and, "Take care, Lloyd," and "Next time, Lloyd." Then they all reclaimed their comas.

Romeo moved on. He went to Balm-of-Gilead Road, to visit Wynetta and old Claude. Wynetta's truck wasn't there though. Had she taken her father back to the hospital?

Was he dead *already*? Shit, thought Romeo, don't let him be dead.

Then he saw that the TV was on.

He went up to the door and knocked, and heard, "Come in."

He opened the door. Claude was lying there naked as a soupbone. "My daughter. Is not. Here."

"Oh. OK. Where is she?"

Ghost of a shrug.

"You all right here, Claude?"

"Never been. Better."

Claude's eyes were not rigorously beholden to each other. Where one went the other would follow, but at its own stately pace.

"Come in," he said. "What's? Your name again?"

"Romeo."

"Oh. How could I. Forget? I'm watching TV. Get yourself. A beer."

Romeo got a PBR from the fridge and sat in the motel-style chair beside the bed. Claude was watching an episode of *The Honeymooners*, and Romeo watched it with him. Took him a while to focus, but once he did he thought it one of the best programs he'd ever seen. The story concerned the purchase of a vacuum cleaner. Ralph Kramden had bought an old secondhand vacuum cleaner for his wife Alice, and of course right away it broke down. His friend Norton offered to fix it. *Did* fix it—but it sprang to life so suddenly that it nearly pulled Ralph's tongue out. Romeo couldn't remember when he had laughed so hard. The tongue part was hilarious—but the funniest thing, and the saddest, was the shame that Ralph felt for buying his wife a secondhand vacuum cleaner.

Claude liked the show too—his laughter emerging in a slow pant. But during commercials he would lift his eyes to the pictures of his wife on the wall.

Romeo asked, "Does that bag need changing?"

"Oh. Don't. Trouble yourself."

It was no trouble. Romeo had tended his father's IV when the old man was dying from testicular cancer. To attach the new bag of morphine took only a minute. Then together they watched the end of the show. An election at the Raccoon Lodge: Ralph was in the running, but lost by one vote. He was certain it was Norton's disloyalty that had sunk his candidacy, but he was wrong: Norton had been faithful all along. When this faithfulness was revealed to Ralph, there was no laughter from Romeo and Claude. They were both on the verge of tears. Loyalty, loyalty to a friend in the face of adversity: this was the great thing.

The credits rolled. Claude said he'd seen enough TV, and Romeo shut it off.

Sitting in silence, listening to the old man's breathing.

Then Romeo asked, "You really dying?"

"So they. Tell me."

"You in pain?"

His rubbery grin. "Well. Keep that bag. Full."

"You want a beer?"

"I can't. Swallow so well. But you. Have another."

"Water?"

"Well. Just to. Wet. My whistle."

Romeo filled a cup at the sink, and held it before the old man's lips. A tongue appeared, shyly. The dragon lady bathes alone. Romeo looked away till Claude was finished, then rinsed the cup and took his seat again.

Claude said, "You're not. From Brunswick. Are you, son?"

"Ohio."

"May I ask. Why you're here?"

"Oh, just a business deal. Me and my buddy."

"Oh."

"Well actually, it's *his* deal. I'm just like, here if needed."

"I see."

They sat a while. Then Romeo said, "Can I tell you a story?"

"Sure."

"One time there was this dude, this grad student from OSU? And he got on my buddy's nerves. We were working at this tech place, my buddy and me, and one night we met this guy, and he was such an arrogant asshole, but our friend Amber really liked him. And Shaw got pissed off at the guy, and they had a quarrel. And later Shaw asked me would I help with what he wanted to do. And, you know, he's my buddy, you know?"

"Yes," said Claude.

"What he wanted to do was break into the shitstain's apartment and put a little nest of vipers into his computer, you know? So I did it. So then Shaw could read all his emails, and know everywhere he surfed, and fuck him in every which way possible. You know? I mean we owned this poor guy."

Claude nodded. He looked uncomfortable.

"I mean, I can't tell you I didn't have fun, because it was OK, because I was doing this with Shaw. We intercepted the emails the guy sent out and changed them just a little to make them sort of insulting. We got him fired from his job, and we made the dean of his college think he was like a psycho child molester, and we made Amber come to hate the sucker. And I said to Shaw, 'This is enough, right?' But Shaw said, 'Are you with me or not? We're going all the way.' So we did. We went all the way with that shitstain."

The old man said, "How far. Was that?"

"Oh God," said Romeo. "I mean *all* the fuckin way. And now Shaw's got me on a similar ride. And I'm scared. I don't want to do this shit."

But Claude's distress was evident, which made Romeo feel awful. He wished he'd never started this story.

The silence grew oppressive.

Romeo said, "Tell me again what your grandfather said. OK? About the old rooster?"

But Claude had fallen asleep.

Romeo settled the blanket around the old man's shoulders, and patted his head like an infant, and went outside. He leaned against the hood of the Tercel. He thought he could still hear the rhythm of Claude's breathing, and he listened to that for a while, comforted—until he realized that all he was hearing was the heave of the a.c. condenser.

Then his alarm buzzed: it was time to make his check-in call.

Shaw took the call outside, on the deck. He murmured, "Hey, how's it going?"

"Good," said Romeo.

"There's a press conference in the morning. Eleven o'clock, at the Plantation House Inn. That pimped-out sleazy dump on Gloucester? You know the one I'm talking about? Right off 17?"

"Wait. A press conference?"

Shaw could hear his fear. "Uh-huh. You win the jack-pot, you have to do a press conference."

"With cameras and shit? And you're going?"

"Of course. Why not?"

"Why not?" Romeo sounded stunned.

Shaw softened his voice, brought it down close to a purr, and said, "It'll be good for us." That was how you had to talk to Romeo. You had to cosset and coddle him, and tell him you understood his fearfulness, and never let him see how much it pissed you off. "This is the way we've got to do this, Romeo. Everything out in the open. No secrets, no skulking around. You know?"

"I think it's insane," said Romeo. "Who's going?"

"Everybody."

"The whole family?"

"So I'm told."

"Cousin Alfred? Vanessa and Henry?"

"I guess."

"Shelby and Miriam and the kids?"

"So I'm told."

"What about their friends? They're coming too?"

"Uh-huh."

"Then who've I got?" said Romeo. "If everybody's at that press conference and the place is filled with pork, I can't touch any of 'em. Who's our hostage? Who've I got?"

"You've got Nell. Nell doesn't care for crowds, so she won't be coming."

"Just Nell?"

"That's all we need."

"Shaw, they'll fuck us!" Sounding panicky.

"No they won't," Shaw murmured. "We're fine. The Boatwrights are fine. They're making their adjustments. They don't want trouble, Romeo. And I've got a little surprise planned for this event which'll be beautiful. You need to trust me on this one."

"What am *I* supposed to do?"

"Just keep close to Nell. And don't worry so much. Have some faith."

SATURDAY

Romeo, early in the morning, went to Trudy's Café and got himself a fried-egg sandwich.

The place was brimful of pork. One big booth against the wall was nothing but bacon. Even that paunchy old cop was here—the one who had confronted him yesterday about the burial. Looking kind of hang-dog though. Sitting there all by himself, while the cops at the big booth were joking and laughing with each other. Romeo thought of going over and joining the poor guy, but didn't. Talk to a cop? Shaw would have a fit.

Instead he got his egg sandwich to go and drove to Nell's house. He parked a hundred yards down Egmont Street, tilted his seat back, and tuned to WICK 103.9. Hoping for news of the upcoming press conference. What he got was a steady stream of treacle: "Ebony and Ivory." "You Light Up My Life." *"Sometimes when we touch, the honesty's too much."* And the egg sandwich was just as greasy and unpalatable as the music: he ate three bites and put it aside.

Thinking, if I start driving now, I could be five hundred miles from this town before dark.

Back in Piqua before morning. Mom'll make me breakfast. Eggs and hash browns. No more scum-colored grits for as long as I live. Call Carla, tell her I'm really sorry for what I said, how would she like to spend the weekend at Lake Loramie? Borrow Burchie's cabin. We're pretending it's Trinidad and dancing calypso by the lake, under the moon which is so fat it looks pregnant. Carla, laughing at my two left feet. God, look at that moon!

Then he opened his eyes. He'd fallen asleep—and when he looked up he saw that Nell was right out there on the street, getting into her car. She was dressed in a pantsuit and wore earrings, and Romeo *knew*, instantly, that she was going to the press conference. From the chambers of his heart, terror came shooting up. I knew it. I could have told you. I *did* tell you, Shaw. They're gonna fuck us.

Shaw was so excited he felt light in the head. Riding to the press conference, he wore his faded brown corduroy jacket—the only one he owned—and a tie he'd borrowed from Mitch. He had the .32 tucked into the thunderbelt behind his back. Prepared for whatever comes. This is the way to live, he thought. Been trying to live some other way, but this is the only way: everything into the fire. He was in the passenger seat of the Boatwrights' SUV—a battered '02 Jeep Liberty—and Tara was driving, and the others were in the back. Tara's expression was grim but determined. Shaw was sure she'd be all right. And she'd lead the others through as well. We're all going to soldier through this.

But then his phone buzzed, and when he answered Romeo barked at him, "Nell's going to your press conference!"

"What?"

"She's heading there now!"

"How do you know that?"

"She's all dressed up and she's in her car. Where else would she be going?"

"Hold on," said Shaw, and he looked to Mitch. "You said Nell wasn't coming."

Mitch said, "I thought she wasn't. She changes her mind a lot."

Shaw told Romeo, "Mitch says she changes her mind."

"*She changes her mind?* Shaw, if she's at the press

conference I can't touch her! I can't touch anyone! They can fuck us at will!"

"OK. Try to calm down."

"This is a *mutiny*! They're gonna kill us!"

"I really can't talk now. I'm in the car."

"We're dead!"

"We're fine, Romeo. Let me go."

He snapped his phone shut just as they pulled into the parking lot of the Plantation House Inn. A Georgia Lottery guy, Mr. Creave, eyes as small as jumping-beans, greeted them and briskly escorted them through the swarm of reporters and into the hotel by way of a side entrance. Took them to a kind of greenroom. Tara and Patsy were installed in aluminum folding chairs, where a couple of local beauticians applied their makeup. Jase sat in a corner and cut down the enemy hordes. Creave kept chattering away. "The Announcement will take place in the Vince Dooley Room! The local Savannah TV station is covering us live, and so is Jax, and there'll be feeds for CNN and Fox! This one's going *around the world*, folks! So it's not just the biggest day of your lives—it's the biggest thing ever to happen to this city! Since Brunswick stew!"

Nobody answered him.

Shaw was trying to think: could Romeo be right about

the Boatwrights? No sign of them plotting—no whispering, no meaningful glances between them. They all just looked exhausted. And they knew he had a gun. They knew if they tried anything, they were all going down: they *knew* that. They weren't *insane*.

But when he looked at Mitch, and saw his fat lip hanging sullenly, he thought, well, maybe a *little* insane.

He took Mitch off to a corner of the room, straightened his tie for him. "Everything all right?"

"Oh sure."

Creave called out, "Five minutes! How we doing? Five minutes! Lives are going to change!"

Tara led her mother to the bathroom, and Shaw let them go. I have to, he thought. I believe in this family now. He whispered to Mitch, "All right, my friend, when did you save me?"

"March of '03."

"And where were we at the time?"

"Greenville, South Carolina."

"And what were you doing the night we met?"

"Working the crisis line at the church."

"What was *I* doing?"

"Passing through."

"All right."

But Mitch kept staring straight ahead, at nothing.

Stupid man, thought Shaw. I'm putting my fate into the hands of an idiot. "Look elated, Mitch. Don't look glum."

"OK."

"Everyone's well-being depends on you looking elated."

Tara went to the Ladies with Mom, and there she pulled a Diet Coke bottle from her handbag, and said quietly, "Gin. Take a sip."

Mom waved her off. "Oh pumpkin, that's sweet of you, but you know I never drink at this hour."

Tara shut her eyes. Just drink it. Don't pose now. We don't have time.

She said, "Mom. Gotta make sure you're relaxed up there. You can't seem frightened or nervous or worried at all."

"Oh, I'll be *fine*."

"Take a sip."

Mom looked off to one side. Then gave a little one-shoulder shrug, and brought the bottle to her lips and neatly polished off a shot and a half. Afterward she drew her chin back the way she always did after her first drink of the day, that smug-turtle look. She resisted a little when Tara took the bottle back. But Tara said firmly, as she led her back out into the storm, "Just keep thinking of how rich we're gonna be, Mom. Rich. Really *rich*. That's all you have to think about."

Burris and a couple of other cops were turning cars away at the entrance, trying to keep control of the chaos. But people kept pulling rank. The mayor arrived with a limo full of councilmen. Some bloated bullying congressman showed up; then some guy who said he was the Secretary of State for the State of Georgia—whatever that meant. A crush of praying-mantis satellite trucks. Burris was in too black a mood to contend with any of them. He hung back and let the young cops take charge. Truth was, he didn't give a damn who got to park and who didn't—why should he?

The hotel manager came out and scolded: "There's no more room! Make 'em park on Bartow!" Came out again and said, "Make 'em park on G Street!" Came out two minutes later and said, "Make 'em park on

Goodyear!" In opposition to him was this Lottery guy who kept wailing, "That's the congressman! Let the congressman in!" Or, "That's WICK 103.9! Let WICK 103.9 in!" Or, "That's the president of the Sea Island Company! For God's sake! Let him come in!"

Burris didn't give a rat's ass about any of it. Horns, curses, bedlam—none of it touched him. He was just trying to stay out of everybody's way.

In the midst of all this, Nell appeared.

In her old white Cadillac. She was out on Gloucester Street, wanting to turn into the lot. One of the young cops tried to shoo her away.

But then Burris stepped up. "It's OK! Nell! Come on through."

The young cop was miffed at the interference. He started to bitch but Burris cut him off: "I said let her *in*."

Nell heard this. She laughed, and called, "That's the way I like to be *treated*!"

Burris told her, "You can park by the front entrance over there. You see where my cruiser is? Park right there."

She said, "Thank you, Burris. I love you, darlin'."

She said it skimmingly and carelessly, but still.

Burris knew that Nell wasn't beautiful, nor had she ever been. She had the haircut of a schoolboy playing hooky, and the shoulders of a stevedore. But her laugh was so musical it could melt iron; in fact long ago it had melted the chains that bound him to the codes of propriety and proportion. He didn't give a shit about the young cop who was now glaring at him. He didn't care about the Lottery guy complaining, "There's no *room*! You can't let just *anybody* in here." He didn't try to explain himself. He didn't say, "That's the mother of the winner," or anything like that. He just stood there gazing moonily after Nell as she pulled into the special place he'd saved for her.

Romeo was in the Tercel right behind Nell. He'd followed her here to the inn, and watched her pull in. They wouldn't let *him* in of course, so he drove to the next street and made a right, and went one block to G Street and found parking at a dentist's office. He leaped out of the car and started running toward the hotel. The air was so damp he felt he was kicking through water, and by the time he reached the rear of the hotel he was wiped out. There was a hurricane fence covered in morning glory. He jumped up and gripped the wire and pulled himself to the top. On his way over, he scraped a pair of parallel gouges into his wrist, but he felt this only distantly. He dropped and rolled, and as he rose he was already into a sprint again.

Around the swimming pool. Trying doors one after another till he found an open one. It led to a laundry room. Old woman roosting amid dunes of unwashed sheets. She squinted up at him. "I'm lost," he said. "You know where they're having the press conference?"

She kept squinting. Clearly she didn't understand a word.

He said, "Jackpot?"

That worked. She led him to a narrow hallway and pointed out a door. As he approached, he heard a clamor beyond. He opened the door and found himself in a big conference room full of people. He was near the front, by the stage. No one cared about his entrance—there was too much going on. Lights ablaze, cameras whirring. On the stage was a microphone stand and two outsized checks, one made out to *The Boatwright Family*, one to *Mr. Shaw McBride*. The amount on each of them, written in folksy slapdash cursive, was *One Hundred and Fifty-Nine Million Dollars*.

Romeo scanned the faces of the audience. Who was here? They all were. Old cousin Alfred, looking distinguished. Patsy's brother Shelby and his wife Miriam. Vanessa and Henry. And up front was Nell—ensconced in her folding chair as though upon a throne. Romeo saw a small patch of standing room by the wall near her, and he went and claimed it.

Nell was the star here. Everyone wanted to be close to her. Folks kept coming up to pay their respects, and she'd smile and call out, "Well, hel-*lo*!" or, "Hello, *ba*-by!" or "Drew Wilson, I been *look*-ing for you!" She kept reaching to touch their hands. Once, when she noticed a camera aimed her way, she posed and batted her eyes, and said, "I'm ready for my close-up now, Mr. DeMille."

Someone asked, "Nell, how come you're not up on that stage?"

"Well, I don't *know*. I guess they're trying to cut poor Grandma out of the deal. Ungrateful wretches!"

She turned to a nearby matron. "Anita, you got kids?"

"Not yet."

"I'd advise *against* it," she said, and cackled. She had no worries, no baggage. If there was an insurrection brewing, she wasn't in on it.

Suddenly the room erupted into applause. The Boatwrights were marching onto the stage from the wings. The kid first, then Tara and Patsy and Mitch.

Lastly here came Shaw with a great sunny grin on his face.

Tara looked down at the crowd. Everyone was cheering—even the TV crews, even the policemen and the reporters: all whistling and woof-woofing shamelessly, and melting before the radiance of her family's good fortune.

Then Mr. Creave stepped up to the lectern, settled the audience, and introduced some congressman, who gave a long dull speech about American values and reward for hard work. Nell, up near the front, said aloud to a friend, "*Work*? What is he *talking* about?" That got a big laugh. The congressman chuckled as though he were truly amused—then went right back to his thudding bromides. Tara stole a glance at her mom. She seemed all right now. The drink had done her a world of good. Her eyes were glossy, bright; she was lapping up the attention. She'll keep, Tara thought, for an hour or so—long enough to get us out of here. And Jase was afloat in his usual dream world but so what?—so long as he keeps his mouth shut.

But then Tara turned to her right and saw Dad's little clenched smile. That scared her. The muscles twitching in his jaw. She took his hand and squeezed it. He squeezed back, too hard. The congressman was getting down to business now, the moment everyone had been waiting for: the presentation of the mock checks. Flashbulbs sputtered. The applause was renewed. Creave summoned Shaw up to the mike.

Shaw's jacket was too small and his tie didn't match his shirt, and he stood there looking kind of embarrassed, as silence took hold around the room. Finally he leaned into the mike:

"Well, are you, um, I guess you're wondering how *I* got cut into this deal?"

A swell of laughter.

Shaw turned to Dad. "Mitch, maybe, maybe *you* could tell it?"

Dad went up to the mike. He seemed to totter. Running two fingers under his shirt collar. He said, "Well. I guess, um. What happened? Is that a couple of years ago, I. Was, um, doing some business training in Greenville? Up in South Carolina? And the church I went to, it had a crisis line? And, well, I was working in there one day, and this young man comes in, and that's, um, this young man here. And well—"

He ground to a stop. He turned to Shaw.

"You should tell it."

Tara was terrified. But the audience seemed to see nothing amiss. They were laughing; they loved watching these two shy yokels passing the baton back and forth.

Shaw came up to the mike again. He said, "Well, I guess, I guess the rest of the story is that I was sort of *nuts*." This won him an immense laugh. "I was having some troubles with the law, and I guess I was doing too many drugs. Well. For *sure* I was doing too many drugs. And this was, um, '03?"

He looked at Dad. Dad nodded.

"And I was driving one night and I was in a strange city, in Greenville, South Carolina, and I was kind of lonely and I, I was, well, I have to say it: I was thinking about ending my life. Because I was, just, in despair. And I went past this church, and it had a sign, that said, if you needed help? So I, I went in, and there was a guy in there. I tell you what, I didn't think I was gonna like this guy. I mean at first he seemed kind of, well, kind of *mean*."

He had to wait for the laughter to fade.

"'Cause you know why? 'Cause he wouldn't put up with any bull from me. None of my, I guess you'd say, *evasions?* And. So I, like I wrestled with him. I mean, I put up a *fight*. Like, you know how a smallie will fight you? Well, I know you guys down here get bigger bass than we do up north, but I like the way our bronzebacks won't ever give up. They'll fight all day, they really will. You're in a boat, they'll pull *you*. And that's what I was doing—I was fighting with all my might, but Mitch here, Mr. Boatwright, he just held on. Till he kind of reeled me in. Through the grace of our Lord Jesus Christ. And saved my life."

The crowd was still. Tara glanced down again at Nell: her eyes were glistening. She was the farthest thing from sentimental but Shaw was being so plain and straightforward and unadorned in his delivery, that she was on the verge of tears. So was the whole room. The stillness they were offering up to Shaw stoked his confidence, and Tara felt a deep relief, a moment of warmth in her veins. She thought: he's OK. He knows what he's doing. Maybe he even believes in what he's doing: that he's some kind of Lamp of Redemption sent to shine upon a benighted world. But the important thing is: *they* all believe.

He said, "I'm sure some folks out there don't think there's such a thing as good and evil? But let me tell you guys, I've seen 'em both, and I know which is which.

This man here. This man, this Mitch Boatwright? This man is *good*."

Shaw waited for the silence to close in around him. Then he brought his lips a half-inch closer to the microphone, and dropped his voice, and said, "So. Ever since that day, I've kept hoping to find this man again, this man who saved my life, so I could thank him. And finally I figured out how. You know how I found him?"

He waited a beat. "I Googled him."

The crowd loved that.

"I gave him a call and told him I was coming through Brunswick. And could I see him? And he said, sure. And we went out and had barbecue, and I told him, it don't matter that I'm not a rich man, because now I know what my calling is. Don't matter I'm not so-called successful, because I know about *real* success.

"And then, when he was driving me back to my car, we went past this, well like a gas station? And he was going in to buy some lottery tickets, and I said, Heck, would you get some for me? I guess I was feeling pretty good, pretty blessed, 'cause I gave him twenty dollars, which is more than I ever spent on the lottery in my *life*. And then, well, then you know the rest. But that's how I come to be up *here*."

Someone started clapping. Others took it up and the applause grew into a great wind of adulation which Shaw could feel blowing against his brow and running through his hair. His lungs filled up. He felt the deep scarlet pounding of his blood.

Creave opened the floor for questions.

Romeo's eyes were on Mitch. Mitch was standing on the stage just behind Shaw, and he looked all wound-up like he was about to come unsprung. He had that big fat lower lip which was just perched out there, and sweat dripped off his chin. And watch his eyes, thought Romeo. Those bulgy eyes, like eggs hard-boiling, how they're fixing on Shaw with such resentment. Bad, broken thinking going on in that brain.

A reporter was saying, "This question is for Mr. McBride. Mr. McBride—"

"Call me Shaw."

"Shaw, do you think all this money might change you for the worse?"

"Well. I guess that's, that's what brought this country down, isn't it? That's why we had the Wall Street collapse. Because of greed. And it could happen to me, yeah. I hope it won't."

Another reporter: "What are you going to buy, Shaw?"

Shaw stroked his chin a bit, as though this was the first he'd thought about the question. The audience knew it was being teased. Some soft chuckling, while Shaw held fire, held fire . . . and then: "Well, I'm not going to buy anything. I'm going to give it all away."

The whole room drew in its breath at once.

Had he really just said that? Had he really just committed to giving away a hundred and fifty-nine million dollars?

Then his features lightened. "Actually that's not quite true. I plan to keep back a little bit for myself. Enough to get me a bass boat."

More laughter, though now the quality of the laughter had changed. Now there were notes of amazement mixed in, and crazed ebullience. The audience was over the moon.

But Romeo kept his eyes on Mitch, and Mitch's expression was growing darker and darker.

Mitch was saying silently to himself, I'll kill the piece
of shit.

The piece of *shit*. The way he's twisting the name of
the Lord to his own ends, and spreading his lies all over
the world, and he thinks I'll just stand here and *let him
get away with this*? He thinks I'm such a lamb that I'll let
him drag the name of the Lord through the muck of his
evil lies? He'll soon find out I'm not a lamb. When I take
his gun from him, when I deposit a bullet from his own
damn gun into his own damn eye, he won't think I'm a
lamb then, will he? He'll change his damn mind then,
won't he?

Mitch searched the faces of the audience. One by one
he located the members of his family. All here. Mom,
right up front. Cousin Harry. And there's Rocket; and
Patsy's brother Shelby with Miriam and their kids. And
Alfred. And Will. And all of Jane's kids. Everyone. All
safe. Even my friend Enoch, and Vince from Lions of
Judah: my people are here and accounted for. And
Romeo is out patrolling the streets—so the only thing I
have to worry about is Shaw's gun. If I lunge, and come
into him hard enough, I'll knock him clear off the stage
and into the front rows of the audience. Then I'll leap
after him. Right into the storm, into the screaming and
the chairs flying, and he'll be confused by the fall, so I'll

just grab the gun from his holster and put it to his skull and shoot him, and the bastard won't seem like Mother Teresa *then*, will he? But here you go, watch this, here's a special delivery to *hell*, asshole.

And I will do it. I'll do it now.

You think I'm a lamb?

Your time for thinking that is about up.

Romeo was praying: Shaw, turn around. Right behind you, the fucker's gone psycho; turn around and look at him! *Turn around!*

But Shaw was running on and on about the bass boat he was going to buy, how he wanted it to have a four-stroke Verado engine, a Humminbird Fishfinder, etc. He was oblivious to everything but the sound of his own voice and the love coming back at him from the crowd. Completely ignoring Mitch. Mitch's pop-eyed glare reminded Romeo of the animal in the wheel well. That man wants revenge. He wants his dignity back. He's desperate for some bloodletting here, and he knows his family's safe, and he'll make his move *any second*. He'll rush Shaw and knock him down and take his gun from him and kill him. And then I'll have to kill Mitch, and the porks will have to kill *me*, and everything will be pointless and blacked-out and waves of shit forever.

A reporter asked: "Mr. Boatwright?"

It took Mitch a moment to realize the question was for him.

"Mr. Boatwright, you saved this boy's soul, and now he says he's going to give away all this money—do you, would you call this a miracle?"

Slowly Mitch approached the mike. And muttered into it, "A *miracle*?"

Then he fell silent. Scarily silent, like he couldn't even *speak*, he was so full of venom.

And then right there in front of everyone, he turned and glowered at Shaw. Shaw's grin evaporated. A hush fell over the audience. It was like a shadow, a huge cold shadow descending over this hall. And Romeo knew he had to do *something*, anything, and right now.

He found himself stepping forward:

"CAN *I* ASK SOMETHING? I GOT A QUESTION!"

Mitch was taken aback.

Romeo shouted: "I GOT A QUESTION FOR TARA! TARA, DON'T YOU THINK YOUR

DADDY'S ANGRY? AT HAVING TO SHARE THIS MONEY?"

Tara turned to him. And recognized him.

The Lottery guy was scolding from the corner of the stage, "Sir, there's a line here! There are questioners ahead of you—"

But there was nothing in Romeo's thoughts except the message he was sending to Tara: *I'm here*.

He boomed out: "YOUR DADDY'S GOTTA BE PISSED! HERE'S ALL THIS MONEY, AND THIS STRANGER'S GONNA THROW IT AWAY, AND IF IT WERE ME I WOULDN'T LET ANYBODY SHARE *MY* MONEY!"

None of it came out with any coherence, but he didn't care. All that mattered was: *I'm here. I'm ten steps from your grandmother. Stop him now.*

And he saw her starting to get it. She shot a look at her father, and she got it. There was a long moment when it felt as though the world was tottering, and then Tara put her arm over her father's shoulder and drew him toward the mike and said, "No sir, my father's not angry at all! He's just, well, we're all kind of *stunned*, you know? But we're happy to share this prize and it *is* a miracle and I'm just so proud of my daddy!"

She embraced him. There was a smattering of

applause, as she spoke a few private words into his ear. Romeo thought: she's telling him who I am.

Mitch looked down at him.

Romeo gave him a little wave. And pointed at Nell.

Mitch saw this. The fight drained out of him. Right before Romeo's eyes, he seemed to slump—but Tara still had her arm around him and she held him up, even as she extended her other arm to Shaw. Then the three of them were arm in arm in a row, and Tara was beaming and weeping, and the applause really got going and flashbulbs lit up all over the room. Patsy and Jase came over and the whole family was standing there with Shaw right in the middle. The audience got to its feet, and everyone was clapping and whooping, and there's no question, thought Romeo: this *is* a miracle, we're still alive and it's a genuine fucking miracle.

Tara drove on the way back. They pulled away from the crowd at the inn's parking lot, and went down G Street. Deathly silence. Nobody spoke. When Shaw sent a text message, the clicking of the phone keys was perfectly audible.

She turned onto Norwich Street. The storefront churches, the ghost-town façades. After a minute Shaw got a text reply—and instructed her, "Turn here."

She pulled into an abandoned minimall. Florist, beauty salon, dance academy: all forsaken. The only store that still survived was an H&R Block, but since this was Saturday even that was shut.

"Go around back," said Shaw.

Behind the stores, under a live-oak tree, was a huddle of dumpsters.

"Kill the engine."

She did. He opened the door and got out, and walked away, leaving them to roast in the heat.

No one said anything.

Flock of grackles presiding in the live-oak tree. Now and then one of them would drop down into a dumpster, peck around, fly up again.

When she saw Romeo she got so scared she thought she might black out. Tears came pouring out of her eyes. No one in the car could see this though, so long as she didn't turn.

Romeo was standing with Shaw by the back door to the old beauty salon. They were having a discussion, except it was only Shaw doing the talking. He was gesticulating, impassioned; his face was flushed. Too far to hear anything though. All Tara could hear was the spitting of the grackles in the oak tree.

Romeo stood there as Shaw told him, "You were right. I was a fool. I keep having faith in people, and then they fuck me over. Every *time*. These assholes. They don't even value their *own family*—how can you work with them? I'm through. I don't care what you do to them. I tried to protect them. But that's what people are like. It's kind of a pure, animal selfishness. If you hadn't been out in that audience, they'd be dead! The whole family! Fuck them. You have no idea how much I hate them. They've turned my life into a nightmare. They want to fuck us? Fuck them right back."

In this hell of noontime heat, with such a weight of malice pressing in the air, it was a struggle for Romeo to say anything. But he finally managed: "I could try to talk to them."

"*Talk* to them? We have to *punish* them."

"Let me try to talk to them."

"Oh, do what you fucking like," said Shaw, and he turned away.

Romeo fetched his broken saber from the trunk of the Tercel. Then he was headed for the Boatwrights' van, but Shaw stopped him. "Romeo."

"Yeah."

"Make them believe you this time."

"Yeah."

"Make them believe you've got nothing to lose. Make them think you're completely psycho."

"Yeah."

"Believe it *yourself*. Then they'll believe you."

Romeo went to the Liberty, and opened the side door. So hot in there you could hardly breathe, and the family was all drenched in sweat and fear, and were as quiet as churchmice. Tara sat behind the wheel. Mitch in the middle seat, Patsy and the brat all the way in back.

They had their eyes on the blade he carried.

Romeo said, "Mitch."

"Sir."

"What were you thinking up there, Mitch?"

"Sir?"

"You wanted to jump him, was that your plan?"

"No sir."

"Stop lying."

Mitch hung his head. "I don't, I'm not sure *what* I was thinking."

Said Romeo, "You know why your mother is still alive? Because of Tara. Because of what she told you, up on that stage. What did she say to you?"

"She told me you were out there."

"Yes. That's why your mother's still alive. But you almost got to see her brains go whomping around the room. How would that have been?"

A strange wailing started up, disembodied and far-away. At first it sounded like a siren—it took Romeo a moment to realize it was coming from the kid. The sound just leaking from him.

Said Romeo. "You *have* to shut up."

But the kid kept wailing. Finally Romeo grabbed him by the collar and lifted him from his seat and held him there, pushing the broken tip of the saber against his Adam's apple. That got him quiet.

Romeo said, "You people, you gotta stop fucking around. You need to understand this. You don't *ever* know where I'll be. Wherever you think I am, I'm somewhere else. I got a dozen of your people on my list, and when Shaw sends an alarm, I'll start killing. Or if I ever call Shaw and he doesn't answer, I'll start killing. I really will. I'll do whatever needs to be done. My buddy is out of his fucking head, I know. But I've got his back. OK? Believe me?"

It might have been more effective had it not been so obvious he was beating back tears. When he said "Believe me," his voice cracked a bit. He roughly shoved Jase away from him, and walked off.

Shaw was waiting for him. "How are we?"

Romeo walked past him and got in the Tercel and drove off.

Burris came home from his shift and heated a can of Progresso chicken minestrone soup, which tasted, he thought, like oiled sawdust. He turned on some baseball game. UGA vs. LSU. He cared for neither team—nor their mascots nor their cheerleaders nor their fans in warpaint: he only wanted the noise. The quiet in this house was a rebuke to him. It was an extension of the long silence of his wife Barbara, which had been a commentary on his faithlessness. Not that he'd ever cheated on her, not *physically*—but she'd known from the beginning about his feelings for Nell Boatwright, and in return she'd given him years of muteness. And he'd come back at her with his own silence, and for forty years they'd strung out this wordless debate, and now there were two grown kids and seven grandkids, all scattered, and Barbara was gone but her silence still thundered, and Burris left the TV on to drown it out.

The UGA pitcher faked a throw to first. Maybe a balk. The crowd felt certain it *had* been a balk. Burris ate his soup. A replay was shown. In the opinion of the color commentator, it had *not* been a balk. Today Nell had said to Burris, I love you, darlin'. She had waggled her fingers while sitting in that big Caddy like she was Hollywood royalty, and she'd said, for the world to hear: I love you, darlin'.

He chewed his toast. He pursed his lips, and unpursed them. He tried to figure things out. He wondered if, in the last forty years, he had ever gone more than four minutes without thinking of Nell Boatwright.

Could he do it now? Now that it was nails-in-the-coffin hopeless, could he finally let her go?

Balk or no balk, mused the color analyst, you can be sure of one thing: this moment will be talked about for years to come. This is a key moment—not just a key moment in this particular game, but really a key moment in the history of the UGA–LSU rivalry . . .

I love you, darlin'.

Could that have been true? If only for an instant? You could have a renewal of affection for someone you were once fond of, couldn't you? Sudden resurgence of feeling, as though a part of your heart that you'd completely shut down was open for business again?

Once, back in high school, Nell had told him, "You're amazin', Burris." It was only on account of his prowess at throwing a wooden ring over the neck of a milk bottle, but she really had meant it. It hadn't been just flirting or flattery. In that one moment she really had been falling in love with him.

Or such was his belief, his best guess, after forty years of pondering the thing.

He heard a burst of rough music. It made him jump.

Where had it come from? Not the TV. Not the phone or the microwave. So what the hell had it been?

It sounded again.

Then he realized: the front doorbell. It rang so seldom now, he'd forgotten what it sounded like.

He went through the parlor and opened the door. A girl was standing there. Twenty or so, blonde, slender and shapely but plain-featured. She said, "Officer Jones? You remember me?"

"Of course," he lied.

"My name's Cheryl. Faith Renewal?"

He did remember. The girl from church. "It's that time again?"

"Sir?"

"The Heart Drive?"

"Oh, no sir." Her tone was grave. "I just need to talk to you."

"What about?"

"I called at the station but they said you'd gone home. Am I bothering you?"

"Not at all."

"I gotta talk to *you* because you're the only police officer I know."

He felt awkward about inviting her in. Bring a young girl into your house you'll get tongues wagging. But then what did he care if tongues wagged or not? Mercy. He stepped aside and she entered. The living room was straight and clean—since he never used it—and he offered her the lime-green couch with the matching pillows, while he took one of the frilly armchairs. The last time he had sat in this armchair was the day of Barbara's funeral.

"Well, how can I help you, Cheryl?"

"You remember where I work?"

"You used to work at the I-95 Chummy's. You still there?"

"Yes sir."

Seemed like she'd been there a really long time. Couldn't she find anything more worthwhile to do?

Though after all, who was he to judge anyone's career? Considering the state of his own.

She said, "Well anyway, sir, I think I might know something."

"Know something?"

She'd been in Barbara's Bible study class, he remembered that, and he wondered if she was about to spring some kind of religious thing on him. Like, Sir, I think I know that Jesus was resurrected in the flesh, but how can I be sure I know? If she asked something like that, he'd be useless.

But then she said, "It's something about the jackpot."

"I'm sorry?"

"The jackpot. We sold the winning ticket at our store."

"Oh. Yeah."

"And the guy who won it? Not the Boatwrights, but the other guy?"

"What other guy?"

"Shaw McBride."

That name meant nothing to him.

She said, "You didn't see the announcement? On TV?"

He shook his head. "I was there, but I was working. Security. Out in the parking lot. I didn't really see anything. There's another winner?"

"Uh-huh. The Boatwrights are splitting the jackpot

with this guy Shaw McBride. Supposedly he's a friend of Mr. Boatwright. Supposedly he gave money to Mr. Boatwright to buy tickets."

"Oh."

"But the thing is," she said, "this guy? He was in our store on Thursday morning. OK? The day *after* the drawing? I remember, 'cause it was when the TV people came to the store. And he asked me, he said, like, what's this all about? He didn't even know there *had been* a jackpot. I had to tell him about it."

Burris held up a hand. "Wait."

She sat quietly.

He said, "I'm trying to make sense of this." He wrinkled his brow. "This guy came in . . . when?"

"Thursday."

"*After* the drawing?"

"That's what I'm telling you. And just now I was watching TV? And I saw him up on stage, that same guy, but now he's saying how he's Mr. Boatwright's old friend. And like, half the jackpot is his. But I, I mean, *I* think . . . ." She trailed off.

Burris prompted: "You think he's lying?"

She nodded.

"But why would Mitch Boatwright go along with that?"

She shrugged.

But the answer was self-evident, and he spoke it: "You think Mitch is scared?"

"I guess, yes sir."

All over Burris's brain, lights were flickering on, doors were creaking open. Some of those doors led directly to Nell Boatwright (of course everything led to her eventually). But there was also a voice inside him that was saying, Whoa.

Don't just leap into this, Burris.

This is how he had screwed himself every time—leaping too damn fast. Thinking he'd been given some kind of private window on the truth. In the past, this had led him to big errors. This is why he was just a corporal when he had once been a detective in the Coastal Area Drug Abuse Task Force, when he could have made captain inside of five years—but no, he was hungry for instant glory; he was susceptible to con men who led him around by the ring that hung from his snout, and so he wound up with nothing. And now he was the object of derision and would be for the rest of his ignominious career.

So slow down here. Proceed with caution.

Ask yourself: what might this girl want that isn't showing? Does she have an ax to grind? Look for the hidden motivation.

He said, "OK. Well now, Cheryl, when this guy was in your store, how did he act?"

"Kind of weird. He was using our tire thing, like for the air pressure? And he comes back and says something about how his tires had like led him to the store or something. I don't know, I didn't know *what* he was saying."

"Did it get personal?"

"Huh?"

"Did he say anything about you personally?"

A thoughtful tug at the corner of her lips. "No, sir."

Burris wondered, had she been flirting with the guy? And somehow gotten her feelings hurt? And was she now retaliating? That happens all the time. There's an injury; injury festers; false witness is born. Better proceed with light paws. There's thin ice here, and if you go stomping along in your usual manner you'll break through, you fat idiot, and who will come to your rescue? Nobody.

Shaw rode in the Liberty, still marinating in his fury. He said nothing though, and soon they were back at the Boatwrights' street. That's when he saw the three

satellite TV trucks and all the reporters and rubber-
neckers.

Tara pulled up the drive to the carport. A baby-faced
man was awaiting them beside his motorcycle, which
was big as a bison. He wore dreadlocks and ikat trousers.
He looked like a hippie assassin.

Shaw got out. The reporters shouted at him from
the edge of the lawn. But the baby-faced man said,
"Them insects, I told them they had to stay off the
property."

"You told them?" Shaw asked.

"Yes sir."

"Who are you?"

"My name's Trevor Miller, sir. I'd like to serve you, if
that would be possible."

"Serve me? How?"

"Any way you like."

Shaw kept his hand close to his hip, ready to reach for
the .32. Was this a setup? Could this guy possibly be for
real?

Said Trevor, "I been up in Hinesville. Fort Stewart,
but I got discharged in February. Working Pantry
Pride? A butcher? But I come down here for the beach.
I was in a bar and you was up on the TV. I asked 'em
who you was, and they sent me over here. I got a feeling

about you. I know you don't know me from Adam but I bet there's a way I can serve you."

Trevor had a searchingness in his gaze, and seemed to be carrying some hurt, some deep wound. Shaw relaxed a little. Thinking, an apostle? Do I really have *an apostle* now?

"Trevor, you were in the army?"

"Yes sir. Third Infantry."

"Iraq?"

"Yes sir."

"Did you kill anyone?"

"They carry their dead with them, sir, when they can. But I would surmise that I did."

Such formality of speech! And the look he was giving was kin to that abyss-black adoration that Shaw had faced at the press conference. This is what he needed! This was the personnel the cause required. He glanced back at the Boatwrights. They were standing there meekly: heads bowed, gazes averted, awaiting his pleasure. And the reporters at the end of the driveway were calling to him, and the crowd waved its fronds and gave praise.

He turned back to Trevor. "Tell me, those that you killed, you think they're at peace?"

"I don't know, sir. I thought *you* might know that."

"I do," said Shaw. "They are."

"Well. OK then."

"You can serve me as long as you like. You hungry, Trevor?"

"A little."

"Patsy'll fix you something. Then let's talk about security."

Romeo was on 17, supposedly on his rounds, but this time he didn't take his usual left turn at Chapel Crossing Road. He just kept heading up 17. Northward. As if breaking for home, as if returning to Piqua, Ohio. He passed the Humane Society, then an old rice plantation, and then a sign that said DARIEN 6 MILES. A shut-down garage: Chancy's Auto Painting and Refinishing. The missionary girls had said this was where you could get a "body suspension" if you needed one.

Next he passed a cemetery with no headstones, just little brass markers on a vast lawn. The sign had Saturn and the moon and shooting stars, and the name: HEAVEN'S VIEW.

The shooting stars reminded him of an event a few years back: a summer night, a little party.

Shaw had organized it. Everyone was supposed to gather at the spillway to watch the meteor shower, the Perseids. Shaw said the spillway was situated over a 'ley line of power'—whatever that was—and from that vantage point the meteor shower would spell out some essential truth about the universe. He said forty people had agreed to come. He said there were pretty girls on that list. Romeo went with him to the liquor store where they bought six quarts of Johnnie Walker and a lot of beer, cups, ice, and Doritos; then they climbed up onto the levee above the rushing water. It was a perfectly clear August night. But nobody showed except Chris and Pissboy and Ricky Cobb's cousin from Toledo.

The five of them sat there and drank. Looking up at the sky, making comments about the bitches who hadn't shown. The meteor shower was disappointing. It wasn't like a fireworks show; it was just occasional pale streaks in the sky. But the watchers were patient, since they had nothing else to do, and finally there came a sky-crossing that was worth the wait. Slow and pompous, a fiery strut, a star that knew it was a *star*. The boys on the levee cheered and whistled and were sad to see it burn out.

Then they got quiet. Romeo was trying to figure out why nobody had come. Obviously, Shaw wasn't as popular as he'd been in the old days. The stupid tech job was eating him up. He was doing too much chronic and too much dex, and the years were elbowing past him. Maybe he was getting a little weird. Restless, too strident, a surfeit of visions. These days he scared away a lot more girls than he scored. You started to think he'd be doing tech support in the Piqua/Dayton area when he was sixty—unless he got adventurous and moved to Cincinnati.

And me the same, Romeo thought.

One by one Chris and Pissboy and the guy from Toledo passed out. Then it was just Shaw and Romeo. Shaw said that, in his judgment, nobody in southwestern Ohio knew how to fucking *live*. He talked about the need to live passionately. "Which of our friends lives passionately? Not one. Not *one*. I mean there's a difference between existing and really *living*."

Then he told Romeo, "Now what *you* do, is you live. If it weren't for you, I believe I might fucking kill myself." He was serious. And drunk, and in a state of agitation.

He said, "I don't know if anything lasts or not. Give it a thousand years, does anything count for shit? I don't know. You look up at those fucking billion-year-old stars, could anything down here count for shit? Does anything last? But I bet one thing lasts. This thing *we* have, between the two of us. This friendship? This will last. In some form. Because this is the only worthwhile fucking thing in history."

Romeo was too moved to say anything.

Shaw went on, "No, I mean it, you and me, we're gonna keep reverberating through this universe. When all the dull assholes who didn't show up tonight have been reduced to their fucking muons and quarks, you'll still get an echo of *us*—this I guarantee."

And now, remembering all this two years later, Romeo didn't feel like driving anymore. He couldn't go home to Ohio. He couldn't leave Shaw.

Just short of Darien, at the entrance to the Two-Way Fish Camp, he turned around and drove back to the Wick.

Tara was made crazy by all the calls. The calls came in from Fox News, from the *Bombay Times*, from some megachurch evangelist who begged an audience. Various unknown Boatwrights called. The Faith Renewal Church of Greenville, South Carolina, called. Senator DeWine's office called. Mom's friends called to say they were organizing a big Jackpot Party for tonight.

By now nobody in the family was bothering to pick up, but the recording kept playing. The voice of Jase: "Yeah, you got the Boatwrights, but we're too lazy to answer," then the *beep,* then importunities from all over the world. This routine growing more and more unbearable till finally Tara said, "Hey, could we shut that off for a while?"

Shaw was at the little faux-empire desk, studying Mom's Bible, marking key passages in yellow. He looked beaky, owlish, fevered. "What?"

"The message machine. Do we have to keep it on?"

He said, "What if Oprah calls?"

Tara knew she was supposed to smile, but she was too weary. She lowered her eyes. He relented: "Yeah, sure. Turn it off. Oprah knows where to find us when she's ready."

She pulled the plug. Then they just sat there, listening to the squeak of Shaw's magic marker, and the dying on Jase's Micro, and the accumulating hubbub out on the street. You'd think all this might disturb a man trying to pull off a hundred-and-sixty-million-dollar extortion.

But Shaw kept serenely highlighting that Bible. If anything, the fuss seemed to please him. He chuckled when he heard some woman outside insisting: "We're from the *Today* show! Don't tell me you don't know what the *Today* show is!"

Then Trevor: "The family's not giving any interviews. But I'll give them the message."

"Just two minutes! If you could let Matt Lauer have two *minutes*—"

"Ma'am, I gotta say, you're trespassing."

"Think of the good that Shaw could do with an appearance on—"

Trevor: "You see the number I'm dialing here? I'm dialing 911."

Romeo got back to the trailer and found that Claude was still by himself. Looking wretched and smelling like a pot of fermented cabbage. Romeo gave him a few pumps of morphine, and straightened up the trailer. He washed the dishes. He took out the garbage. He vacuumed. Then he gave the old man a sponge bath.

At Hermann's Candle Shoppe in the mall, he'd

bought a true sponge from the ocean. Now he found an enamel pot under the sink—which reminded him of the bedpan his mother used to set out whenever he was sick—and he scrubbed out the grime and the cobwebs, and filled it full of hot soapy water. He set down clean towels on one side of the bed, and rolled Claude onto them. In turning him on his belly you had to be careful not to bruise him, and make sure he was breathing OK. Bear in mind you've never handled anything so perishable before.

Claude groaned when the sponge touched his back.

"Too hot?" said Romeo.

"No no. It's. Good."

Romeo started at Claude's shoulders and worked his way down. Where the skin was pocked and mottled, its texture resembled the sponge, but Romeo didn't find that repellent. Even Claude's swollen calves didn't bother him—even that horseshoe-crab mockery of a pelvis, even cleaning around the withered asshole. When he had finished the feet, he turned Claude back over, and did his front. The old man's testicles were prodigious: a brace of quail in a leather sack. Everything else had shrunk up, but not his nuts.

But his stomach was ticklish, like a little child's.

Romeo had made it all the way up to the gossamer

ribcage when he heard a car outside. He looked out and saw Wynetta's pickup, and the sight dismayed him.

"Your daughter's here."

"Oh." Claude made a gesture: cover me. Romeo got the sheet pulled up just before Wynetta came bursting in. She went right to her father's side and spoke with unnatural volume, as though a court bailiff had just told her to speak up: "Oh, Daddy, I'm sorry! I haven't had no fuckin cell phone! If you knew how crazy everything's been!"

Claude gave her his sweet wobbly toothless smile. "It's OK."

"I'm so *fuckin* sorry."

"No. Problem."

Now she regarded Romeo. Her lips curled into a sneer. "Oh, shit, the stoned elf. What *you* doing here?"

Claude explained, "He's taking. Care of me."

She said, "Oh, no. Oh, no. Were you giving him medicine?"

"Yeah," Romeo admitted.

She said, "You an RN?"

"No."

"Then you can't give him medicine. God. Daddy, he didn't make you mess with your *will*, did he?"

Claude shut his eyes.

"God," she said, "Where the hell is Joanie? She's supposed to *be* here. God damn it to hell. I knew I shouldn't trust that bitch."

"It's OK," said Claude. "I'm good."

"Daddy, you know where I was? I was in Tifton. I went to Tifton with that Greek fucktard? And it's like, I lost my cell phone, I don't even know the number of my own father, 'cause all the numbers were on my cell phone. And then I was trying to get that shitwad to give me a ride home like he said he would, but he's like Numero Uno Selfish Cocksucker of the Universe, oh, Jesus, and I keep telling him, my *daddy*! My poor daddy's *sick*. God fuck it."

Claude smiled at her, with all the forgiveness he could bring to bear.

Wynetta turned to Romeo. "Hey, fucktoad. I know what you want, but you ain't gonna get it. My daddy is not your meal ticket. You can clear the fuck out of here. Right now."

Claude said, "Wynetta."

"What?"

"He's been good. To me."

"Oh, Daddy. If you knew. I been crying all the way back here. I 'bout had a wreck in Nahunta. Is there any beer?" She opened the fridge. Stuck her head in, and moved things while she searched. Her voice came out flattened. "You didn't drink the PBRs in here, did you?"

Claude took Romeo's hand and whispered, "I'm sorry."

But Wynetta had already pulled her head out of the fridge, and she heard this. She said: "Uh-uh. No sir. You come between me and my daddy? I'll make you bleed outta your *ass*."

Patsy set up her laptop in the kitchen, and went to BibleGateway.com, to spend some serious time with Scripture. Vowing to herself to go easy on the gin today, and keep far from the temptations of Malibu. Just let me find some gentle parable to give me strength. Sweet Jesus? I'm in your hands. This is your little lost lamb Patsy. Please, Lord. Deliver me from Evil and from these Demons who have come into my life!

But while scrolling through the pages of the Holy Book, she felt more lost than ever. What the hell was all this gobbledy gobbledy? The massacres of Chronicles, the oppression of Kings, the merciless butchery of Judges: where was the comfort? Pretty soon her eyes began to glaze over. She sighed, and huddled herself closer to the screen. And sneaked a quick trip over to Google. Keying in:

luxury homes

Just for one minute, she thought.

But the houses she found seemed too generic and suburbs-of-Fort-Worth, so she amended her search to:

luxury homes ca

That was better—she got some very nice pictures of estates in Brentwood and Bel Air. The residents were maybe not the cream of the A-list, but they weren't warmed-over reality stars either. They had respectable properties. Cobblestoned drives, box hedges. Still, there was something missing. Everything looked kind of stodgy and lonely, and she surfed from one house to another without satisfaction until finally she gave in and added that magic elixir:

luxury homes ca Malibu

Just for one bittersweet minute!

The first place she came to was a twenty-two-million-dollar hideaway in the Colony that looked, she thought, like the concrete-block rest-room station at the Welcome Center on I-95. I can't *believe* this; these places can't cost this much! I bet I could get this for *half* what they're asking! If I even wanted it, which I *don't*—

Shaw came into the kitchen.

"What you looking at, Patsy?"

She touched her way back to BibleGateway.com just in time, just before he came to peer over her shoulder.

She said, "I'm looking at The Book of Nehemiah. The Word of Our Lord. Is that permitted?"

"Sure," he said. But then he grinned and reached down and checked her History. It was all right there— luxury homes, luxury homes ca, luxury homes ca Malibu—and he laughed. "More like The Book of Brangelina. What a comfort in times of stress! What're you drinking, darling?"

"I'm not drinking."

"Well, let's get to it, girl. This is a time for celebration. How about a couple of g&ts?"

"Oh, not for me," she said.

"All right. Make me one?"

She shrugged. She got up and fixed him a drink so strong it smelled like Christmas. An aroma so endearing she changed her mind and made a little one for herself as well.

She came back and handed him his drink, and sat. He said, "You think I'm messing with your dreams, don't you?"

She gave her ice a swirl.

He said, "I just want you to understand, I'm not going to cost you money. I'm going to *make* you money. You'll be much richer because of me. This I guarantee. You're going to make a billion dollars. One *billion*. You think I'm insane, but I'm telling you the truth. You know how I'm gonna make you a billion dollars?"

She kept her eyes down. Thinking, one *billion*?

"Because you haven't just won the jackpot here. What you've done, you've become a receiver of God's power."

She had no idea what he was talking about. She was wondering how much a billion was.

He went on: "There's all this power passing through us, every second. Radio waves, TV waves. Messages from distant stars. Currents of pure healing. All the power in the universe just passing through us all the time—except not through you, Patsy. Because when the power gets to you, it stops. You *receive* the power. Which everyone is starting to notice. Everyone's in awe of you, because the power of the Lord is with you. And I'm going to make sure it stays with you. Everyone will read your books. Everyone will watch your videos. Everyone will come to hear you speak."

"Me?" she said. "Are you kidding?"

"They'll pay you not millions, but tens of millions."

Was he *toying* with her? Was this just a string of lies to amuse himself? But he was looking right at her like he really meant every crazy thing he was saying.

"Within two months, I guarantee, you'll be having lunch with Oprah. Dinner with Regis. You'll have weekends with Montel Williams and Dr. Phil. And when I say a billion? I'm dead serious. Actually, I'm lowballing it a little. You could wind up with more money than Bill Gates. The only question is what're you gonna do with it once you get it?"

She didn't mind hearing him talk, even if it was all baloney.

But she noticed that her drink was down to just ice. He noticed it too, and prompted, "Go make yourself another, girl."

"What about you?"

He'd scarcely touched his, but he said, "Sure. Bring me another too."

She made two more g&ts, giving each glass a sawtooth lime wheel. When she returned to the table, she saw that he'd placed his chair close to hers, so they'd both be able to see the computer screen. Which at just that moment was conjuring up an image of the Earth in deep space.

He murmured, "I want you to get to know this planet. I mean since you're about to own *so much* of it."

She couldn't help but grin. He was smiling too, and his smile was so goofy. When she handed him his glass, their fingertips touched for an instant. A little jolt.

"Sit," he said.

She did. On the screen, the Earth kept getting bigger and bigger—she felt she was gently falling, and Shaw was falling beside her. They were falling right toward New York City, but then things kind of blurred out, as if they'd entered a cloudbank. When everything came into focus again, she found herself not in the city but somewhere in the countryside, near the sea. She was hovering above a landscape of engraved shadows and oblong swimming pools and trellises and dovecotes and shapely gardens.

He said, "See this house?"

"Uh-huh."

"This is Gwyneth Paltrow's house."

It was a proud thing but not preening. It was perfect. She took a drawn-out swallow of her g&t.

They drifted over the treetops. As though they were riding in the gondola of a hot-air balloon.

He told her, "This is Vera Wang's house."

It was severely graceful, the soul of elegance. They floated on, and she sipped, and he showed her the homes of Larry Gagosian and Barry Diller and Diane von Furstenberg. He told her who these people were, and they seemed somehow more *serious* than the celebrities of Malibu, their lives more significant. He took her over Ralph Lauren's dreamlike estate. She couldn't believe that Ralph Lauren was an actual person, that this was *his actual home*. That pair of shadows on the lawn—could that be Ralph and his dog? Could that be Ralph Lauren walking his dog this very moment, and maybe wearing one of those shirts with the horse and rider?

Grace of God.

Then came Paul McCartney's house; then P. Diddy's house.

Then the 'cottage' where Arthur Miller had spent a summer with Marilyn.

"Some say the Hamptons are over," Shaw said. "But you know what? They'll never be over. Because this is where so many lines of power converge. The Hamptons go on and on, and beauty is drawn to them as though by a magnet. And this is where you must preside. Not Malibu. Forget Malibu. Malibu is for common entertainers. You're not an entertainer, Patsy, you're a visionary. We'll get you a quiet estate off to the side. Not on the beach or Georgica Pond, nothing melodramatic, but just something quiet and magnificent that will suit you. You can spend your winters in St. Barts. But during the season, here is where you'll preside. Everyone will come to your house, because they'll know that Patsy Boatwright is a receiver of the power of God."

They didn't speak for a while; they just coasted.

"Shaw?"

"What?"

"You're a lunatic."

He smiled. "I've heard that before."

She said, "You gonna live here too?"

"Well, you know, the Hamptons really aren't for me. They're for you. I'll need something a little simpler. You know?"

"Oh sure," she said. "Like a little *hut* somewhere?"

"Exactly."

They laughed together. She swirled her gin and it was all ice again, so she got up to make herself one more little one.

Clio kept telling herself *no*, she wasn't going over there. Never. Never debase herself by showing up at Tara's house. That place that was now like some kind of Bible camp crossed with a Jaycees' barbecue? I mean I refuse to kneel down and beg her to be my friend. Do I even care what the stuck-up bitch thinks about me? I'll be OK without her. I'll drive around a while. I'll go to the island. That dude Zach Collins who supposedly likes her so much? He'll be getting off his shift soon at Southern Soul. Let's go see who he likes when his sweet dick is in *my* mouth. Right?

But she didn't go to the island. She was on Rt. 17, ready to take the turn—but instead she pulled into the McDonald's parking lot and turned around and headed for Tara's. She had to see Tara, she *had* to. She had to tell her about how Manny's check for Cindy's abortion had bounced three times. And that she had met the manager for Drive Fast & Shut Your Eyes, and he was a screwy little nutbag but kind of cute. She had to tell Tara—who else would understand?

She thought, I'll just stop by for a second. I mean after all we've been through: she can't have forgotten me overnight! Right? It's not possible! Not *overnight*. Give her a chance.

The cops made her park three blocks away from the

house and walk. The place was swarming with cult people, some of them singing hymns and others cooking on grills, and so much smiling it made your teeth hurt, and there were TV trucks and the scene was totally bizarre. When Clio tried to walk up to the house, she got stopped by a couple of goons who told her she couldn't go any farther.

She said, "I can't go to my own frikkin best friend's house? Like what, like she's got a velvet frikkin rope now?"

One of the goons went to check, and then came back to escort her to the carport. Making her wait there till Tara came out to meet her.

Then suddenly here she was. She looked terrible.

Oh, Tara, thought Clio. Oh my God. Jesus.

She looked drawn, ghostly-pale, lumpy around the eyes, nervous. And Clio instantly forgave her everything and just wanted to take her into her arms.

Tara thought: finish this. Make it quick and show no mercy. If you show mercy you put her in danger.

Clio said, "Hey, Ratface. Sup, bitch?"

Tara gave her nothing.

They stood there like that, until Clio said, "So what's it like? Shit. All that money."

"It's . . . fine."

"Yeah? But what's with all these frikkin zombies?"

"These are my friends."

Give her nothing, and make it seem like I'm a thousand miles away.

Clio said, "Bitch, they're staring at me. They're like, undead."

That's *exactly* the word, Tara thought. A laugh tried to surface but she smothered it.

Said Clio, "How come you haven't answered my texts?"

"Been busy."

"Too busy for *me*?"

Rip this, thought Tara. "Look, Clio, I have other friends now, OK?"

"What do you mean, other friends?"

"I don't know. I guess better friends. Like more in common. You know? Maybe we're like, it's like time to give each other some space. All right?"

Clio's face went splotchy. "Sure. Absolutely. Have fun with your zombies."

"I'm sorry," Tara said. But she was thinking, stop it,

shut up, just get away from here quick as you can. "OK," she said. "See ya." And turned from her just in time, before the tears broke.

Romeo slowed the car as he passed Cousin Alfred's house. It was a grand affair, a Queen Anne Gothic with turret and eyebrow window, and a gray-misted garden to which Romeo felt powerfully drawn. He slowed the car to a full stop, the Tercel sitting in the middle of dead-quiet Union Street, with the windows wide open because the a.c. was useless against this heat. Keep moving, Shaw had said. Keep moving at all costs. But the garden was calling him, and finally he parked, and walked up to the iron palings. Tangled and fragrant and dark in there, and the stone bench looked perfect for sleeping. Voices came down to him from the house. The verandah was swaddled in vines, so Romeo couldn't see anyone, but he heard one older cultivated male voice (he guessed this was Alfred himself), and several younger male voices, languorous, and now and then the cackle of an old woman. They were exchanging gossip. The tinkle of ice cubes, the pour of bourbon, laughter. Romeo didn't know anyone they were speaking of, but he loved the suggestion of soft malevolence in their tone; and the fragrance of the vineflowers was ravishing, and he stayed there a long time, clinging to the palings, trying to follow the talk. Only when a knot of rude kids came up the sidewalk, and one of them said, "Dude, you drunk?" did he finally manage to quit that spot and totter away.

He got back into the Tercel. He drove on.

What the hell, he wondered, was that about?

All I have to do with Alfred is kill him. Not get mired up in his life. Just be ready to behead the man when called upon to do so.

The Tercel crept through the stately streets. His thoughts spun slowly. He went past Nell's. Nell came out of her potting shed wearing a big hat and carrying a long-handled shovel. She seemed sufficient unto herself, like a desert prophet. Her garden was as enticing as Alfred's. He wished he could do some hoeing for her. Happily he'd have worked all day for nothing. But he had to keep rolling, keep going round and round on his carousel.

His problem, as he saw it, was a lack of hate. Not enough hate. The brain of a revenge killer, he thought, should be spiky with hate. He should be hating Nell, and hating Alfred, hating them all. He should make himself dizzy with hate, should work himself into the same whirling froth he'd been in that time in Hollow Park, when he was ten years old and he'd beaten the hell out of Shaw's mutineer.

Burris drove to the station house and went online, went to Accurint, to find out what he could about Shaw McBride.

Precious little.

City of residence: Dayton, Ohio.
Breaking and entering '94.
Suspended license '97.
Civil claim for unpaid rent '98.
Misdemeanor possession of marijuana '00, probation.
Passing bad check '03, probation.

That was it—except for his pretty face on the mugshots, which looked glum in '97 but by '03 devil-may-care, with pinned pupils and a slippery grin.

It surprised Burris that the sheet wasn't longer.

He took the cruiser up Rt. 341 to the I-95 Chummy's.

He asked for the manager, but the clerk said not today. Saturday was Mr. Hu's day off.

Burris flashed his badge. "Just get him."

The clerk made a phone call, and Mr. Hu came in a hurry. He was Korean or Laotian or something, and struggled with the language, but was as obliging as could be. Burris explained that he had questions regarding the jackpot winner. He asked to look at the security tapes.

Mr. Hu said, "You mean when jackpot winner buy ticket?"

"No, from the *next* day. Thursday."

"Oh. OK."

Mr. Hu didn't ask questions. He took Burris back to his little office and slipped the disc into the drive. It was an old cheap system. Fisheye videos, herky-jerky. The customers came lurching into the store, rushed around, paused before the cash register for a few hummingbird heartbeats, then flickered away again. One large couple came on with such a ludicrous waddle that Mr. Hu burst into a deep malignant laugh—before he caught himself and got all smiley again.

Abruptly, on the screen, Shaw McBride made his entrance.

"Slow it down," said Burris.

Then the frames came one at a time. McBride looked sweaty, tired. He stopped to groom himself before approaching the cash register. All that could be seen of Cheryl the clerk was the back of her head. She handed McBride something: what was it? He didn't pay for it; he just walked out of the store.

"What did she give him?"

"For tire," said Mr. Hu.

"Pressure gauge?"

Mr. Hu nodded.

"Skip ahead," said Burris.

Mr. Hu jumped to McBride's re-entry. Now it was Mr. Hu behind the counter and Cheryl at the window. McBride handed the gauge to Mr. Hu, then went to talk to Cheryl. You could hardly see either of them. After a minute, McBride went out.

A moment later, a couple of guys with TV cameras came into the store. And that was it. Show over.

"You remember that guy?" said Burris.

"No remember."

"You have a picture of his car? You got an outside camera?"

Mr. Hu tried another tape. It was from a camera focused on the pumps—but during the time in question, there was no car to be seen. This wasn't surprising

218

though—McBride hadn't come for gas. He'd have been parked over by the air pump.

But Burris and Mr. Hu did get a glimpse of *something* passing through the frame and driving out of the lot. Blurry and inconclusive but it might have been McBride's car. Sedan. Kind of boxy.

Burris shook his head. "OK. You can turn it off now."

Mr. Hu complied.

"Hey, aren't you getting some money for this? For selling the winning ticket?"

"No money," said Mr. Hu. He smiled some more.

Said Burris, "I thought the store that sells the ticket was supposed to make a lot of money."

"No for me. I just manager."

His grin was not rueful at all, but truly content. He seemed quite pleased to be taking no part of this pie—altogether pleased that winged megafortune had chosen to alight on some other poor bastard's shoulder, and not his.

Shaw went with Mitch to visit this big financial guy, Henry Lonsdale. Lonsdale lived in a parvenu mansion in the Black Banks neighborhood of St. Simon's Island.

Tabby walls and cold beetling balconies, windows of smoked glass. From the driveway you were led by the maid beneath a columned pergola to the 'office', which had a twenty-foot-high vestibule. One wall was adorned with trophies and plaques for bass-fishing prowess.

Lonsdale came in and introduced himself. Shaw asked him, "You really won the Bassmaster Southern Open?"

"Which one? Oh, yes. '06."

"Wow. What'd you haul?"

Lonsdale shrugged. "Oh, I think 59, 3. Something like that."

"God. What were you throwing?"

"Well, I started spinner but swimbait filled my bag. If memory serves I used a King Shad."

"That's soft?"

"That's a hardbody. It all depends on your throw. I saw you on TV, Mr. McBride. I take it you like to fish?"

"Just, well, up in Ohio. Where I'm from. Never largemouth. I'd love to cast for largemouth."

"Well, there's not a lot of that action here on the coast. But I'll gladly take you jigging for redfish, if you'd like."

"I would like that very much."

It was plain that fishing was Lonsdale's passion in life. He told Shaw he didn't do finance full-time anymore. "A few clients, just to keep my hand in," he said, imperially.

At the man's great stone desk, three factotums awaited. Banker, Accountant, Lawyer. They all wore shimmery suits, and looked you in the eye when they shook your hand, and imagined they were big movers and shakers. But Henry Lonsdale in his tennis shoes and chinos outclassed them easily. While they chattered amongst themselves, he flopped into his chair behind the desk and took up the twelve-page memo of understanding, and leafed through it—and then when he was ready, he simply launched. It was a joy to witness. The way he just *shredded* the thing. Slicing out one phrase and transplanting another, X-ing out extraneous dross, peppering the poor fools with questions and complaints, brooking no dissent and contemptuous of any hesitation. What a show! Shaw, transfixed, said not a word but once or twice he laughed out loud. And only after the thing seemed to have been settled to everyone's satisfaction did he dare to inquire:

"Oh, Henry. By the way. Do you think I could have some cash?"

Smiles all around. Lonsdale finally saying, "Cash?"

Shaw nodded. "I could use a little bit of cash."

"Shaw. It'll *all* be cash."

"It will?"

"The whole shebang. What we're talking about is

getting you *out* of cash the moment it lands—and into securities, into long-term investments, so you can start earning some return on your capital—"

"But I want to start giving it away."

"So I understand," said Mr. Lonsdale. "But you know, we'll need to set up a foundation—"

"I don't want a foundation. There isn't time."

"There isn't? Why not?"

"Because the world is coming to an end."

How gravely and stupidly they took in his words. The Banker, the Accountant, the Lawyer: they all had the mien of grieving cattle. Shaw broke into a wide grin. "Look at you guys!"

Still the grave faces.

"I'm *kid*-ding."

And then, one by one, they began to chuckle.

"No rush at all," he assured them. "And hey, can I tell you something? You know how I said on that TV show that I'm giving it all away? Well. Slight correction. Not *all* of it."

More laughter, which grew quickly into barks and wheezes of relief. Understandably, thought Shaw: the thought of me giving away my fortune must have seemed an insult to their very natures. Shaw waited patiently for the laughter to fade. Then he said: "But I really could use a bit of spending money."

"Of course," said Lonsdale. "We'll keep a few million liquid. Will that do you?"

"Great."

"Say, five million? Enough for now?"

"Perfect. And when will all this come in?"

Lonsdale turned to the Banker. "Dave?"

"I'm expecting it to land by Tuesday. If we get everything signed today."

"Well, that's wonderful," said Shaw. "That's sooner than I thought. That's just great. Thank you all very much."

Said Henry Lonsdale, "Tell you what. When it does hit? Let's celebrate with a little redfishing."

Tara was in her room, listening to Trevor the spooky ex-soldier organize the world. He'd set up his card-table office right outside her window, and all day he'd been out there snapping commands: planning the kitchen, laying out the camp, negotiating with the cops and with the neighbors. Tomorrow the pilgrims would have to move, but for tonight he'd made a deal with the neighbors, and they could stay.

He was good at all this stuff, a natural *vizier*. She hated him. The sound of his voice grated on her. But where else could she go? Mom was in the kitchen and Shaw in the living room, and the pilgrims had the house surrounded, and if she went outside for an instant they'd mob her.

So she stayed there. She tried to read: she couldn't. She tried to watch *Before Night Falls,* the movie where JCD Jr. was so stunning as Bon Bon the transvestite—but his profile brought up thoughts of Shaw. She killed it. She tried listening to music on headphones but they made her feel too isolated, too vulnerable.

She went online. She looked through the hundreds of new comments on her MySpace page.

Tara I think you're beautiful and I would like to be just like you. I think Shaw McBride is a dream. You're not lucky, you're blessed.

Another wrote:

You're a sign to all of us that the Lord is 'with us' and watching over us.

Another wrote:

i watch u on the video when u win the lotery, and I love
u and want u to be my wife.

She scrolled through them. She didn't answer.

On her photo album was the **CRUNK POSSE!**, that shot
of her and Clio and Cindy and Jennera when they were
so drunk and stoned at Rafters. Someone had written:
GAWD YU GIRLZ IZ SMOKKIN!!

Wasn't that the night she had kissed James? And
thought she wanted to marry him? There was a pic of
the two of them at the Arcade Fire concert: he looked
like a kid. God. They both looked like kids. And this
photograph was taken six months ago?

She stayed away from pictures of Nell.

Shaw came to visit. He knocked politely. She murmured, "Yeah," and he came and sat in the camp chair
and asked her, "So what do you think?"

"About what?"

"This great adventure."

She looked away from him.

He said, "Romeo thinks you're not scared of him."

"I am."

"If he goes off, he'll go off like a banshee. You don't
want to test him."

"OK."

"There was a guy once back in Ohio who made the mistake of insulting us. We just *ruined* his head. We tore him to bits, and he didn't even know who was doing it. He thought we were his friends. Romeo took him for a walk one time, so the poor guy could talk about his problems. They went up on the railroad bridge. You know what happened up there?"

She shook her head.

He smiled. "I don't either. But next day they found the guy's body down on the rocks. With his brains smashed out. Suicide. Do not *ever* test Romeo's love for me."

She kept her eyes low, but she knew he was staring at her.

He said, "I know how scary this is for you. But it's also so fucking exciting. We're going to bring beauty to this world. Beauty like you've never dreamed of."

"Yes."

He said, "Look at me."

She met his gaze. "It will be worth the struggle," he said. "I swear to you."

Romeo took a right off 17 onto Belle Point Road, then a left at Indian Mound Road. He cruised past Uncle

Shelby's. The *snap snap whip whip* of sprinklers, and there was Shelby himself in the driveway, vacuuming the Escalade.

Romeo thought, I bet I could work up some hate for *this* guy.

Not just on account of the Nazi landscaping but also because he's vacuuming his car on a *Saturday afternoon*. Wasting a Saturday afternoon on such cinch-up-your-anus bullshit.

If I got to know him, I'm sure I could come to detest him. Then if I had to I could kill him.

He drove down to the end of Seahorse Drive, turned around and came back. Pulled into the driveway. In his pocket he still had the leaflet that Tess had given him, from her Church of Jesus Triumphant, and as he emerged from the car he took it out and handed it to Shelby. "Hi, there. You got the word on Jesus?"

This only peeved the man.

"Son, I'm a deacon at Faith Renewal. I don't need this."

Offering it back. Romeo thought the visit was going well. The guy was a puffed-up jackass, and that stirred a small resentment in Romeo's heart. He just needed to give this a little juice. Maybe if he got a look inside the house?

"Sir, you wouldn't have anything I could drink, would you? Glass of lemonade?"

"I think we're out of lemonade," said Shelby. His look said, *Enough. Go away now.*

"Not even powdered or something? How about water?"

Thinking, you're a Christian, Shelby: you can't deny a poor passerby a drink of water.

"All right. Hold on."

He meant for Romeo to wait outside. But Romeo followed him right into the garage. Skateboards hung on hooks near the back door, with badminton rackets, lacrosse rackets, skis. Said Romeo, "You guys are so sporty."

As Shelby opened the kitchen door, a golden retriever commenced a low woofing. Shelby called, "MacKenzie! Come hold Lucky. We've got a visitor."

A little girl, radiant and ringletted, came and grabbed the dog by the collar.

Romeo followed Shelby into the kitchen. What a paradise! Earth-tone tiles and seashell lighting and Old Testament magnets on the refrigerator door. "Hey Dad," came a boy's voice from the great room, "you should see the approach Sergio just hit. Oh man, he nailed it. With a three-iron. Six yards from the hole."

"Darn," said Shelby. "How's Phil doing?"

"Phil's out of it."

"Darn."

The little girl was staring at Romeo.

Her father told her, "MacKenzie, would you please give this man a glass of water?"

Romeo said, "MacKenzie. That's a beautiful name." He took the glass from her and drank. The lovely cascading void.

"Thank you," he said.

He gave her back the glass. She rinsed it and placed it in the dishwasher, and sponged the countertop. When she was done, everything was immaculate, just as it had been. You've got quite the system here, thought Romeo.

He said, "MacKenzie, do you like Mew Mew Power?"

She smiled and her eyes grew round. She said, "I *love* Mew Mew Power."

He said, "I have a niece who loves Mew Mew Power."

She asked him, "You see the magnets?" She meant the magnets on the refrigerator. "They're from the Bible."

"That's beautiful," said Romeo.

She pointed to a Nativity. "That's from the Gospel of Matthew."

"Really? What about that one?"

"That's Acts of the Apostles."

He smiled. "This here is a house of true holiness. You know how I know that?"

MacKenzie guessed, "The magnets?"

"Well yes, but more than that, your generosity." He truly meant this. It had been a mistake to come here. He felt no hatred for these people at all. He hoped Shelby would invite him to stay for supper.

But Shelby said nothing. They all stared at him.

"All right," said Romeo. "Well, thank you for the water. Goodbye, MacKenzie. Goodbye, sir."

Shelby told his daughter, "Honey, hold Lucky, I don't want her getting out."

Romeo got back in the Tercel, and returned to his circling of hell.

Shaw and the Boatwrights went to St. Simon's Island for the Jackpot Party, arriving at 7:00 p.m. It was still light out, but the place was already packed to the rafters. *Hoo-aws.* Bear hugs. To get through the crowd Shaw had to give everyone a shake or a tap. Some guy hung an elbow over his neck and introduced himself as Skeet and asked what he was drinking. Shaw said shyly, Johnnie Walker

Red? Rocks? Then a girl with a tightly strung midriff murmured into his ear how much she liked what he'd said on TV. She murmured more than that, but there was an old-timey band playing, harmonica and fiddles and banjos, and he couldn't hear. Her lips brushed his cheek as she spoke, though, and her message came through.

Henceforth all the world would be coming to him like this? On a platter?

The scotch was placed in his hand. He pulled out his wallet but Skeet said, "No, *I'll* get this. *You* get my mortgage."

When Shaw laughed, everyone around him also laughed.

Also he found that wherever he looked, girls would lower their eyes bashfully, pretending they hadn't been staring at him.

Skeet was a tax preparer three months of the year and a beach bum the rest. He advised Shaw to steer clear of sharps and grifters. He said, "Success is a peak—soon's you get up there you start sliding down. Anyway, that's what I did."

Shaw laughed and they high-fived.

Then he worked his way through the crowd to the Boatwrights' table. There was supposed to be a no-media, no-pictures rule, but flashes kept going off. Oh, let them, he thought. Are we hiding something? No, we're as open as church doors on Sunday. He asked Patsy for a dance. She was already pretty drunk, so to absorb her clumsiness he took something off his own moves. He twirled and jitterbugged and rock-a-bye-babied her, and made her look almost graceful, and she seemed to enjoy herself, and locked eyes with him as they spun.

But he saw Mitch glaring at the floor with his bug eyes.

So while the musicians tuned up for another song, Shaw went over to sit by him. Saying into his ear, "I'm not getting it on with your wife, OK, Mitch? I just want everyone to survive. Remember in a week I'll be gone and you'll still be the richest man you know. You don't have to love me, but make 'em think you do. OK?"

Then he bought a round for everyone in the bar.

Romeo, following Shaw's orders, left the car on Redwood Street, and went on foot from there to the Boatwrights'. A pig-rig was blocking Oriole Road, which made him nervous. But he walked right past it, and they didn't try to stop him. They were just there to keep vehicles out—there were already too many SUVs and RVs and TV trucks.

At the Boatwrights', he found twenty people, whites, blacks, and Latinos, sitting in a circle under a big oak, singing songs of praise. Their smiles were unwithholding. One pointed to a cooler full of soft drinks, and Romeo nodded thanks and took a Stewart's Root Beer, and listened to the music while he steadied himself. Then he went up to the front door.

Waiting for him was a taut, drawn-looking guy in tie-dye pants.

"You Trevor?" said Romeo.

The guy made a small acknowledgment—a circum-scribed tilt of the head. "Romeo? Shaw said you were coming. I'm supposed to help get you settled."

They went into the house, to Jase's room, where Shaw was staying. Trevor pointed to one of the two beds and said, "Take that. We'll find somewhere else for the kid." Then he left Romeo alone.

As soon as his footsteps faded, Romeo slipped across the hall to Tara's bedroom.

It had the fragrance of a small-town college girl. Humbly sweet and fresh but with a faint pull of sexuality. He wondered if Shaw had been in here yet. Had he tried to seduce her? Well, he would. This was just the kind of girl he went for: skinny and feisty and nice-haunches-no-tits and loves her grandmother.

On her bookcase was a Stephen King and an Edgar Allan Poe and *The Uncanny*, by Andrew Klavan. So she liked terror? Though she also had *Wind in the Willows* and *The Borrowers* and *The Bell Jar*, and a glowing Jesus and a cross-eyed rhinoceros. And an Edward Scissorhands bobblehead doll.

From outside came the praise-singing: "Even when the flood starts rising, Even when the storm comes, I am washed by the water."

He sat before her laptop. Turned it over, opened the mini-PCI slot, installed his keylogger card and transmitter. It took him two minutes. Then he went to the master bedroom and impregnated Patsy's laptop the same way. The system was rigged so that Shaw's computer would hijack the transmissions and email them directly to Romeo.

Then he went out to the carport and found Trevor. "Hey, listen," he said. "Thank you, but I just can't take that kid's bed."

"Oh, that's no problem. He can sleep on the couch."

"Tell you the truth, I'm kind of freaked out by the singing. But tell Shaw to call me, OK?"

He went down the driveway while the folks were singing "El-Shaddai." He got to his car and fed Drive Fast & Shut Your Eyes into the CD player, and drew another slow circle around the city.

He went by Hazel Ramsey's house. Shaw said that Hazel was Patsy's friend—that's why she was on Romeo's circuit. But her house was dark. Of course it was. Any friend of Patsy's would be at the Jackpot Party.

He went by Enoch Emery's office. Enoch was a 'Point of Interest' because his business had been mentioned a few times on Mitch's website. But the office was closed, naturally. It was Saturday night. Enoch would be at the Party.

The neon signs along Rt. 341 made Romeo feel lonely as hell. So did the sodium-arc streetlights on MLK Boulevard, and so did the hoarse songbird when he stopped for a red light at J Street. Then on Rt. 17 he saw a line of claret taillights, waiting to turn onto the St. Simon's Island causeway. Saturday night! *Everyone* was going to the island, everyone but Romeo. He got gas at El Cheapo, and drove on. He wanted to scream. He wanted to batter his fists against the windshield. Driving around and around trying to figure out how he could ever kill these people. How did anyone ever scrape up that much insanity?

Shaw danced with old Nell, buckdancing and high-stepping. The two of them brayed out "Rocky Top" like a pair of broken-hearted hounds, and anyone could see they were madly in love.

Shaw had another Red-and-rocks. Then he danced with Cousin Vanessa.

He didn't ask Tara to dance. That would have been too loaded—everybody was watching him as it was.

He had another Red-and-rocks.

There was a new girl. Over by the fireplace. Tall, strong-boned, tragic, gazing at him with fierce interest. She wore a strange ornament: a spiral snake that wound through her cheek, and he knew who she was from her MySpace pics.

He made his way over to her. "Hello, Clio."

She gave him a sidelong squint. "The guy on TV?"

"Uh-huh. How'd I do with that?"

"Want the truth?"

"Yes."

"You were kinda cheesy."

"Aw. You didn't see the light of Jesus radiating out of me?"

"I saw a cheesy poser-ass on drugs."

"What kind of drugs?"

"I don't know," she said. "What kind you got?"

"What kind do you like?"

"Depends on my mood," she said. "Amytal? Percs? Dems if I'm *really* depressed. Like today."

"Why are you depressed today?"

Clio drew a breath and let it out. "My best friend just dumped me."

"Why'd she do that?"

"She thinks she's too good for me."

"No she doesn't."

"How would *you* know?"

He smiled. "Cup your hand."

She did, and he pressed a little round pill into her palm.

"What is it?"

"Just a little old-fashioned dexie. It'll lighten things for a while."

He passed her his Red to chase it with. She kept her eyes on him as she drank. Then she had a thought: "Hey, how do you know my name?"

Tara saw Clio flirting with Shaw and ceased to breathe.

She thought, everything I did to protect her has only made things worse. Because now she thinks I deserted her. Now she's furious with me. She might have fucked Shaw anyway, but now she *surely* will—just to hurt me.

She saw Clio break into a laugh, and though it was drowned out by the bar noise, she knew just how it sounded: cutting but playful. Tara had one like it in her own arsenal. You put the boy down cleverly and use the laugh to throw him off balance, then soften it into a giggle at the end. She could see it was working for Clio. She could tell by Shaw's expression—kind of confused but beguiled at the same time. He was caught.

Aunt Miriam came up to Tara and started chirping: "Oh, child! That was the best news ever! We're *so* proud of you. I believe God truly has a purpose for your family. I think when He gives so generously, it's because He has a purpose, don't you? These things don't just fall out of the sky for no reason. There's nothing that happens in this world without a *reason* . . ." And on and on, but Tara hardly heard, as all her focus was on Clio and Shaw. He was showing her that cocky little smile of his. She stood on tiptoe to speak into his ear, to share some intimacy, and he reached up and traced the serpent on her cheek with his fingertip, audaciously zigzagging down the coils.

Tara felt something give way then, in her vitals.

A tiny snap of jealousy.

He's *my* demon, *my* hell; leave him *alone*.

The thought was gone in an instant. But she could feel its poison lingering in her mind, and meanwhile Aunt Miriam kept twittering: "I mean don't you think this Shaw boy is just a jewel? He's truly *devout*, Tara. That part's very real. I think he's an absolute gift from God, if you want to know what *I* think . . ."

Romeo knew he wasn't welcome at the trailer. He knew if he stopped there, Wynetta would come after him with a kitchen knife. But he wasn't planning to stop—he just wanted to drive past, for a glimpse of Claude.

But when he saw that Wynetta's truck was gone, he pulled right in. He went up to the door and pushed it open. Claude lay there with no blanket. His eyes lifted slowly. "I feel. *Great,*" he said. Then turned away with a gypsy-dog look of remorse. There was a sour smell, and the sheet around his ass was stained a rich walnut.

Romeo asked him, "Where's Wynetta?"

Claude attempted to shrug.

Romeo went to the linen closet and found sheets, threadbare but clean. At the sink he rinsed out the sponge and filled the enamel pot with warm water. Then he went to work.

So long as he was taking care of things, he felt light-hearted.

But as soon he was done, the moment he had Claude all cleaned up and resting peacefully in fresh sheets and pillowcases with a new bag of morphine seeping into his system, Romeo felt the weight of all his troubles again.

He lay down on the bed, next to the old man. The two of them gazed up at the spiderwork cracks on the ceiling. Claude's lips were moving, and he seemed to be struggling through some train of thought. But maybe that was wrong. Maybe he wasn't thinking at all—maybe he was just suffering.

Romeo said, "Has it kicked in yet?"

Long pull of silence. Then Claude said, "I think. I know what. You're doing here. You're supposed. To kill someone. Right?"

Romeo took a breath. "Yes."

"But you're not. Ready?"

"I'm not."

"Well. Then. You should. Practice."

"What do you mean?"

"Killing," Claude whispered.

"Practice killing? How would I practice killing?"

"On me."

"I don't . . ."

"Please," said Claude.

"Oh my God. Claude. Wait for the morphine. It'll work in a minute."

"Can't you give me *all* the morphine? Give me the whole bag."

"It's on a pump, Claude. You can't get it all at once."

"Help me."

The look on the old man's face—all selfishness and weakness—was crushing to Romeo. That this pillar of strength should be crumbling right before his eyes.

"Claude. I can't do that for you."

"Just. For practice."

"Try to understand, Claude."

"To get. In shape. For the real thing."

"I can't! You don't get it. I gotta get worked up for this shit!"

"Please," said the old man. He was begging. How could he be so weak? Romeo wondered. How could he have fallen so low?

"I'll see."

"Please," said Claude.

"I'll see. Later. But I gotta go now."

Romeo arose from the bed and walked out. He shut the door behind him. He got into the Tercel and drove. He didn't know where he was going. Without thinking he started making a circuit.

No. I don't want to make a fucking circuit.

This time, when he came to the turn for the St. Simon's Island causeway, he took it. He crossed the marshes and came to the island, which he found to be well-manicured but dull. Retirement condos, offices for osteopaths, phony-looking palm trees. But he followed a sign to the village, and found an old and kind of sweetly run-down settlement, a last gasp of character and grace. Murphy's Bar was easy to spot. So many folks were milling outside the Jackpot Party.

He pulled over on a side street. Under a spreading oak. From this vantage he had a clear view of the bar, the partygoers flowing in and out.

This misery he was feeling, couldn't he use it somehow? Work it up into some kind of rage? That was the key, a little rage.

Then he noticed someone coming out of another door, a back door.

It was Shaw. Trying to slip away without being spotted by the crowd. Hovering near the dumpster, waiting for someone. He didn't see Romeo parked in the shadows down the street.

Then Clio drove up in her Miata. Shaw got in, and they drove away. Romeo's heart went slamming around in his chest.

Clio. She's mine. That was *Clio*.

She's all I care about in this fucking town. He *knows* that. He must. Doesn't he give a shit? It doesn't even matter to him? My best fucking friend!

He followed the Miata. Allowed it a generous lead, and kept his headlights off, and pursued the car down a few back streets and then a little unpaved lane that led to the ocean.

The Miata stopped. Romeo stopped.

He got out quietly—carefully clicking the door shut—and went back to the Tercel's trunk, and took the cavalry saber from its nest. He started toward the Miata. Oak branches were twined above his head. His footfalls were deadened by the sand. My best friend, he thought, my best fucking friend. He could see that the Miata's windows were open. He heard passionate breathing. In the dark, he could just make out the lovers' silhouettes.

But he noticed, as he approached, that his rage was quickly fading. Was, in fact, gone. Now he didn't know what he felt. There was the pain of Shaw's betrayal, but this was indistinct against his general background pain. What he was mostly aware of was loneliness. And the thought occurred to him that at least Shaw was happy now.

Shaw's fingers roamed from Clio's breast to her thigh, then made a shrewd horseshoe turn and came gliding back up toward her pussy. She made a half-hearted attempt to stop him, clamping her thighs together, but didn't stop kissing him. And he retreated for only a moment and then was back right away—his fingers circling their quarry closer and closer, and he knew she wouldn't hold out long.

"Jesus," she breathed. "You just swoop down, don't you?"

She was here to be taken, wasn't she?

Soon he was pressing into her through her panties which were already soaked; his fingers pleading, insisting, till she sighed and relaxed a little and then he moved quickly, slipping under the elastic and into her, one finger, another, cupping her pubic bone against his palm. Her breath coming ragged, her musk, the smell of the sea, a mockingbird overhead. And the other girl in the bar, the one with the brightly burnished midriff—she'd be available for him later, wouldn't she? And finally: Tara. Tara would be sleeping in the next room tonight, and every hour would bring her closer to him. He grinned. He had three fingers inside this one, and when her breath seized up he thought she was coming and he increased the pressure. Then she screamed.

She was pushing him away and staring at something.

He wrenched himself around to see. Someone was there. A figure, a man. Retreating. Carrying some kind of a long knife that glinted in the thin moonlight. Shaw was scrabbling at the car door, searching for the handle, and he found it and got the door open and barrel-rolled out, propelling himself into the dark.

But the man was getting into a car. Headlights, and the car backing away violently, vanishing.

Shaw turned back to Clio.

She was sobbing. "He had a fucking knife! He was watching us! Who was it? Who the fuck! *Was it?*"

Shaw didn't say a word.

Romeo parked where he had a clear view up Mallery Street to Murphy's Bar. He waited, and soon enough Clio's car appeared—stopping near the back of the bar—and Shaw got out, and the car drove off.

Shaw snapped open his cell phone and jabbed at it with his finger. The phone in Romeo's hand trembled like a frightened animal. He lifted it to his ear. "Yes."

"Where are you?"

"Turn around," said Romeo, and when Shaw did he flashed his lights.

"Come here," said Shaw. "Now."

Romeo pulled up and Shaw got in and shut the door hard. "Drive."

Romeo eased past the crowd in front of Murphy's.

"*Drive!* Before someone sees me. Get the fuck out of here."

A T-shirt store, then a souvenir shop, then a frilly ice-cream parlor. Shaw said, "You know, I really thought we'd done this thing. I thought we'd made these amazing lives for ourselves. You stupid shit."

Trying to keep a lid on his anger. But his mouth didn't work right. An electrical hiss at the edge of his words. Finally he said, "So what is the *matter* with you!"

"I don't know," said Romeo.

Shaw demanded: "Tell me! Why the fuck were you standing there?"

Romeo sniffed. "I don't know."

Again Shaw said, "*Why were you standing there?*"

"Isn't that what I'm supposed to do? Supposed to be the watcher, right?"

Now Shaw blew up.

"From a distance! You dumb fuck! You're supposed to be invisible! You're not supposed to be standing there when I've got my hand down some bitch's pants!"

Romeo said, "Is she just some bitch?"

"WHO PUT YOU IN CHARGE OF FUCKING UP OUR LIVES?"

Romeo bore down on the gas at the very moment that a platoon of frat boys, in flattops and green golfing pants, came strolling across the street. They were disinclined to yield till they realized their lives were on the line—then they hotfooted it, shouting obscenities after the car. Romeo hardly saw them.

He drove to the village pier, parked, and walked off. Leaving Shaw with the car. Who needs the fucking car? He walked along the sea wall, past the miniature golf course and its rinky-dink music, past families ambling along in the heat. Everyone was eating—ice cream, chili dogs, cotton candy—and everyone was dull and fat and waxen. He came to a sandbox with two big gray blobs that looked like the swollen corpses of fat kids. When he got closer he realized it was supposed to be a sculpture. A sculpture of swimming whales. God. Everything was so ugly and wrong here. What was he *doing* here? He needed to keep moving, find an ATM, get a taxi to the bus station and a bus back to Piqua, Ohio. Start right now.

He sat on a low wall beside the whales.

In a minute Shaw came up and sat next to him.

"OK." Shaw's voice was full of remorse. "I think I just got it. You *liked* Clio. Didn't you?"

Romeo didn't answer.

"Oh Jesus. I'm sorry. I should have seen that. Why didn't I see that? That was your backyard. You must hate me."

They stared out at the black swells of the Atlantic Ocean.

Shaw said, "I'm just, I mean I've just been so keyed up, I'm not thinking straight. My God, if you'd *seen* them tonight. The Boatwrights, back at that bar? They're all trying to submit. Even Mitch. He *wants* to submit. He wants it so much. And the wife wants me to fuck her. And, God, you went by the house—

you see that? See all the people there? The whole *world* wants to submit. You know why, Romeo? Because of you. Because of you being out there in the darkness."

A horn buoy moaned offshore, just as Shaw was saying *out there in the darkness*. The harmony of it took Romeo's breath away.

Shaw said, "You know what I've been thinking about? About the history of the world, about how this is always the way. Anything good, or original, it's never just someone with a plan. There has to be an enforcer too. Caesar had to have legionnaires. Thomas Jefferson had to have the Continental soldiers freezing their fucking feet off. Joseph Smith had that great story about the Golden Tablets, but he also had to have the Danites, to skulk around and murder his enemies. That's how the good comes into the world—with a dark escort. Always the light is guarded by darkness. Always. Every great idea has a Romeo patrolling just outside. Every great idea is enforced by great terror. All right? I mean, if you want something else besides the shit they hand you? You want to make room for love or beauty or anything? You've got to be fearless and you've got to be merciless. You've got to make them kneel before the divine right of ravens. It's a hard thing to accept, but it's the way the world works. And what we're doing, you and me, this adventure of ours? This is the best idea anyone's had in a thousand years. But it all comes down to you. To you suffering in that darkness. To my knowing that you won't let me down. You see what I'm saying?"

"Yeah, I do," said Romeo.

Really he didn't see it very well, but it didn't matter—what mattered to him was Shaw's passion. The fact that sometimes in his presence Romeo felt OK about the strange meshwork-trap of his life.

When I'm with Shaw, he thought, the rest of the world can go fuck itself. Fuck itself or not fuck itself, it's not important because the world doesn't *exist*. It only seems to. The so-called 'world' is here for our amusement only.

Two young pigtailed sisters in cutoffs were coming off the pier, lugging a big ice chest between them. Their T-shirts were streaked with shark blood. And Romeo felt bold enough to say: "Hey, check out the meat puppets. They fuck each other, right?"

"Only every night," said Shaw.

Romeo put a little leering growl into his laugh. "But what's that on their shirts? Could that be menstrual blood?"

"Oh yes," said Shaw. "They're pigs for it."

"They have no idea how disgusting that is?"

"Kids today."

Then they both were laughing. They walked back to the car and took a drive. They cruised aimlessly. They went down some street with a lot of real estate offices and brokerages and big touristy restaurants: Crab-daddies, the Crabshack, My Crabby Aunt Sally. They found another road that ran parallel to the ocean. A lighthouse flashed away in the dark. Rowdy boys were setting off roman candles. Romeo was almost smiling. It was as though he and Shaw were finally on the vacation they'd intended. Now there would be girls and margar-itas and softshell crabs, and the whole Southern night spreading out before them.

But in fact they drove for less than ten minutes before Shaw said he had to get back. "I'm worried about the Boatwrights."

So Romeo took him back to Murphy's, and left him there.

He was alone for the trip back across the cause-way. He looked out at the vast black marshes, which made him think of death, which made him think of Claude. Jesus. He still had to do something for poor Claude.

Patsy had fallen into a nostalgic mood. It was after midnight, and she and Shaw and Tara and Mitch were in the Liberty on their way home from the party. Shaw wouldn't let them put the a.c. on. He said he wanted the ocean air, so they kept the windows down which reminded Patsy of high school days, of riding around in Danny Duggan's El Camino. Danny hadn't liked a.c. either. Or maybe the a.c. just hadn't worked in his crazy old pickup-car? Anyway, in those days you could still drive on the beach late at night, and if your windows were open the ocean air would come rippling in at you just the way it was doing now.

"Mitch," she said, "you remember Danny Duggan?"

Mitch grunted. "What about him?"

"Remember that thing he drove?"

"I never hung out with Danny Duggan."

"Oh, right," she said. "Danny Duggan wasn't in Bible Club. He was *e*-vil."

She was aware of the sharpness in her tone but she didn't care. She was drunk and she didn't care about that either. She proclaimed to the whole car: "Danny Duggan taught me how to dance. He might have been *e*-vil but he sure knew how to dance."

Nobody answered her.

She added, "Though he never danced like you, Shaw."

Does that come across as provocative? she wondered. And do I give a rat's ass? "Shaw. Don't you want me to tell you how you dance?"

"OK."

"Like a *lun*-atic."

She laughed. He didn't laugh with her, though. Nobody did.

Tara was doing the driving and staring at the road as cold as stone.

Well, probably she was jealous.

Though there was no way to know for sure. Patsy couldn't see her face, and anyway, Tara always buried her feelings; she never shared with her mother. Which was sad. My own daughter is at war with me, she thought. She knows me not. She thinks I'm as churchy as her father. If she knew the wildness in my soul it would blow her mind. If she knew for example the mischief I got into on that trip to Spain when I was her age; oh my Lord in heaven.

And who *did* understand that part of Patsy?

Well. This was nuts but she thought Shaw did. A little. Was she sick to think that? About her captor? Was that quite inappropriate?

Maybe Shaw was attracted to Tara—but Patsy was sure he was closer in spirit to her. Because he was in love with adventure. True, he was a criminal, a son of a bitch, and hanging would have been too good for him. *Castration* would have been too good for him! But it also had to be admitted that he had blood in his veins. He had the heart of a swashbuckler, which Patsy's daughter couldn't possibly appreciate and which her poor sad husband with his soul full of ashes couldn't *stand*. Patsy wasn't excusing him or forgiving him in any way, ever— she was just saying Shaw McBride had blood in his veins.

Romeo had prepared himself to do what Claude had asked, to be of service. If all he needs is death, I'll provide it, and in return I'll just ask him to tell me again, one more time, about the old fisherman.

But when he got to the trailer he found he was too late. Claude's eyes were open but no one was there. Romeo touched his cheek: it was like something in a museum. And Romeo's own heart went cold inside his chest.

He thought, I should close his eyes, shouldn't I? That would be the proper thing to do. But which eye first? He chose the right. He tried forcing down the lid with his thumb, but it slipped free and sprang open again and his thumb skidded onto the cold vitreous humor—the iris rolling away, averting its gaze from a botched job.

Oh. Fucked this up. I'm sorry, Claude.

Shaw was astonished, when they got back to the house, by the increase in his flock. Cars were parked along the curb of Redwood Road nearly as far as 17, and on Oriole Road two police cruisers had their roof lights flashing. The pilgrims were cheering and waving palmetto fronds. Some of them had come in RVs and had brought kids and dogs and Frisbees. Some seemed to be derelicts. They showed the black roots of their molars when they grinned.

Trevor's crew of bodyguards held the crowd back as Shaw and the Boatwrights emerged from the Liberty.

Shaw murmured to Trevor, "Too many."

Trevor nodded. "I paid off the neighbors for tonight. Tomorrow we go to the fairgrounds."

An old woman reached between two bodyguards and touched Shaw's shoulder, crying, "Father! Help me! Father!" She was tiny and frail, but she wouldn't be

denied, and finally he made a sign to the bodyguards: let
her approach.

"Father," she said, "can you heal the sick?"

"Who's sick? Not you."

"My husband." She clutched his sleeve, pulling at him.
"Please, Father."

He let her lead. The crowd eddied and purled around
them. She brought him to the end of the driveway, to an
old man sitting in a wheelchair, who cast a skeptical eye
as Shaw approached.

All I need to do, Shaw thought, is use the power that's
already here.

He asked the man, "What's your name?"

"Bill Phillips."

"And why are you crippled?"

"RSD. Ever heard of it?"

"Tell me."

"Reflex sympathetic dystrophy."

"You're in pain?"

"Oh, yeah. Around my knee here. So much pain I
can't use the leg."

Shaw said, "But that's not the pain you need to be
awakened from. What you need to be awakened from is
this dream of life. You understand this?"

Bill Phillips squinted at him. The crowd had fallen

silent. A TV camera whirred, in harmony with the crickets, and cell phone flashes reflected off the oak leaves.

Shaw said, "You dream that you're alone in the world. You dream that your Father is not with you. But in truth He's right here beside you, and if you could awaken, you'd see Him as bright as day."

"Right here?" said Bill Phillips. His eyes were tearing up. Soon he began to weep. Shaw set hands upon his withered legs, till the spasms of weeping subsided—then turned from him, and walked toward the house, and the crowd parted so he could pass.

Romeo went out looking for Wynetta, to give her the news. One redneck dive after another: Duke's, the Oleander Inn, some nameless cinderblock bar out by the airport. But she wasn't to be found. He even tried a titty bar called the "VIP" Lounge in an old brick warehouse downtown. The sign had it just like that, with quotation marks around VIP. She wasn't there, but when Romeo glanced up at the dancer working the pole, he found to his amazement that it was Tess! Tess the missionary girl!

GEORGE DAWES GREEN

Seeing her up there was as disturbing to Romeo as looking up into that wheel well had been. She clomped
through her act in black suede boots and a silvery g-
string, with her big forehead and the allure of an
industrial robot. Luckily she didn't notice him, didn't see
him wincing.

But when her song was done, and she came trolling
for a "VIP" lap to fill, she recognized him—and broke
into a wide grin. "Romeo!"

"Hey, Tess."

"What are you doing here?"

"What are *you* doing here?"

She shrugged. "Paying my rent."

She took the stool next to him. The bartender was a
dour old dyke. Romeo bought Tess a drink and asked
her, "What happened to the missionary deal?"

"Oh. Guy who sent us? Kind of flaked."

"And the other girl?"

"Megan? She's working at the bag plant. Up in
Darien. Last I heard."

"Sounds fucked," said Romeo.

"Yeah."

"You still love that guy who hangs people on hooks?"

"Sort of. But he don't love me back so forget it."

They were watching the next dancer, who wasn't any

258

golden beauty either, but at least her performance made a stab at coyness and come-hither.

Tess asked him, "So how's your vacation going, Romeo?"

He shook his head. "Not so good. My friend just died on me."

"Oh, I'm sorry. That guy, the one I met?"

"Uh-uh. Old dude. Lived in a trailer. Old fisherman."

"Oh."

"His grandfather was an old fisherman too. His grandfather used to call him the little rooster."

She smiled. "Really?"

"I was taking care of him. Do you know Balm-of-Gilead Road?"

"Yes!" she said. "We witnessed out there."

"Find any converts?"

"You gotta be joking."

The DJ said: "Frankie, to the stage."

"Well, that's me."

He said, "That's like your dancing name? Frankie?"

"It's short for Frankenstein. I make 'em use it. It's my nickname from back home. They don't want me to use it, but I tell 'em I'm not gonna be your damn Tabitha or Crystal or Charmaigne, you know? I gotta go now. Wait for me?"

"I wish I could."

However, he did take a five-dollar bill from his wallet, folded it lengthwise, and when she held her garter open he placed it in the space provided. That small transaction occurred between them; then he went.

Back on the road, he remembered that Wynetta had mentioned some bar she liked out on Rt. 341. He couldn't quite remember the name. Some kind of bird name. He drove out there anyway. Rt. 341 was dark for a long time, then came the blindingness of the lights around the State Police Barracks, then darkness again. Finally he saw a dismal neon sign: Pigeon's, with a dismal tavern beneath it. And there was Wynetta's truck sitting in the lot.

He parked and lowered his seat and waited for her.

One by one, drunks came two-stepping out. Driving off.

Finally, here was Wynetta on the arm of some turkey-neck codger who leaned her up against her car and started sexing her. Trying to fit his hand down between her tight belt and her fat belly, and he had to bend his elbow like he was bowling. After a minute he seemed to have taken his fill of this awkwardness: he pulled his hand free and gave her belly a pat and staggered away.

Wynetta called names after him but he was done. He drove off in his pickup.

Then Romeo got out of the Tercel. "Hi, Wynetta."

She was confused. Trying to recall how she knew him. Was he a former boyfriend? Cop or something? But the gears turned slowly.

He said, "There's a problem about your dad."

Now it came. "Oh shit. The fucking. The fake nurse. Get away from me. I scream, the goons will be in your face in ten seconds."

He said, "I just want—"

"In your face! In your face!"

"All right. I just want to tell you about your dad."

"What about my dad?"

"He's dead."

"What?"

He wasn't going to say it twice. "I'll give you a ride home."

"I got my truck," she said. "Did you say my daddy's dead?"

"Better let me take you."

She shrugged. He escorted her to the Tercel and they drove back down Rt. 341.

She said, "How do you know my daddy's dead?"

"I went to see him."

"Oh," she said.

More dark road went by. She said, "You didn't drink all the PBRs, did you?"

What a piece of work, thought Romeo. "There are no PBRs. The PBRs are all gone."

"You drank them?"

"No, you drank them, Wynetta."

"I didn't drink 'em *all*."

"OK," he said. "What's your point?"

"My point? My point is, you took something that wasn't yours."

It stressed him to be sharing his car with this callous vacant alcoholic middle-aged brat. She had made Claude's last days on earth such a living hell he had begged a stranger to set him free. She'd done that to Claude! Romeo hadn't felt such a purity of disgust in a long time.

He wondered, can I make something of this?

Wynetta was still whining: "Take me to Lonnie's? Lonnie'll loan me a sixpack."

"It's pretty late."

"I'll wake him up. When I tell him my daddy's dead, I bet he'll let me have one beer from his precious stash."

Romeo said, "No, I'm taking you to your father's."

"Why? To see him dead? I don't *want* to see him dead."

They turned onto Balm-of-Gilead Road.

She said, "It's not something I care to enjoy."

Concentrate on the indecency of her indifference, thought Romeo, and the horror of her breath, and the sadness of this road. Think about all these things at the same time and see how much anger you can scare up.

She said, "I want one beer. You're saying that's not OK with you? One cocksucking beer?"

He let his left hand drop to where the saber was waiting, between the seat and the door. He curled his fingers around the handle. He could do this. He'd needed inspiration; now he had it. Get me mad enough, bitch, and I'm as dark as any motherfucker on the planet.

"Wynetta. You know what I do for a living?"

"You sell insurance."

"No, I made that up. What I really do is, I'm an angel of vengeance. You know what that means?"

"Uh-uh."

"It means, like, I dole out just deserts. That's my job."

Her mouth was slightly ajar, but not from fear. It was just her normal expression.

He pulled in at the trailer and said, "Shall I make it clear to you?"

"Nah. I got shit of my own to worry about."

She opened the door and got out.

Romeo got out on his side, saber in hand. Keeping it shielded behind his leg as he came around the front of the car. This was the place to strike, out here. Inside would be too cramped. Also Claude was in there with his eyes open, and Romeo knew he could never do this with Claude watching him, even if Claude was dead.

But he could do it out here. Let it happen now. Let this anger take over. Get to that whirling place. He visualized a sharp coppery *whoosh* from the blade. Then her shout—then her shout cut short.

But even as he was conjuring this, she stepped up to the trailer door and said, "Hey, leave me alone with my daddy, OK? I'll handle the ambulance and everything. Thanks for the ride." She went in and shut the door behind her.

The whole time, he just stood there like frozen mud.

Wondering, why hadn't he acted?

Well, for one thing, she wasn't worth it.

There was also the saber. The saber had been such a bad idea. He could have done it with a gun. With a gun you just needed to pull the trigger, but with a saber you had to go leaping and slashing like a buccaneer and no way was he ready for that.

He stood there for half a minute.

Then he got back in the Tercel and drove off. On Rt.

341 he came to some kind of nursery school, and pulled around to the dumpster in back and tossed the saber. Then he got the scabbard out of the Tercel's trunk and tossed that as well. Thinking, what I need is to kill coldly. To climb out of my soul and kill *coldly*. How the hell did I think I could kill her with a fucking pirate sword?

SUNDAY

Burris, as ever, sat six pews behind Nell. As ever, Nell didn't take her own seat till the last moment, but floated from crony to crony, cackling and wisecracking, the loudest most boisterous soul in church. He tried not to look at her, but he was helpless. Her least movement drew his eye. Even while he mumbled hello to his pew mates (they spoke tenderly to him, as he was still a fairly fresh widower), he could see her at the margin of his vision. He leafed through his hymnal, but was aware only of her laugh. He adjusted his tie. He smoothed down the unruly patch of hair on his forehead. He pursed his lips—a thing he often caught himself doing these days, which he hated because it was something an old man would do. Well, he *was* an old man. It was too damn hot in here. The air-conditioning couldn't begin to keep up with this crowd. He stole another look. She was chatting with one of the elders, and of course flirting. As ever. But then came a murmur and swiveling of heads, everyone turning because the Boatwright family was coming up the aisle.

Shaw McBride was with them.

The girl, Tara, was saying something to her mother, and she had her hand on her father's shoulder. Then she murmured some private joke to McBride, which he smiled at. When her little brother lagged too far behind, she went back and took his hand firmly and guided him forward. The whole family seemed to orbit around her. She looked into the pews and nodded to friends and relations. She smiled radiantly at her Uncle Shelby and Aunt Miriam and their kids. She bestowed a kiss on the furry cheek of Mrs. Briggs, her teacher from Glynn Middle School. At last she reached Nell. When those two embraced, it made the whole church feel buoyant, sunny, storybook.

Burris was thinking, could this family really be the target of a hundred-million-dollar extortion scheme?

It sure didn't look that way.

McBride wore an ill-fitting jacket, and seemed shy and uncomfortable. A stranger congratulated him and he gripped the man's hand as though holding on for dear life. He seemed overwhelmed by all this fuss. The last thing you got from him was *mastermind of terror.*

Burris started to worry: had he gotten this all wrong? Had he screwed up *again*? He was sweating, and with no handkerchief he had nothing to wipe his brow with but the sleeve of his jacket, and as he raised his arm to do that, he caught a whiff of his own pungency. Dear Lord, he prayed, let this service be over quickly.

But it went on and on, world without end.

First came Rev. Dave's sermon, pumped up with weepy little stories and zings of corny humor. The parishioners sniffling and laughing on cue, shouting out affirmations like this was some kind of real estate seminar. Next, a batch of praise singing. Next, Marie Kingsley had blessings for the infirm and ailing. She read out a list of all the poor souls in hospital, and as always it was a wrenching and horrific tale, and Burris thought, Lord? What's Your purpose again in this? Why exactly do You put us through this every week?

Next, everybody fell to their knees for a round of prayer.

After which three guys from Valdosta, hair piled up softly on top of their heads like haystacks, sang "Awesome God" and "Hallelujah! (My Chains Are Gone)."

Knees again.

And all this time, Burris noticed, no one so much as mentioned the recent deluge of gold.

No one alluded to the jackpot. Or to the parking lot full of reporters and TV trucks. Or to attendance, which was at Christmas level today—every pew packed and even standing room in short supply, the rafters ringing with thank-you-Jesuses. The cause of all this excitement went unspoken. As though the Max-a-Million jackpot was so holy its name was never to be uttered.

Everybody up for singing.

Down again for praying.

Finally, somewhere near the end of time, the service was done and people were shuffling out to the aisles and milling around—and Burris was headed toward Mitch. A little crowd was already gathering around the Boatwrights, so he had to push his way through. Then he spotted Nell, standing right beside her son, and she happened to be looking Burris's way. He froze. Gave her a frail lockjaw smile. She seemed not to notice him though. She turned away and went off to one side with her granddaughter and Shaw McBride, and the three of them made a little huddle.

Oh god, Burris thought: is she talking about me?

No, stop it. Don't be so paranoid. She didn't even see me. She's not being deliberately cruel. Remember how yesterday she said, I love you, darlin'? She has no conception of the pain she's causing, of how much I'd like to curl up at her feet right now and die like a poisoned wasp. Forget it. Just do what you came to do.

He took a breath and pressed forward. Walked up to Mitch and gave him a big embrace.

Inasmuch as they hardly knew each other, this took Mitch somewhat aback. But Burris held on, saying softly, "Hey, I gotta see you. Right away. Police business."

Then pulled back so they were looking eye to eye.

Mitch muttered, "What do you mean?"

"Meet me at Huddle House? Alone? In two hours?"

Clearly Mitch was disturbed by this request. But what did that tell you? Out of the blue a cop declares he's got official business with you: wouldn't that rattle anyone?

Still, Mitch's eyes were buggy and furtive and he did look *very* worried.

Burris insisted, "It's important."

Mitch finally shrugged and conceded, "OK. Huddle House. What time again?"

"Two-thirty."

"Tell me what this is about?"

"Two-thirty, Mitch. OK?"

Shaw discovered that just being around old Nell made him happy. Just hearing her laugh. He adored her little self-involved dramas and her frankness. He was pleased particularly now, as she took him and Tara aside and said under her breath, "Oh, kids, you gotta save me."

Tara asked, "From what?"

"Deppity Dawg."

"The cop?"

"He's got this *thing* for me."

Shaw couldn't hide his amusement. He laughed out loud.

"I swear," said Nell, "he's about to *invite* me to something. I know it."

"Which one is he?" said Shaw.

"Don't look!" said Nell. "The one talking to Mitch. Can't we get out of here? He's always giving me these moony looks. Come on, we'll slip out through the rectory. Will there be cameras out there? I'm getting weary of those cameras, I tell you that. This celebrity thing, how long is this gonna drag on?"

Shaw shrugged and smiled.

Said Nell, "I thought you're supposed to be famous for fifteen minutes. Fifteen minutes I wouldn't mind. But this is driving me crazy. It's your fault, Shaw. It was that 'I'm giving it all away.' That was such a damn fool thing to say. You want to get rid of your money, let me do it. I'll make it *disappear*. Ha ha ha! Come on, let's go, don't dawdle. The vultures are right behind us."

Tara drove on their way home from church. Shaw rode in the passenger seat. They had a police escort now: pinwheels of dancing light, both ahead and behind. But a bold photographer, chasing on a motorcycle, managed to slip into the next lane—suddenly he was right beside her, snapping away.

The world was closing in on her.

And just then Dad said, from the backseat, "Hey Shaw? Something I got to tell you."

"What?"

"Cop back at the church? Says he wants to meet with me."

Shaw turned in his seat. "What are you talking about?"

"At the Huddle House. In two hours."

"Why?"

"He didn't say. He just wants to meet me."

Shaw was glaring. "A *cop* wants to meet you?"

"Yes."

"What the *FUCK*?"

It was too much for Tara. Shaw's anger, the paparazzi, the cops: she was overwhelmed. At Redwood Street, the cruiser ahead of her slowed to turn, but she didn't notice this till the last second, and had to hit the brake hard. Shaw was pitched forward. Nearly thrown into the windshield.

"WHAT THE FUCK ARE YOU DOING?"

He drew out his pistol and held it low where the cops couldn't see it but Tara could. "WHAT THE FUCK IS HAPPENING?"

She said, "I'm sorry! I just, I wasn't, these lights are confusing me!"

"YOU LYING CUNT!"

She tried to focus on her driving. She managed to make the turn, and then crawled along. As Redwood was only a two-lane street, the motorcycle had to fall back. Shaw got on his cell phone and screamed, "*SHIT GOING DOWN. FIND A TARGET!*" A pause. "WHENEVER I GIVE YOU THE WORD! JUST START KILLING. KILL EVERY BOATWRIGHT IN THIS COUNTY!"

He shut the phone and turned to the backseat: "WHO TOLD?"

Nobody spoke.

"JASE, YOU GAVE US UP, DIDN'T YOU, YOU LITTLE FUCK?"

Jase was bawling. "No sir."

"YOU READY, JASE? READY FOR THE KILLING TO START? READY FOR THE PUNISHMENT? I'M READY!"

"I swear I didn't tell! I swear to God."

Shaw turned to Mom. "WAS IT YOU, BITCH?"

She had her face in her hands. "No, I wouldn't! I wouldn't! Ever!"

"THEN WHICH ONE? WHO'S THE FUCKING PSYCHO WHO WANTS ALL THE KILLING?"

I have to calm him, Tara thought. "Shaw, it wasn't us."

He shifted his eyes her way.

She said, "There's lots of things that cop could want. Maybe he just wants to complain about the size of the crowd. Maybe he wants Dad to hire him for security. I don't know, but I mean none of us would say anything, really, Shaw, we're not that crazy, we wouldn't—"

"Shut up."

He was staring out at the street. They were already back at Oriole Road, which was lined with pilgrims. "Just shut the fuck up. I have to think."

Romeo sat in the Tercel across the street from Cousin Alfred's house, awaiting Shaw's command. He'd taken the Phoenix .22 from the trunk, and had it handy, wedged down beside the parking brake. He had the phone in his hand, and he was looking up at the grand façade of the house. Waiting. As soon as Shaw gives the word, I'll make the word flesh. I will not let him down. Get ready. Any second. When he says go, don't hesitate.

Finally the phone buzzed, and he answered: "Yeah."

"It's OK, you can stand down. We're still alive here."

Mitch slipped out through the backyard, climbed over the fence into the Lumbachs' yard. The Liberty was waiting for him there, and he got away with the paparazzi none the wiser. Headed for the mall.

A line from Scripture came to him: *If your sinful nature controls your mind, there is death.* It seemed not to apply. Then he thought, *If the Holy Spirit controls your mind, there is life and peace.* Still didn't pertain. There was no coherence to his thoughts. He passed the Arby's and the Payless Shoes, and pulled into the parking lot at the Glynn Place Mall.

He sat there. In two minutes Romeo approached the car. He got in beside Mitch and shut the door and said, "Unbutton your shirt."

Mitch did. Romeo taped a Radio Shack remote mike to his chest, and a transmitter to his back. The little bastard trembled as he worked. He was unshaven and pasty and looked like a wreck. If he weren't such a nasty runt, Mitch thought, I might even feel sorry for him.

For a few minutes Romeo fiddled with his laptop, testing the connection. Mitch watching intently. Till Romeo snapped, "What're you looking at?"

Mitch lowered his eyes. "I'm sorry."

And heard his own echo out of the laptop: *"I'm sorry."*

Romeo asked into the air, "OK. Can you hear us?"

Shaw's voice replied, from the computer, "Yes. Hey, Mitch."

"Answer him," said Romeo.

Mitch grumbled, "Hey."

Shaw said, "Mitch, I have a question. Do you think we're afraid to kill your family?"

"No, sir."

"You know that if you fuck up, everybody dies?"

"Yes."

"If you falter for even an instant?"

"I know."

279

"Look at Romeo. Look how insane he is. He doesn't give a shit about anything. You see that?"

"Yes."

"So tell me you won't fail us."

"I won't fail you."

"Tell your wife, because she's right here beside me."

"I won't fail you."

"Jesus. Say her *name*, Mitch."

"Patsy. I won't fail you."

"Tell your daughter."

"Tara, I won't fail you."

"Tell your son."

"I won't fail you, Jase."

"OK. So. Make us proud. We'll be with you every second."

Burris arrived at the Huddle House at 2:27. He knew the difficulty of the task he faced, and that he wasn't the cleverest cop in the world—but he also believed, as he swung his feet out of the cruiser, and stood, and straightened his aching back, that he was a pretty good man for this job. Someone who cared,

anyway, and someone who knew the lay of the land—
you could've done worse.

But as he was passing the big glass windows, he
caught sight of his reflection, and thought, mercy. What
a paunchy shambling loser. Wouldn't you think, when a
man goes bald, that at least the little hair he did retain
would do as it was told? Not for Burris. The sides stuck
out like a clown's; the patch in front was as sassy as pubic
hair. And why the hell wasn't he in uniform? At least the
uniform would have commanded some respect. But
instead he'd chosen to wear the paisley shirt that Barbara
had given him for Christmas twenty years ago. It had
seemed stylish at the time. But now he looked like a
Polynesian Rent-a-Clown.

OK. There's no remedy for any of it. Leave it alone.

Mitch was already in a booth. When he saw Burris he
started to get up but Burris waved him back down. "Sit
down, Mitch. How are you?"

"I'm good."

"I believe *that*," said Burris, squeezing into the booth,
aiming for breeziness. "I guess your life has changed
completely, hasn't it?"

"I guess."

"Has it all sunk in yet?"

"Not really."

"Them TV people, they getting kind of intrusive?"

"You said it."

The waitress came over. They both ordered coffee.

Burris said, "You fixing on keeping the business?"

"Don't know what else I'd do."

"Get yourself some quail land?"

"That's an idea."

"Couple thousand acres might suit you well."

"Mm-hm."

Mitch was being terse, withholding, and he kept plucking nervously at the top button on his shirt. Now's a good time then, thought Burris—before he gets comfortable. Watch him closely, particularly those fingers, and let's get to it.

"Mitch, I need to talk to you about Shaw McBride."

For a fleeting instant, the fingers hardened into claws. Just a quick clasp though—then the hand relaxed, and when he spoke, he sounded OK. "What can I tell you, Burris?"

"Well. Start with, was Shaw McBride with you when you bought that lottery ticket?"

"You mean, was he in the store with me? No, sir. Why do you ask?"

"Where was he?"

"I guess headed back to his motel. I'd invited him to

dinner, to meet Patsy and the kids. So he was gonna, just get changed or whatever. I was proud of him. You should have seen the kind of man he used to be—and then, how he turned out? I like to think maybe I had something to do with that."

It all came flowing out so smoothly. It seemed so genuine. Burris felt the ground giving way beneath him.

Mitch went on, "I mean that man is just full up with love. When he says he's gonna give all his money away? He *means* it. My gosh. He tracks me down to say thank-you for a kindness I showed him years ago? And next thing, we're winning the lottery together. You say whatever you want, but I think there's the hand of God in all that. *Has* to be."

He *couldn't* be making this up, Burris thought. He couldn't. This wasn't some fancy Hollywood actor. This was just Mitch. Just Nell's kid, who had a real spiritual way about him and went to church every week and Lions of Judah on Wednesday nights, and how in the world could he be pulling this off and looking Burris in the eye unless what he was saying was true?

Ah Christ. Well, let me lay it all on the table, then.

Burris took a sip of coffee. Looked around to be sure no one was listening, and said, "Mitch, I want you to tell me something."

283

"OK."

"McBride putting any kind a squeeze on you?"

"Squeeze?" Raising a brow to show how peculiar he thought the question.

Burris held his gaze steady, and spoke with slow, deliberate weight. "Listen to me. I don't know what the guy's told you. What kind of fear he's put into you. But I guarantee you, if you talk to me, I'll protect you. I'll protect your family. We'll put him away forever. You hear what I'm telling you?"

Mitch lowered his eyes. All he wanted was to give Burris a sign. He even seemed to hear a voice: *Take their help, let them rescue you.* Could this be the voice of the Lord?

But the duct tape was tugging at the hair on his chest.

He knew they were listening.

They'd kill his family in an instant. If he said a single word.

But—I could *write* something, couldn't I? I could just reach back and take the pen from the waitress station and write a note on this napkin: *Help me. Two of them.*

They're listening. Wouldn't that be enough? Burris could take it from there.

But then Burris pursed his lips to suck in some coffee, and Mitch thought: What the hell am I thinking? This is *Deppity Dawg.* I write that note on a napkin and he'll probably read it *out loud.* He'll say, "Help you in what way, Mitch?" And then everything will be lost. Everything. My whole life. My wife and children, my mother, all lost forever and for what? I can't risk it. I can't even afford this silence right now . . .

Shaw was in Jase's room with Tara. The voices from her laptop sounded tinny and washed-out, but still you could hear most of what was being said. He looked at Tara. Her lips were moving slightly as she listened. He knew she was trying to project a message to her father; something on the order of, *Don't screw up, Dad, don't give us away, please don't screw up* . . .

There fell a long scary silence. Shaw reached back and wrapped his fingers around the handle of the .32.

But then they heard Mitch clear his throat. He said, "Something I'm trying to figure out, Burris."

"What's that?"

"Are you *kidding* me?"

A smile began to crawl up Shaw's face.

Mitch went on, "You're saying Shaw McBride's trying to *steal* from me?"

Voice of the cop: "Well, I'm not saying. I'm just asking."

Mitch: "But how would he do that?"

Cop: "Threaten your family?"

He put it as a question. Weakness had seeped into his tone. Mitch pounced. "Shaw *McBride*? *Threaten* me? Burris, are you out of your mind? The *Lord* brought that young man into our lives!"

Mitch wasn't just defending his position—he had a full head of indignation going. It was a thing of beauty. Could it be, Shaw wondered, that he was starting to *believe*? In Shaw's dream? In the warmth of it, the sunny big-skied beauty of it?

Shaw leaned back in his chair and grinned irrepressibly. This was no time to celebrate, he knew. There were still a thousand things that could go wrong. For example, this cop Burris: who the hell was he? What did he know, what did he suspect? But Mitch had come through! That was a triumph right there. We've got Mitch fighting for the cause. If Mitch himself is fighting for the cause, then really, how can we not succeed?

Shaw told the family, "I think the old man has done it."

But his gaze was on Tara. She was trembling, and her lashes were wet, and she was sitting so close to Shaw that he could smell the sweetness of her breath. He put his hand over hers. When he squeezed, he felt a tiny pressure of reciprocation. This day, he thought. This day is the most dangerous and the most rapturous that anyone has lived for *centuries*. It was an absurd notion and it made him laugh at himself, but still: who else had ever lived the way he was living this very day?

Tara in pieces in her room, the tears pouring from her.

She had squeezed his hand.

Within her was some creature who wanted *his* comfort.

She sat at her desk, before her laptop, and looked at her photo albums. This time she was too weak to resist: she went right to her favorite shot of Nell. Nell and Tara and the cat Horace Jackal on the swinging bed. With those yellow roses climbing all over the screen—

though you couldn't see them well in the picture. What you saw was Tara laughing and Nell laughing even harder.

What had she done? What had she done to bring this hell smashing down on her?

She fell to her knees, as hard as she could. My Lord! Why are you doing this! Why are you so angry with me?

What did I do to you?

Then she thought about that time on the porch, the time she had told Nell about winning the jackpot, when she was so drunk on dreams of coming loot: shoes and a BMW and a trip to Paris and a new apartment. When she'd still thought winning the jackpot would be some kind of blessing.

How could she have ever thought that? What was it she had thought she needed?

The only thing she wanted now was to be back in that swinging bed looking out at the chili pepper plants and the crepe myrtle and the bathtub. But that was gone now. She thought, *I will never get back there.* The Lord had seen her greed and arrogance, and to punish her had exiled her forever from Nell's back porch. She knelt and clutched the bedclothes and sobbed, and when she thought of the Lord the face she saw was Romeo's—she couldn't help it! She couldn't help it! Though she knew that this was another way in which she was betraying God and was deserving of her banishment and of all this horror and of this grinding wheel of terror.

Romeo strolled toward the Kroger supermarket, like he was going in to buy groceries, like this was an everyday thing.

A thirtyish mom with two kids was also heading in, and was much closer to the door than he was. But she paused to get a shopping cart, and then had to hold the hand of one of her kids while piloting him toward the door. Romeo had already guessed she'd do these things. He'd factored them into his pace. He had everything meticulously timed, so that he got to the door at the same instant the woman did. For a moment everybody froze—then Romeo graciously stood to one side, and signaled: you go ahead.

The woman gave him a big smile. She and her kids went past him and headed to Garden Produce.

He bought a bottle of water and went out, and was

embraced again by the heat. He leaned against the Tercel, and waited.

He knew he should get back to patrolling. But patrolling didn't seem possible now. Not even *possible*. He thought, I have to do this. There was a new woman coming through the lot, and he guessed she was a career woman. She was wearing flats, and her legs were strong. He predicted she'd move briskly. She might not even stop for a cart. She might be content with one of those baskets you pick up inside the door. When he moved to meet her, he moved quickly.

But unexpectedly she lollygagged, gazing at the patio suites. He had to cut his speed down to an amble. But then she went quickly again, and he had to hurry, and altogether their duet was ratchety, graceless. At the door, they nearly collided.

She stepped back to make way for him.

He said, "No, please."

She not only gave him a smile—her eyes lingered appraisingly. Then she went in, and he went in after her. He bought a can of anchovies.

But he didn't take it right to checkout. He thought maybe he could find a way to talk to her.

He found her in Dairy. He thought he might ask about how to read expiration dates. He put his head down and approached, but at the last moment he knew he couldn't go through with it, so he veered off. He grabbed a half-pint of sour cream and booked it out of there. These doorway encounters he could handle pretty well—but *talk* to these women? No chance. Anyway, who had the time? No time for socializing and romance. He had work to do.

Shaw decided to give the Boatwrights a little R&R, in honor of how smoothly Mitch had handled the cop. He asked them what they did for fun, and Jase spoke up: "You know what's cool? Seining. Can we go seining?"

So they all got into the Liberty, with Shaw behind the wheel. He eased through the crowd of folks, and then down Oriole Road, with Trevor and a couple of body-guards right behind them on motorcycles. Trailing the bodyguards were the photographers. It made for a strange slow cortege: Liberty, bodyguard, paparazzi, cruising down Oriole Road.

They took Robin Street, to Altama Avenue. They passed the bowling alley and Willie's Wee-Nee Wagon and Tiger-Wheels Customizing.

Then abruptly Shaw turned onto a side street.

The bodyguards blocked out the photographers, and Shaw stepped on the gas and took a hairpin curve fast. Jase laughed and Patsy's eyes lit up. The Liberty squealed down Cate Street onto Habersham and suddenly they were free.

They drove over to Nell's. She came out on her front portico with a cat in her arms, and Shaw called to her, "Hey, come on, we're going seining."

"I better not. Me in a bathing suit? I'd scare your dinner away."

But he cajoled and got the Boatwrights to cajole as well, and at last she said, "Oh, what the hell. Just give me a second—lemme feed these devils."

Sunday afternoon in the deep South. Pair of black bugs on the windshield, getting it on. Nell's garden had an old clawfoot tub for a birdbath, wheelbarrows and cats and yellow blooming roses, and Shaw told Tara, "I see why you love this place so much."

Tara wouldn't look at him.

Nell got in and they drove over to Uncle Shelby's to borrow a seining net. Shaw got to meet Shelby's little girl MacKenzie. A little dimpled charmer, with the same huge voracious gaze as her cousin Tara had, as her grandmother had. Shelby's big house was impressive.

Shall I buy it, Shaw thought, when the money comes in? Or better, buy the house next door? Then on Wednesday evenings, Tara and I can take our kids plus Shelby's kids to Bible study in a single car. And on Saturdays we'll play golf, Shelby and I, and in the evenings he and his wife Miriam will visit us on our back porch, and drink Madeira or mojitos, and watch the sunset over the marsh. And discuss real estate and school board elections.

I could do that. I could be content with a life like that.

They borrowed two seine nets from Shelby, and took the causeway over to St. Simon's Island, and went to a little beach near the village. The Boatwrights carried the nets toward the water, while Shaw hung back and removed his thunderbelt and .32, and stashed them under the driver's seat. Then he followed the others over the sea wall to the narrow strip of sand. The tide was perfect. Tara had already stripped to her bikini, and she and Nell were unrolling one of the nets. Shaw watched as they hauled it into the water. Nell with her get-it-done grace. As she kicked into the sea, she called out: "Crabs and shrimpies! Trust your Aunt Nell! Get into this net and I promise I'll make a tasty sauce for you!"

Tara held the far end of the net, taking the deeper route. Compared to her grandmother, she seemed fragile. Tall, thin, a reed in the water. The swells were strong and she struggled to hold her pole straight. Shaw thought her beauty unbearable.

He asked Mitch, "Should we take that other net?"

"You go with Jase. I'm kind of wore out."

"All right. You up for it, Jase?"

"OK."

So Shaw and Jase walked the net a hundred yards down the beach, then headed into the ocean. Soon Shaw was above his waist. He slipped once in the wet sand and went under, but managed to keep his grip on the pole. When he came up sputtering, Jase was laughing. "Shaw, can you even swim?"

"Pull! Let's go!"

After they had dragged the net a hundred feet through the ocean, Jase held up and became the pivot; Shaw turned the arc and they waded ashore. They'd done OK. A dozen brown shrimp and three softshell crabs along with a couple of throwaway puffers. Jase showed him how to disentangle the crabs without getting pinched. The sky reared up above them, rose and lavender, a paradise of thoughtlessness.

Meanwhile, down the way, Nell and Tara were picking through their own net. Shaw could hear Nell addressing the crustaceans: "Fools! Suckers! I can't believe I talked you into this! Bet you'll be more careful next time, won't you?"

As soon as the net was clear, they took it back out again. Shaw watched them.

Jase said, "Can I ask you something?"

"Sure."

"How come you always answer when he calls?"

"Who? You mean Romeo? I have to."

"Why? 'Cause he's your friend?"

"It's not about that. If I don't answer he'll think something bad's happened. Then he'll do something bad right back to your family."

"Would he kill us?"

"Why do you ask?"

The kid spoke with a fierce intensity: "Because we'll do what you want anyway."

Shaw just looked at him. Honored by the kid's devotion—but also a little wary of it. "Well Jase, I know I can count on *you*. But the others—"

"They won't fight you," said Jase. "Even Dad. He won't fight you no more."

"Romeo thinks he will."

"Romeo doesn't know us! You should stop talking to him. Tell him we don't need him. We're fine by ourselves, so tell him to go away."

Shaw was thinking of how to answer, how to be gentle but still let the kid know that Romeo wasn't going anywhere. But just then he saw Tara come out of the ocean, dragging the net, carrying the last sunlight on her skin, and his powers of speech left him.

Tara caught him looking at her. It was no surprise: she knew he wanted her. So now he's a lewd son of a bitch; who cares, so what else is new?

What she wasn't prepared for, however, was the little thrill that his watching gave her. A needlelike pleasure in her stomach, just below her ribcage. And she realized she was arching her back a little as she came out of the water, to show off her figure.

She dragged her end of the net out of the surf. She and Nell dropped their poles, and squatted and went to work, tossing their catch into a bucket. She'd known this was coming. She'd felt the tremors a while ago, and now it was opening up inside her, and in this way also she thought she betrayed the Lord; defied Him and grew apart from Him.

Burris went to the station to begin his shift, but as he passed the dispatch desk Rose Whittle declared—with offhand cruelty, not even looking up from the trimming of her cuticles, "Chief wants to see you, Burris. He's in with the Lieutenant. Good luck."

The Lieutenant's office was a century old, and the ceiling was sixteen feet high. The smells were of ancient varnish and stucco and moldering police files, of termite crap and generations of tobacco smoke. Generally Burris liked coming here. The Lieutenant was fat and moved slowly and was nearly as old as Burris himself, and remembered far more. And he loved to talk; you could wallow in his talk. You might come to discuss some little complication in a DUI case and then wander out a couple of hours later with a headful of details about the '71 Cal Humphries murder, or the mad misrule of Chief Carswell in the eighties—and then realize you'd forgotten even to mention the case you went in for.

But today it wasn't just the Lieutenant. The Chief was there too, and he had a nasty twinkle in his eye. "Hello, Corporal."

"Hello, sir."

"Guess who called me a little while ago?"

A guessing game. Great.

"Sir, I just don't know."

"Mitch Boatwright called me."

"Oh."

"Wondering why the hell you were harassing him at his church."

Christ. Better hunch my shoulders. Get low here, try to get as gray and mouselike as possible. "Well sir. I just—"

"At his *church*? You couldn't wait till the service was over?"

"Well, I *did* wait, yes sir, but—"

"I'm sorry, is he a liar? I wouldn't have thought Mitch Boatwright was a big liar."

"If I could explain. I did go up to him at church this morning—"

"I thought you just said you didn't."

"I came up *after* the service. So if he says—"

"In front of three hundred parishioners, you accosted the man—"

"I spoke privately, sir."

"Corporal." Sharply, crisply, as one might admonish a wayward pup. "You intend to keep interrupting me all day?"

"No sir."

"I'm trying to ask you a question."

"Yes sir."

298

"I'm trying to ask you, Corporal, why you couldn't wait until Mr. Boatwright was at home?"

"At home? Well. There's all those people there. There's TV trucks and all. I didn't want to raise a ruckus—"

"You ever think of using the phone?"

"Well, the business I had with him was kind of delicate."

"Delicate? He says you grilled him."

"I wouldn't say grilled."

"Oh no?"

"And we didn't talk at church. I arranged to meet him later, at the Huddle House."

"I understand that, Corporal. I've been informed of that. I think it's terrific. Great police work, taking your interrogation out of the church. Although the Huddle House, now, is that really your best choice for a 'delicate' interrogation?"

"Well I didn't feel—"

"Please don't interrupt. Mr. Boatwright says you wouldn't let him leave? He says you made all these accusations, and you weren't even in uniform, and you were acting a little crazy, he says, and you were—"

"I didn't make any accusations, sir. I was trying to *protect* him, not to—"

"May I *finish*?"

"Yes sir. I'm sorry sir."

Long pause, harrowing. The Chief glanced at the Lieutenant. The Lieutenant hung his head sadly.

Said the Chief, "Mr. Boatwright says you've got this notion that Shaw McBride is extorting money from him. Is that what you think?"

"That's what I *thought*."

"But now you've changed your mind?"

"Well, now I'm not sure what—"

"This was another of your little half-cocked schemes?"

"I did have genuine reason for concern. I had a tip."

"Ah," said the Chief. "A tip! And what might that tip have been, Corporal?"

"Well, that Shaw McBride didn't even know about the jackpot till *after* the Boatwrights won it."

The Chief glowered. "That's it? That's what you got?"

"Yes. I thought I had to check it out. But, well, I talked to Mr. Boatwright and now I think there was probably no merit to it."

"You mean your 'tipster' was lying?"

"It's possible. But still I had to check it out."

The Chief let out a sigh of exasperation.

"Burris, let's get something straight. Have I ever told you *not* to check out tips?"

"No, sir. I didn't mean that. I meant—"

"I sometimes wonder, Corporal, when I'm talking to you, if I should even be in the room. I mean, as you seem to be able to carry out the whole conversation without my help at all. You *imagine* I say something, and you answer, and then you *imagine* I say something else, and you reply to that. I'd appreciate it if now and then you'd check in with me, to see if what you think I'm saying bears any correspondence to what I really *am* saying. How about that?"

"Yes sir."

"In this city, Corporal, we're very big about checking out tips. But we try to do it without making one of our oldest families feel like they're the subject of some kind of crazy witch hunt."

"Yes sir."

The Chief then turned to the Lieutenant. "What are your thoughts here, Jim?"

The Lieutenant looked uneasy. His eyebrows flew out jaggedly from his brow. He said, "Chief, I think you hit the nail right on the head."

"Good," said the Chief.

"Though in fairness, it was a sticky situation, and Burris was only trying his best, you know, and—"

"Oh, that's true," said the Chief. "I have to give you that, Corporal. You always do 'try your best'."

"Thank you, sir."

"You try your damnedest."

"Thank you, sir."

"But next time? How about consulting with one of us or one of the detectives before you follow these leads. OK?"

"Yes, sir."

"'Cause if you don't? I will fire your ass, and I don't give a damn if you've vested your goddamn pension or not. Do you understand me?"

"Yes, sir."

"You can go."

"Thank you sir."

"Catch some drunks for us, OK, Deppity Dawg? That's something you do very well."

Tara took a shower to wash the sand off, and then retreated to her room. She looked at her email. More of the deluge. Kudos and congratulations by the thousands. She kept scrolling through the list, though she didn't know what she was seeking. A note from Clio? Though had she found one, she wouldn't have been able to read it.

Then an address caught her eye.

A message from Dad. Posted just a few minutes ago. She tapped OPEN.

```
Hon I'm going to tell the fbi. Ive
been thinking a lot. I don't trust
that burrus. I know i did the right
thing lying to him, but the fbi wont
be fools. Theyll track the calls that
Shaw makes. They got gps on cell
phones now so therfore theyll find
Romeo easy and catch him. And shaw
too. They'll kill them clean. But if
we wait till soembody makes a mistake
or Romeo goes crazy or some reporter
guesses something we will all die
can't sit and wait for that. I love
you more than the world.
The BIBLE says watch ye, stand fast in
the faith, be strong.
```

It wasn't just fear that rose up in her then, but anger also.

She hit REPLY and wrote:

Dad,
The FBI, they screw up all the time.
People get killed. If you tell them,
you'll get US killed! Daddy, dont! if
they make one mistake! we will LOSE.
But if we play along with Shaw and let
him have the money we'll be OK. He
wont hurt us. If he hurts us, he knows
he'll lose everything, but if we push
him he'll have nothing to lose.
Dad, I know how much you hate him. I
hate him worse. When he opens his
mouth I get sick. He thinks now hes
some kind of prophet but people only
love him for the money and hes a
coward. But once he gets the money
he'll try to run and that's when we'll
call th4e FBI. He won't get away!
I know its frustrating doing nothing,
but please, Dad, please don't try to
tell the FBI. Please please please.

She reread, made a few corrections, deleted the number 4. She put *please please please* in caps.

She knew that by writing this she was doing exactly what Shaw would want. She was even starting to sound like him: *I know it's frustrating.*

She pressed SEND.

She waited. Every few seconds, a new email came in from one of her fans. She didn't touch them. She stared at the screen.

Finally she got a reply:

OK

As she was looking at this, she heard some commotion outside. A flurry of flashbulbs.

She cracked the curtain. A crowd had gathered around Bill Phillips, the man with 'reflex sympathetic dystrophy'. He was no longer in his wheelchair; he was walking—sort of. With someone on either side to steady him. And he went only a few steps before they eased him back into the chair.

The folks loved it though. They shouted "Praise the Lord!" and looked toward the house and called to him, "Shaw!" "Father!" "Father, come see this!" "Praise the Lord!"

Tara felt another wave of anger.

Now they *worship* him?

She lay down in her bed. She felt as though she had not slept in weeks. But as soon as she shut her eyes she had a vivid picture of herself stepping out of the ocean, with Shaw McBride watching her.

She forced her eyes open again.

Out in the yard the pilgrims were calling his name: "Shaw!" "Shaw!" "Father!"

Her eyes fell shut again. She was on the beach, coming into Shaw's arms. She had no strength to resist him. The power he held over her life had damaged her. She imagined him lifting her up. She wrapped her legs around him, with her head against his chest so she could hear the beating of his heart, and his cock was inside her. She started touching herself, feathering her clitoris with two fingers. She couldn't stop; she needed to touch herself while she thought of his strength, and she was trembling and bathed in sweat, and as she started to climax she could hear all those voices outside.

"Shaw!" "Father!" "Lord!" "Father, heal me!" "Heal me!" "Praise the Lord!"

Romeo sat in the McDonald's on the Scranton Connector Road near the mall. He'd come for the Wifi. He sat with fries and a Coke while he consulted the key-logger he'd planted. It had picked up an email from Mitch to his daughter.

Now why should Mitch be sending an email to his daughter? It gave Romeo a bad feeling, even before he read it. And after he read it, he was crushed. It broke his heart.

He stared out the window at the kids tumbling in the playhouse.

Trying to summon some strength. That he had known this was coming didn't help. He thought, *Why* are you so stupid, Mitch? Is it that you can't see the horror that's looming over us? This is your *family* you're risking. How can you risk the lives of your family for the sake of your wounded pride?

And Clio! How can you do this to Clio?

He forced himself to turn back to the laptop and read Tara's reply.

Shaw had seen Diane Sawyer on TV a thousand times, and what had attracted him the most was the sense that beneath all her sweetness and generosity were the depths of the Arctic Sea. But close up it was different—it wasn't iciness he felt from her, but a kind of steady imperial radiance. She sat on one of the wing chairs, with Tara and Mitch and Patsy on the couch, and Jase on the floor. Shaw sat across from her in the other wing chair. Her gaze floated from one Boatwright to another, and finally back to him, and she spoke in that dry murmur:

"Shaw. All these people outside. All these . . . *people*."

"Yes."

"They keep coming."

"Yeah. Too many now. We gotta move tomorrow. Going to some kind of fairgrounds."

"And I understand you've had a few emails?"

He dipped his head. Amiable beleaguerment. "A few."

"How many?"

"Um. Thousands."

"Thousands?"

"Yeah."

"Shaw, what do they want?"

"Well. I guess they want to think there's some meaning to all this."

"To what?"

"To life."

Her smile was impeccably composed. She was a planet in a perfectly elliptical orbit, with the cameras gliding like moons behind her. It was a spellbinding show. "And they're coming to you. Why? Because of your luck? Because of your money?"

"Because of the Lord."

"You think the Lord is calling you?"

"I think the Lord's calling everyone. Maybe we don't want to hear Him. Too busy thinking about money. All this mortgage stuff and market stuff, we can't hear nothin'. But sooner or later, He's gonna get through."

She turned to Tara. "Tara, when your father told you that your family would have to split the jackpot, what was your first thought?"

Tara considered. "Well. I guess, I guess for a second I was thinking, Daddy, do we *have* to? Does this guy even have to *know*?"

One of the cameras sneaked over to take in Shaw shaking his head and laughing.

Then Tara said, "But then . . . I got to know him . . ."

She sent him a quick glance—misty-eyed, with a note of yearning. He knew she was doing it for the cameras, for the sake of the people she loved—but still, wasn't it a little bit real? Her blush, that was real. And the look of contentment on her mother's face—he knew *that* was real. Patsy was pleased to put her life in his hands. And Jase belonged to him, he was certain of that. Even Mitch seemed almost at ease now. And the pilgrims were out there waiting for him, with legions more ready to come. I've woven this whole world out of pure faith. It's a kind of magical tapestry of faith and love and power, and it's come alive now—

Vibration in his pocket. Romeo was calling.

Diane Sawyer said, "Tara, when Shaw says he's going to give away all his money . . . do you believe him?"

"Yes."

"You don't think he's a little crazy?"

Tara softly bit her lower lip. The camera closed on her.

"No. I think he's beautiful."

And Diane Sawyer was beaming. Beaming! She must be wondering, is this love? Has Tara fallen for Shaw? If this is love, it's the love story of the year! But again Shaw felt the trembling—the fucking phone. Romeo's second call. Which meant some emergency, which probably wasn't anything at all—but still, he *had* to answer it.

Diane Sawyer was asking Tara about all the money, what the money would do to her family. The cameras left Shaw for a moment, and he pulled the phone from his pocket and held it low and flipped it open. Romeo had sent him a text:

```
Mutiny. Tara & mitch. Emails. Going to
cops. Plan to kill us.
```

He shut the phone, and looked up.

Tara was telling Diane Sawyer, "Well, the things that Shaw is talking about, I think they're true. Money *should* be about what good you can do with it. If you keep it for yourself? You'll be miserable. If you show love with it? You'll be happy. I think he's right about that. You know, he keeps saying how much my father has taught him? But now he's the one teaching us."

Her most dazzling smile.

Shaw wondered, How can she do it? How can she be so glib? Such a liar, such a heartfelt liar down to her bones! And her father next to her! That weasely cunt of a man. Lying to the world. The hypocritical *liars*!

Diane Sawyer turned to him: "This family seems to like you, Mr. McBride."

He gathered himself, and forced a grin. "Well, they're sort of *my* family now. They have to like me."

Everyone laughed.

But he was thinking: How do we make you suffer?

There's been no dream in history but fuckers like you have torn it apart with your lies, treason, and selfishness. But this time there'll be a price. A price you'll be paying for the rest of time, you cowardly shits. Who did you think you were dealing with?

The moment the interview was over, he signaled the producer, who came over and detached him from the mike. He went to the little bathroom next to Jase's room and held down the number 7 on his cell phone.

Romeo answered. "Took you long enough."

"Just tell me," said Shaw.

Romeo read him the emails.

Shaw said, "Listen, I don't have any privacy here. I'm in this cramped little shitbox. It's like the shitbox in Wendell Redinski's trailer, you remember that? Like it's made out of cardboard. But, God. My God she's gonna suffer. Her whole family. They'll suffer like they didn't believe such suffering was possible."

"Shaw, we don't have to—"

"Don't tell me we don't have to. You know we have to. We have to shove the suffering up their spines like electrical current."

"Shaw—"

"I mean pity these fuckers."

Patsy got to talk to Diane Sawyer for a few minutes after the show, just one on one, chatting while the crew took what they called B-roll footage. She asked Diane about her favorite charities, and Diane mentioned the Robin Hood Foundation. Patsy said she'd like to make a little donation. Saying it so Diane would know she didn't really mean *little*.

She wished Shaw were here to see her. But he'd gone off somewhere.

She walked Diane out to her hired car: a somber black Lexus LS hybrid. The pilgrims lined the driveway and applauded, and Diane was kind enough to stop for a moment and chat with them. A woman that Patsy detested, a Mrs. Riley, came up and started flapping her jaw, making derogatory comments about Ellen DeGeneres, as though Diane wanted to hear that! As though Diane Sawyer were as catty and mean-spirited and competitive as Mrs. Riley! Patsy told Mrs. Riley, "It's too bad we're in such a rush because we'd love to talk." Not harsh, not unpleasant, but *whap,* it did shut the woman up.

As Patsy and Diane walked on, Diane murmured, "Thank you."

And they chuckled together and Patsy thought, maybe it's true, what Shaw says about me: I *preside*.

She thought, there are qualities you can possess that

those closest to you can't really see. Even you yourself may be blind to them. It takes someone with a fresh eye to discern them and bring them out and make you shine. God, I wish he were here. Where is he, what in the world is he doing?

Romeo bit down on his knuckles as he would an apple; then he rubbed the back of his bloody fist against his tears. Then he slammed his foot into the gas pedal. Since the engine was shut off (he was parked on the outskirts of town, near the pulp mill, under a lone streetlight that turned the pavement into snakeskin), nothing happened. He couldn't cry out because he was on the phone with Shaw. Shaw was telling him what he wanted done. Telling him step by step, and after each step waiting for Romeo to say, "OK. I got it."

Shaw suggested, "You want to write these things down?"

"No. I got it."

"You remember what to say?"

"Yeah. There was a price. The price was posted."

"You have to do it all, Romeo. I can't do any of it."

"OK."

"You have to be merciless. I can't because we need them to love me. They have to love me or all this goes to shit. You understand?"

"Yeah."

"I know you're upset. I know you don't want to do this. But everything depends on you."

"Yeah."

They hung up.

It would have been OK to cry out, Romeo knew, there in that empty lot where no one would have heard. And he did *try* to cry out, but no sound emerged.

Burris made a space amidst all the crap on the kitchen counter. He started writing a letter to make clear his position on things.

First he wrote *Dear Nell.* Then he canceled that. He started on a fresh page, and wrote *Dear Nell* again.

Then he wrote:

You do not want anything to do with me because you think I am an idiot. You are right. But as you probably know I have loved you every minute of every day since our first date which transpired in Archies Restaraunt in Darien which was the most exiting night of my life I think so even when I was married to Barbara. I guess you know and she probably too.

By now you may have heard about my meeting with your son Mitchel.

He stopped. Did Mitchel have two t's?

He couldn't look it up in the dictionary because it wasn't a word.

Well, why not just say Mitch then? Just because this is a letter doesn't mean it has to be so damn formal.

He stared at the page.

What *is* this?

This is the stupidest thing I've ever done in my life. What in God's name is the point of writing this?

Well, to be fair, what was the point of any of the dumb things I've done for that woman?

For example, that night forty years ago, a few months after the breakup, when he'd appeared under Nell's window, sobbing and begging her to give him another chance. She'd been gracious in her refusal—but not *too* gracious. It wasn't oh-my-love-come-into-my-arms. It was more like, I'm-flattered-but-get-over-it. Or that day twenty years ago, after her son Mitch had wheedled her into joining the church, and Burris had run into her in the supermarket and she'd told him frankly that Faith Renewal felt more like a seniors' bingo room than a church; whereupon he'd confessed that he attended only because Barbara made him attend—and they'd laughed all the way to the checkout counter, and after that he hadn't slept for a year. That was the year he'd screwed up on the Coastal Area Drug Abuse Task Force with his overeagerness, charging that city commissioner's kid with dealing crack and then being unable to quite prove it, getting demoted. But that was also the year he'd felt most completely alive, because he'd carried inside him that memory of Nell in the supermarket, laughing at his little jokes. But then, at the Jaycees' barbecue, he'd acted maybe a little too affectionate and she'd cut him short. Also there was the day when he had come to talk to her students through the Community Policing program, and afterward she'd told him what a triumph it had been. And over the years there had been several more chance meetings at the Winn-Dixie and the Heart Drive picnic and Trudy's Café; plus the occasions (about seven hundred of them) when he'd seen her car go past his stakeouts; and several phone calls when he'd invited her to one event or another (she'd always declined); and three times at the July 4th fireworks on St. Simon's; and Barbara's funeral. And the whole time, throughout the whole forty years, day in and day out and even in his sleep, he'd been nursing this hopelessness in his head. The merciful thing about being an idiot is that you're too dumb to know what an idiot you are. But suppose you get a bit smarter for just a second and the whole picture comes to you, almost like in a vision, like now. A whole lifetime's worth of boneheadedness crashing down like a shelf full of shoes, all around your head at once: isn't that too humiliating to bear? How could you possibly survive such pain? Also why would you want to?

Clio was hanging out in her room, listening to Bat for Lashes and staring at the wall, when she got a call from that bizarre little dude she'd met at the tattoo parlor— that guy Romeo, the manager for Drive Fast & Shut Your Eyes.

He told her he'd found this guy up in Darien who did body suspensions. "You want to go see how he does it?"

"OK." She tried to sound ambivalent but actually she was happy to get out of the house.

"I already called him," said Romeo. "I'll come get you."

He picked her up and they went north on 17. His music was loud and razory, but she was OK with it. She was happy just to ride. A few miles north of town, they passed that old rice plantation. It was so hot today that steam seemed to be rising from the fields. An egret or some such bird was standing there on one leg, not moving, just standing there in the warp of heat.

Then Romeo did lower the volume, and said, "I can't believe they did that. Did your family do that?"

"Do what?"

"Own slaves."

She shrugged. "Oh. I guess. My great-great-grand-father or something. He was like a Confederate major."

Romeo was thoughtful. "But he wasn't a bad guy, right? I mean, I guess his buddies were telling him, like don't worry about it, owning slaves is cool. People believe anything their buddies tell them. That's how you become a soldier. You say, these are my buddies, I love them, I trust them. Then you can kill left and right and turn into a fucking troll of death if you have to, and do it happily because it's for your buddies. But it's really all about love. Right? Jesus this fucking planet. How did my soul happen to get assigned to *this* planet? I'm sorry. I'm ranting."

"No, that's OK."

He *was* ranting, but Clio didn't mind that.

She asked him, "The suspension, will it hurt?"

"I guess," he said.

"So why should I do it?"

"Maybe it'll make you feel free."

"You think?"

"Yeah. But vulnerable too. So you gotta be careful."

They drove past the Humane Society and came to the old auto shop where Arroyo lived. Squarish spectacles, soft lumpy shoulders. He led them to his backyard, which was cloistered by an old aluminum fence, and showed off his 'apparatus': just a chain hoist hung from an oak limb, but he was proud of it. He talked about dynamic rigging and 'eight-gauge vs. six-gauge' and 'Suicide vs. Superman' till Clio couldn't take another word. She had an itch she was crazy to scratch but it was beneath her skin—and this jackass was going on about inside-out eyebolting?

She said, "Hey, could you shut up a minute and hook me up?"

He pushed his glasses up to the bridge of his sweaty nose.

Happy to oblige.

She stripped to panties and bra, and lay down on her

belly, and he started throwing fishhooks into her flesh. Matching pairs: scapulars, triceps, wrists, thighs, hips, and calves—till there were twelve hooks in all. The pain was smashing. For a while she tried to fool it by singing to it. "The worms crawl in, the worms crawl out; they crawl all over your face and snout." But singing didn't help.

Arroyo turned the winch, and she was lifted into the air and the pain was magnified tenfold. The pain had its own lighting system. Powerful searchlights that came from inside her and beamed jaggedly out to the world, to her miserable life—bad grades, the scorn of her parents, bad boyfriends, Tara's betrayal, Tara's cruelty, Tara's this and Tara's that: her unsupportable, unquenchable love for Tara. She was hanging face-down and horizontal, the hooks stretching out her limbs till she was a superheroine flying through pain. Or a cross between a superheroine and a bag of hospital waste. She tried to say something exultant, but no sound came out, only a thread of slobber. Arroyo was trying to encourage her. "Just get in the flow," he said. Then she vomited. Something was wrong here. She knew that bursting into a shower of sparks was wrong, and distantly she heard Romeo bellowing: "GET HER *DOWN*!"—then more sparks; then finally Romeo had her in his arms and he was saying, "It's all right,

Clio. It'll be all right. Oh girl, it's gonna be fine. It's all *right*. It's all *right*."

The hooks coming out, one by one.

Then Romeo holding her and talking to her while Arroyo massaged the air out of her skin.

She heard herself screaming, *"I'M SORRY! I'M SORRY!"*

Romeo held her and said, "I know."

He went out to the car to get her some Percodan. While he was gone, Arroyo asked if she'd mind if he bound her and gave her a forced orgasm. She said not tonight, OK? Arroyo said of course not tonight; he wasn't thinking about tonight, but some other time. He said, what would be a good time? Next Thursday?

She threw up again.

Then she was in her own car, in the passenger seat, and Romeo was driving. The sun was setting on the old rice plantation.

"Are you awake?" said Romeo.

"Uh-huh."

"How do you feel?"

"I'm aright."

Next, she was in a sleazy motel room, on her stomach, and Romeo was rubbing unguent into her wounds.

Next, she was above the toilet and Romeo was holding

322

on to her as she retched tiny drops of green bile. She was surprised that he could hold her so firmly; he must be stronger than she had thought. He carried her back to the bed and set her down carefully. He wiped her face with a cloth.

She said, "You know what, Romeo? I could fall for you. I think I could frikkin *falling* fall for you."

At some point she woke up and Romeo was on the phone with somebody, and he was arguing and crying, and then there was a long silence. A light flared in her eyes, and Romeo got her to sit up. He made her drink. Then he placed her laptop before her. She didn't understand what he wanted.

He said, "You have to write something."

"What?"

"You have to write about your pain. Before you forget."

The computer was at her MySpace page.

"Log in," he prompted. "And then go to your diary."

"No, I'm too sleepy."

"You have to."

He woke her again. He spoke more insistently: "Log in, Clio. We have to hurry. It's almost time."

She logged in. Her diary page appeared.

He said, "OK, write something."

"I can't."

"Then I'll write it. Just tell me. How did it feel up there?"

"It felt like I was floating above the Wick."

He typed that. He asked, "Did it hurt?"

"Yeah."

"How bad."

"The worst," she said.

He wrote that. "How does it feel now?"

She wanted to say, "Now it's better." But she fell asleep before she could speak.

When she awoke, he was still writing in her diary.

He said, "I'm writing about the pain."

He seemed to be on the verge of tears. He was the strangest man she had ever met. Also the kindest. Kind and wise and an old soul.

Then she was asleep again, and he was shaking her. "Clio. Wake up. You've got to stay awake."

"Why?"

He said, "It's worse than you thought."

"It can't be," she said. "It can't be worse than I thought."

He said, "Everyone needs for you to die."

She knew this was sad news, but she didn't understand why. She was kind of foggy.

He said, "Tara particularly needs you to die. She *needs* it. I'm sorry. We have to do this."

She stared at him, not comprehending.

"And Shaw?" he said. His voice gluey with tears. "Your lover? He also needs you to die. Oh, God, Clio. He needs you to show them there's a price for what they've done. And you're it. You're the price. It's not your fault, but that's what you are. Come on; let's just do it; let's just make it as quick as we can, OK?"

MONDAY

Tara woke with Shaw standing over her. Still dark out. He told her to get ready; they were going on a 'family expedition'. That's all he said. He didn't say where they were going.

He'd already woken Mom and Dad and Jase, and now he hustled the whole family down to the Liberty. Trevor assigned a few convoy bikers to ride with them, to ward off the news jackals, but the jackals never even stirred. When Tara pulled out onto Oriole Road, it was quiet. She followed Shaw's instructions, and went north on the Rt. 25 Spur. After a few miles, the Liberty was the only car on the road. Clearly there would be no pursuit. So Shaw waved off the bikers. The Liberty went on by itself.

Tara had never been so tired in her life.

Shaw read to her from a sheet of directions. "Take the spur, cross over I-95. Go three miles, then left on 99."

She did that.

"Then right on Cooper Pasture Road."

Here at the edge of town were a few sprawling developments—Oglethorpe Estates, Georgian Majesty Villas—that had gone belly-up in the real estate crash and were now abandoned, choked with weeds, already haunted. After that, there was nothing. A few trailers, quiet as crypts. Scrub pine. Cow pastures. Tara checked the rearview mirror: Mom was sleeping soundly with Jase's head on her lap, but Dad was as vigilant as ever—she saw the gleam in his eyes.

"Left on Green Swamp Road."

Was this going to be some picnic thing? Were they going seining again? Or crabbing this time, or bass fishing? But Shaw kept mum, and the blankness of his features got under her skin. It was a game for him, keeping her in the dark like this. It was too cruel. To be in thrall to this bastard, at his beck and whim, day in and day out—it was too hard.

But she knew she couldn't show what she felt—she needed his mercy. For Nell's sake she had to keep it steady, keep a distance, float above this.

Green Swamp to Butler, Butler to Honeygal.

Then Shaw read, "300 yards to farmer's road on right." Intoning the words as though he had nothing to do with them, as though they were some kind of disembodied decree. But it's you, she thought. It's your plan, you cowardly fuck. Whatever it is, I know it's yours.

They were on an oystershell road that wound through a hummock of pine and palmettos and Spanish moss. Oak branches scraped the roof. The forest closed in, darkened. A banana spider fell onto the driver's side mirror and perched there, defiantly, big as a hand. After a hard turn, and twenty more ragged yards, they broke abruptly into a clearing, a bluff that overlooked a marsh creek. There was a car here already, and Tara recognized it, and her heart became a fist. It was Clio's car. Someone, a woman, was leaning against the front fender. She wore a shawl, and kept her face down—so for a moment Tara could pray that she wouldn't be Clio.

But the woman raised her head, and of course she was Clio.

Standing there looking lost, hugging herself as though she were cold—though the morning was already hot and sticky. Oh, my Lord, thought Tara. Please my Lord I know what I deserve but please don't let it be Romeo who brought her.

"Turn off the engine," said Shaw.

Tara obeyed. Silence. Then Romeo appeared. He went and leaned against the car, next to Clio, and drew her hand into his own.

Tara still praying: please don't let this be what it is.

From the back, Daddy asked Shaw, "What's *she* doing here? Why have you got Clio?"

Romeo called to them: "Everybody out. Don't talk, don't waste time. Just everybody get out of that car."

They all emerged from the Liberty. Clio cried out happily and opened her arms for an embrace. But Romeo held her and murmured, "No, you stay here."

Dad said: "Why is she here? Shaw, what are you doing?"

Shaw gazed at the ground and said nothing.

Romeo said, "There was a price. OK? The price was posted. You knew the price."

A heaviness in his voice, a slogging rhythm, as though he were reciting these words from memory.

Dad asked him, "What do you mean? What are you saying?"

Romeo unfolded a sheet of paper. He read aloud, "Hon I'm going to tell the FBI."

Dad made a guttural moan in his throat.

Romeo kept on. He read like a schoolkid, stressing each word, pronouncing *the* like *thee*, making the a's long as well, and coming to a full stop at the end of each sentence: "I've been thinking a lot. I don't trust that Burrus. I know I did the right thing lying to him, but the FBI won't be fools. They'll track the calls that Shaw makes. They got GPS on cell phones now, so therefore they'll find Romeo easy and catch him. And Shaw too. They'll kill them clean."

Dad said, "I'm sorry. I shouldn't have written that."

Romeo looked up from his paper.

"It was so stupid," said Dad. "I'm so sorry. Oh my God, I'm *sorry*, Shaw. I didn't *do* anything though. I swear to you—"

"Just listen," said Romeo. He read, "Dad, I know how much you hate him. I hate him worse. When he opens his mouth I get sick. He thinks now he's some kind of prophet but people only love him for the money and he's a coward. But once he gets the money he'll try to run and that's when we'll call the FBI. He won't get away!"

Tara knew it was her turn to grovel now. But it felt as though the muscles of her jaw had been fused shut by rage. Now, when she most needed to surrender, she couldn't. She just looked at her father as he implored, "Please! Shaw! It wasn't Tara's fault! It was mine, and I don't know what I was thinking, but Shaw! Please—"

"I can't help you," said Shaw. "I warned you but you wouldn't listen. Now it's Romeo's call."

Dad turned to Romeo, "Oh my Lord, sir, I'm sorry, I'll *never*—"

"There was a price," Romeo repeated. "The price was posted."

Then from his pocket he produced a little amber bottle. He made Clio hold out her hand, and he poured a dozen pills into her open palm. Then he handed her a flask of something. Whispering, "Take them."

Dad said, "*What are you doing?*"

"Do it," said Romeo.

Dad started toward them, but Romeo raised his pistol. "If you come any closer, I'll kill your kids. Which one do I start with?"

Dad's mouth came open. But no sound.

Romeo grabbed Jase by the neck. "This one?"

"*No!*" Dad sank to his knees. "Please, no! Don't hurt my son! Do what you think is right, sir, you know what's right. But don't hurt my boy, please!"

Tara thought she should be doing as he was: kneeling in the dust, pleading. Why couldn't she? She was putting them all at risk. What was the matter with her?

While Romeo kept prompting: "Come on, Clio. We've got to save her. Remember how we save Tara?"

Clio lifted the pills to her mouth. Took a drink from the flask and swallowed them. Dad cried out, "NO! DON'T DO IT CLIO! FOR GOD'S SAKE, YOU'RE KILLING HER!"

Romeo said softly, "That was very brave, girl."

Tara saw the moisture in his eyes. As he drew two more amber bottles from his pocket, and filled Clio's palm again. Twenty or so this time. Blue pills, yellow. Gesturing: take them.

She did.

Mom was sobbing, and Dad made those tortured noises. But Tara just stood there, frozen.

Again Romeo replenished Clio's palm.

But now Clio had turned ghostly pale. She whispered, "More?"

Romeo, holding her wrist, gently raised her hand. "You gotta be brave."

She put them in her mouth. She drank.

Romeo turned to Tara. "Now we wait. Tara, you gotta say goodbye. Say goodbye to your friend who loved you so much that she gave up her own life as a warning to you. Say goodbye to her."

But something snapped in Tara. Those words, *Say goodbye to her*—released her. She told Romeo, "Fuck you." And went up to Clio and said, "Come on, let's go."

Romeo said, "Get away from her!"

She disregarded the order. With everyone watching, she put her arm around Clio's shoulders and helped her take a few uncertain steps toward the Liberty. Clio tried to flow out of her arms, saying, "Honey, if it's OK, I'd rather, I'd rather just, just lie down right here, just, sleep for a little—"

"Sleep later," said Tara. "Come on."

Romeo commanded: "Stop!"

But Tara didn't even look at him. She drew Clio along.

He cried, "I'll start killing!"

She said, "Kill me first. You've already killed Clio. It's my turn."

"I'll kill your brother!" Romeo shouted. "I'll kill your mother! Everybody! Whatever I have to do! I'll kill your father right now!" He pointed the pistol at Dad. Tara saw this movement in the corner of her eye, but she didn't stop. She opened the Liberty's back door, and helped Clio get in. Waiting for the shot. Any second, any second.

Then she heard Shaw say, "Let them go."

Romeo, confused: "What?"

"Put the gun down."

"There's a *price*," Romeo insisted. "The price was posted."

"It's paid," said Shaw. "Now we need mercy. Let's get her to the hospital."

He helped Dad to his feet, and told Tara, "I'll drive."

Everyone climbed into the car. Tara turned to look back at Romeo—one long look into his eyes. Then Shaw started the engine and they roared off.

Shaw pushed 70 mph on the dirt of Honeygal Road, but when he hit Rt. 341 he cranked it to 90. The tires sang on the turns. He tossed his cell phone back to Patsy and said, "Call the hospital. Tell them to be ready for us."

He came barreling down 341 and approached a red light with traffic idling before it. He veered, and lurched up onto the curb and skirted around the line of bleating cars, shooting through the intersection. Every second was precious. Clio's life dangled by a thread, and all that kept her in this world was Tara, Tara talking her through the valley of death. Shaw pounded the horn and slammed the accelerator, and the blocks ticked away. He turned left at Community Road and right on Altama, following the H sign.

A time to punish and a time to forgive.

He took a left at Shrine Road and swept into the ER bay. Nurses were already waiting. They wheeled Clio away on a gurney and allowed Tara to go with them.

337

Shaw checked the clock on the dashboard. Only fourteen minutes since they'd left the creekside. So she ought to have a chance.

He and the Boatwrights went to the waiting room, and sat, and in half an hour Clio's mother came running in, nearly incoherent from fear. Some attendant escorted her into the ER.

Nurses and orderlies kept coming around to gawk at Shaw and the Boatwrights. One even got up the courage to say, "You're the jackpot people, aren't you?"

Patsy nodded.

The nurse said to her, "The spirit of the Lord is upon you."

The receptionist murmured, "Amen."

Romeo was trudging through the white heat. Green Swamp Road had looked cool and shady on the map, but in the event it turned out to be just a straight track of brutal sun and whining katydids forever. And his brain felt swollen, full up with that look that Tara had cast him.

The sun took up most of the eastern sky. Round his

head was a halo of gnats. After a few miles he thought he could walk no farther, so he sat down beside the road.

A long time passed.

I should get up and move out of the sun, he thought.

After sudden wealth there's a rush of demons. Always. Flocks of demons. Wheeling. And he among them. The beast, circling. And who to oppose him, that girl? But she had hollowed herself out, and taken in the suffering around her; and now she was ready to fight him.

An ancient bronze Cadillac eased up beside him. The window was lowered ceremoniously and an old black man asked, "Would you care for a ride?"

"I would," he said. "Thank you."

He got into the car. The man said, "Which way you headed for?"

"Brunswick?"

"All the way to town? Would a been a long walk."

"Yes sir. I had given up."

"Get yourself a drink, son. Reach in the cooler back there."

Romeo thanked him, reached over the seat back and opened a Styrofoam ice chest. There were a few cans of soda floating in an inch of murky water. Romeo took a can of Shasta Creme Soda.

The man said, "I got them sodas for my grandkids."

"Would you thank them for me?"

"Sure. How come you ain't got no car?"

"Well. I went to a party with a girl. In her car? But she went off with somebody else."

"Oh. Well, I know that feeling. You feel bad?"

"Yes."

"I don't doubt. How long you been going with this girl?"

"I wasn't going with her. I was supposed to kill her. But everything got fucked up, because I was afraid, and they knew it. Now I don't know what to do."

They didn't say another word till they got to town.

As they drove, Romeo kept seeing that one thing: that look of Tara's.

Well, OK, he thought. You're so good with suffering, I'll give you as much as you can stand.

Shaw and the Boatwrights waited in the hospital for two full hours. Finally Clio's mother came out from the ER and told them Clio was going to be OK.

Patsy embraced her; they both laughed. Patsy told her how Shaw had raced here so heroically. The woman took Shaw's hands into her own, and kissed them, saying, "When I saw you on TV, I knew you were a good man." Her eyes brimmed with tears.

Jase said, "I never seen no one go faster *ever*. Not even Dale Jr.!"

Everyone laughed. Clio's mother said, "Sir, you are a saint."

They went outside. Already there was a crush of TV crews and reporters:

"Shaw! Why are you here?"

"Shaw! Is it true you saved a girl from killing herself?"

"Shaw! How did you know about her?"

"How did you locate her?"

"Shaw!"

"Shaw! Is it true that the voice of God led you to her?"

Burris went on duty at three o'clock. As was his custom, he pulled up behind the stand of oleander on Rt. 17, and lay in wait for speeders. But he felt drained and whittled-down, and his thoughts were ugly. He recalled his meeting with Mitch Boatwright, and what a fool he'd been. He considered the patch of frizzled hair on his forehead and wondered why he didn't just give up and shave the thing off. Then he wondered why the hell was he thinking about the hair on his forehead? All he ever thought about were stupid things. Did Nell love him, would the Chief ever respect him, should he shave his head, etc. Why couldn't he think about things substantial, spiritual, weighty?

Well, maybe because he was only a joke.

Possibly he was only a joke that the Chief was telling at Trudy's Café—some long pointless story about a clown cop who thought he'd find some dignity in the world but the world kept knocking him down and pissing on him. *You, dignity? Deppity Dawg?* And at the end of the story everybody was laughing their jawbones loose, everybody in town.

He sat in the cruiser. The traffic swam by. He sat there for an hour, and caught no one because he pursued no one.

However, at 4:57 p.m., Rose Whittle dispatched him to a possible burglary in progress at the Jane Macon Elementary School. It was late in the day and he found the school empty, except for an old black lady, a secretary, working in the office. She said she'd heard noises. He accompanied her to check the classrooms, and then the bathrooms. They found nothing. And they were about to quit; they were on their way back to the office, walking through the big gym, when Burris heard whispers. Off to the left. Where the bleachers were. He went and peered beneath them. Eyes. Two pair.

"Come out of there."

Two little girls scurried away. He jogged after them, but he had that big gut to haul, in addition to all the bouncing and clanging cop paraphernalia on his duty belt, and he was aware of how he must look, with his bald head and the shades and the cop shoes. He wasn't really trying to catch anyone.

But one of the girls turned out to be so chubby and slow that he caught up to her anyway. He tapped her shoulder and she crumpled on the floor and started weeping.

Oh, what a fearless crimestopper am I.

The other one got clean away.

He helped the chubby one up and marched her to the office. He sat her in a chair and folded his arms and scowled at her. He wanted to comfort her but knew it was his duty to be cold and mean—for at least a little while.

"What's your name?"

"Kyra."

"How old are you?"

"Ten."

"What did you think you were doing here?"

"Following Shylana."

"Is Shylana your boss or something?"

"I don't know."

"Because she left you holding the bag."

Kyra wept.

"Maybe you shouldn't be following Shylana around. Maybe she's leading you to bad places."

He asked the old secretary for a tissue and passed it to the girl. It wasn't much help. Every time Kyra looked at him, she'd cry with more vehemence. Because of the uniform, of course. Wear a police uniform, and everywhere you went, people got emotional. Children, lovers, hardened criminals. They'd see the badge and the shiny shoes and they'd start bawling their heads off.

But then a funny thing happened. Shylana appeared.

She marched right into the office and sat down next to Kyra and glared up at Burris. She didn't say her name, but who else could it be? She was very tiny but she was beautiful. Her face was delicate and her eyes enormous. She said, "This was *my* idea. So leave her alone."

Burris asked, "What was your idea?"

Shylana didn't answer.

Said Burris, "I mean, what're you doing in school after hours anyway?"

She glared.

She reminded him of Nell. From a long time ago, from fourth grade. Burris had been in love with her even then, when they used to take the bus on Thursday afternoons to Baptist Bible study—which they both hated. He'd sit behind her and tell dumb jokes and she'd laugh her wild laugh. Once, the bus driver had told her to pipe down but she'd ignored him. When he'd complained a second time, she'd said: "You're not my father. You're not my teacher. You don't get a *vote*, mister." Skewering him with her powerful eyes. And fifty years later, here it was again, the same unrepentant alien gaze, from tiny Shylana. As Burris sternly admonished her: "Your principal could get a juvenile warrant, you know that? Then you'll have to go before Judge Parr and he could send you to the juvenile home—you hear me, Shylana?"

Streams of tears broke from her eyes. Two thin cascades, running straight down her face. Yet she kept glaring at him; her gaze didn't falter. Burris was upended by admiration for this girl who'd come back to share her friend's punishment and who wouldn't be cowed by the cop with the gun and the gut and the patch of snaky hair in the middle of his forehead.

He stopped lecturing. They just studied each other.

Then abruptly Shylana confessed, "We came to look at my picture."

"What picture?"

Shylana shook her head. "Picture I made."

"Could I see this picture, Shylana?"

She got up and started walking. He followed her out of the gym and down the dark school corridor, and Kyra and the old secretary came behind them. Shylana went into a classroom, and pointed to a watercolor on the wall. It was a portrait of a schoolbus. The bottom of this bus bellied down in a way that made it seem alive, and gave life to everything around it. Shylana had chosen to make the sun itself the color of grape juice, which made the bus look extra-stunningly yellow. Good God. It was the old school bus from his childhood, with its creaking seats and blown shock absorbers, with sunshine roaring out from its Bluebird heart.

He wondered, how is this possible: such sunniness, after so many years? His eyes were filled with prismatic tears. He told Shylana it was the best picture of a school-bus he'd ever seen. He wanted to say it was the best picture of anything he'd ever seen, but he was afraid that might have sounded insincere. He murmured something about needing to use the little boys' room, and the old woman pointed the way. He went down and pushed through the door. It was truly a 'little boys' room, with dwarf urinals and dwarf sinks. He leaned against a sink, and got down on his haunches, and looked at himself in the mirror. All I've ever wanted was a lot of sunshine, and here it is, suddenly, knocking me down. What's happening to me?

After he collected himself, he drove Shylana and Kyra home. He left Kyra off first, then took Shylana to her grandmother. Before he drove away, she gave him a kiss on the cheek.

He said, "Shylana, you remind me of someone. A little girl. A long time ago I was in love with her."

"Really? Did you marry her?"

"No."

"Why not?"

"Beats me," he said. "You think I still could?"

She shrugged. "How would I know?"

Mitch didn't speak during the migration to the Rotary Club fairgrounds, but held Tara's and Clio's hands the whole time, and kept his eyes low. He knew what he'd done. He'd almost gotten his daughter's best friend killed, with his own family thrown into the bargain. His pride had led him into massive folly, from which others had rescued him, and he felt lower than dirt. He wished he could be a grub so he could lie in filth and be trodden upon and forgotten.

An honor guard of pilgrims walked with the Boatwrights.

It wasn't a long walk. They went down Robin Road and crossed Canary Drive and Fourth Street, and then there was a sign: Rotary Club fairgrounds. The sign had a clown and a Ferris wheel. Mitch remembered the Ferris wheel from the fairs of his youth, but it was long gone; now there was just a big scrubby lawn with picnic tables to one side. A cattail pond. A few cabins (sometimes the place was used as a summer camp). Hundreds of the faithful were already here, and they cheered as Mitch arrived. Such an outpouring of love! He stayed hunched over, looking at his shoes, bewildered. Then he and his family were ushered up to a place of honor, by the card table that had been turned into an altar.

A chant went up: "Shaw! Shaw! Shaw!"

At last Shaw obliged them with his presence.

Someone handed him a microphone. The crowd kept calling his name, but he held his hand up and begged them: "Don't. *Don't*. I'm not important here." For a while they refused to obey him: their love was irrepressible. But finally the chanting died away, and silence settled in, and then Shaw said, "What *is* important is that we rescued a soul today. You all hear about that?"

Another upwelling of devotion, mixed with rapturous laughter. Everyone was looking at Clio, who hid herself in Tara's embrace like a shy baby animal.

Shaw motioned, to indicate the lofty sweet gums and oaks that surrounded the field. A breeze was passing from tree to tree. "And do you feel that? Do you feel that wind?"

"Oh yes!" came the response. "Praise the Lord!" "Yes, yes!" "We feel it!" "Praise the Lord!"

"Do you see how the wind is drawing a circle around us?"

"Yes sir!" "Yes, Jesus!" "Yes we do!"

He said, "And I guess we know what's coming."

"We know!" "We know what's coming!"

Shaw said, "Be a change."

"There's gonna be a change!" "Big change!" "Praise the Lord!"

Mitch could see the spirit traveling from face to face. Already some were on their knees. He glanced over at Tara and found that she—even his beloved daughter!—

was so absorbed in Shaw's words that she didn't notice her father looking at her. Oh Lord. Just a few hours ago the man was threatening to kill us. He's a demon, isn't he? Am I mistaken? Isn't his heart as black as death? My Lord, my Father, help me to see!

Shaw held up a loaf of bread. He said, "Well. It does *look* like bread."

Chuckling from the assembly.

"Except, when you taste it," he said, "it tastes like *light*. You know the taste of light?"

"Praise the Lord!"

"If you don't, you're going to find out," said Shaw.

"Praise the Lord!"

"Because this bread is the body of our Lord."

"Yes it is!"

"And the light comes from Heaven."

"Praise the Lord!"

He made a motion to Patsy: come forward.

She neared the altar. Shaw gave her a nod, and she knelt. He tore off a morsel of the loaf and placed it on her tongue, and said, "You chew this good, honey." He didn't say this into the mike, and only the people in the front rows heard it, but their laughter rolled through the crowd and the folks in back laughed just for the sake of laughing.

Then Shaw held up a goblet of wine.

Patsy's lips parted. She gazed up into his eyes and sipped. Mitch knew that she was imagining Shaw McBride's lips against her own. She was in love with Shaw McBride, Mitch knew. She worshiped him. It was a knowledge that should have filled Mitch with anger, but didn't.

All he felt was shame, and fear, and the looming of some upheaval. Something was about to play out here. He was about to make some kind of journey, and take leave of these troubles. The wind that was kicking up was going to rip him out by the roots from the world he'd been living in, and carry him to some new world, and so be it.

His daughter Tara led him to the altar. He knelt. Shaw touched his forehead, and the touch was scorching. When bread was set upon his tongue, the hollowness inside of him, the hunger, was quelled. His thirst was quenched by the blood of the Lord. He sobbed. He rose and stumbled from the altar. The cry went up, "Praise Jesus! Praise the Lord!" His daughter led him back to his seat. He sat there holding her hand, still with the taste of Jesus in his mouth, and he knew he had journeyed a great long way to this salvation. But all that mattered was, he was here. He'd made it. He'd found the green pastures and the still waters, and he could lay his head down now in his daughter's lap and be all right.

Romeo patrolling on Rt. 17, saw Old Pork in his cruiser, lurking behind bushes. Romeo slowed the Tercel. Slowed *way* down, till he was just creeping along, 10 mph or so, and gawking as he went by.

Still Old Pork didn't notice him. He was looking at nothing, lost in thought, and only by chance did he happen to shift his eyes and spot the Tercel. Then instantly his overhead came on. He burped out a little pig-squeal and in five seconds was perched on Romeo's ass.

Romeo pulled into the parking lot of Tawney's Transmissions. Old Pork right behind. Getting out of his cruiser and waddling up to Romeo's window. "How are you today, sir?"

"Good, thank you. How about you?"

"I'm good. You're still in Brunswick."

"Yes."

"Get that animal disposed of?"

"Yes, I did."

"Still on vacation?"

"Yes."

"Folks don't usually vacation in Brunswick."

"They don't?"

"No, they go over to the island, or Savannah or something."

"Oh."

"There's not much to do here."

"You're right about that." Romeo shrugged. "I guess I just like how it's falling apart and nobody's trying to fix it."

Old Pork studied him intently. Trying to get a read, decide what his angle was. Romeo didn't mind the attention.

Then the cop said quietly, "OK. Could I see your license and proof of insurance, please?"

Romeo handed them over. The cop took them back to his car, and did his little incantations over them or whatever cops did.

Then he came back and returned the documents and said, "Mr.—I'm sorry. I forgot how you say your name?"

"Zuh-DER-ko."

"I got a question for you."

Romeo waited.

"Your license says you're from Piqua, Ohio."

"Yes."

"Would that be anywhere around Dayton?"

Oh! It was coming then. The Truth. It was coming in the guise of a shabby old traffic pig. He wondered what he should do. Should he keep prevaricating under the very shadow of Truth?

"I'm sorry, Officer. Would you repeat the question?"

"What I'm really asking is, you wouldn't happen to be friends with Shaw McBride, would you?"

"Well. Oh. I guess yes. I mean I used to be."

"Used to be? You have a falling out?"

"It's a long story."

"Give me the gist."

"The gist is, he got struck by lightning."

"Sir?"

"I mean he won that jackpot. And became the apostle of all those freaks. And me, I guess I'm becoming something else."

"What are you becoming, sir?"

"Nothing."

"All right."

"Officer, do you sometimes get the feeling we're on the same ride? You and me? The way we both keep driving around and around this city like we're on some carousel together? Me on this ugly old shit-colored pony, you on your porkmobile pony? Jesus. Like we're waving at each other as we go around. You know?"

"Sir, I'm not sure what you're saying."

"I'm not either. It just feels like everything's spinning faster and faster, and we know this ride is gonna crash but we gotta keep pretending it's not."

"Crash?"

"I'm just thinking, why don't we jump off?"

"Sir?"

"I mean I wouldn't mind going home for a while. You wanna come with me? I could use another driver for the trip. You could get a break from this heat. See Ohio. Ohio's nice."

Old Pork looked at him.

Romeo smiled. "I'm *kidding*. I know, we're stuck. We're not going anywhere."

"Sir, do you have any weapons in this car?"

"I have a Phoenix .22 plinker in the trunk. That legal?"

"So long as you keep it in the trunk."

"OK. Could I ask why you pulled me over?"

Old Pork thought a while. "Well sir," he said, "you've got no illumination on your tag. That's a requirement in the State of Georgia."

Stood there just looking at him, with no expression

Romeo could read. But finally he added gently, "So you get that fixed, all right now, sir?"

Clio figured, so long as she was with Tara, she'd be OK. The memory of what had happened at the creekside, though already faint, was still present, and she needed to keep clear of it. So she stayed close to Tara's side; she stayed busy. They worked with the pilgrim ladies on the supper line at the fairgrounds, Clio ladling out barbecued shrimp, Tara dealing the garlic mashed.

Tara had filled a Snapple bottle with Cuervo. Now and then she or Clio would duck down and take a surreptitious pull. That's what Clio was doing when Tara announced, "Oh my God. The Turkeys are here."

The Turkeys were a family of pilgrims from Delaware. The father had this jutting thing he'd do with his chin, and his wife and kids all had identical birdlike stares. And just now the whole family was coming through the chow line, and Clio and Tara had to fight to suppress their laughter.

Soon after them came the Enormous Pious Lady. Tara

gave her an extra scoop of potatoes, and the EPL actually said, "Bless you, my child."

Then some guy came through the line and Tara whispered, "Doesn't he look like that guy on *The Hills*? The poser-ass dickwad?"

Clio groaned. "Oh my God. Spencer! He does!"

They were still laughing over that when the EPL came back for seconds. Tara gave her another big dollop of potatoes and the woman said, "Well, the Lord provides, don't he?"

And Tara said, "Yes ma'am. Provides and *provides*." As soon as the woman was gone Clio let loose with howls. She had to apologize to Mrs. Riley, the old lady who was running this show. "Sorry, Miz Riley. Getting it together now. Going back to work now."

The woman gave her an indulgent smile. Everyone was so good to Clio. Everyone knew how lucky she was to even be alive.

The last ones to come for lunch were Shaw and Trevor. They crossed from the picnic tables, talking quietly, easy in their skins, glowing with confidence. Clio worshiped Shaw and thought Trevor was sort of cute as well, and she was glad to see them. But Tara turned the color of ashes, and put down her big ladle and said, "Come on, let's get out of here."

"Wait. Why?"

"Or stay," Tara snapped. "Stay if you want." She walked away. Heading for the big cabin.

Clio hurried after her. "Why? You don't like him? But he saved my life. Didn't he? It wasn't true what Romeo said! I mean it was you and Shaw who saved me, right?"

Tara kept walking. "I think he's great, Clio. I'm just tired. I gotta lie down. You wanna come with me?"

Clio gave up trying to understand. Nothing clear or honest will show its face to me now, she thought. Which really was OK. She felt helpless, lost; she seemed to see everything through a keyhole; she couldn't tell which of these shadows were angels and which demons and the best thing was to go wherever Tara led her.

Burris drove around Brunswick, considering Zderko.

Had he ever in his career encountered anyone more troubled? No. Back in '87 he'd worked on the security detail that had transferred Leroy Massequa to Reidsville. Leroy had just killed his whole family, believing (correctly) that his girlfriend was cheating on him with his own father. Yet even he had seemed tranquil compared to Romeo Zderko.

And why was Romeo Zderko in such turmoil?

Because, Burris believed, he was under the thumb of Shaw McBride. Because he was the cudgel that Shaw McBride was using to terrorize the Boatwrights.

Though Burris had no evidence for this. He had nothing but conjecture. And since he'd never even met McBride, and had seen him in the flesh but once—in church yesterday—he thought he ought to be careful before laying any judgment on him.

I ought to at least *meet* the lying extortionate snake.

He turned the cruiser around and headed for the fairgrounds.

Romeo drove past Shelby's house and saw, through the great-room window, that the Braves were on. Somebody in that house liked the Braves. But he had no idea who. The boy? Uncle Shelby? MacKenzie? Or maybe they just left the TV on when they went out; maybe the house was empty?

As he drove away he thought, what a useful visit. I'm learning so much on these patrols.

He went over to Vanessa and Henry's house on Poinsettia Circle. Just as he passed, Vanessa came out to her mailbox, and when she went back in, she opened the kitchen door without using a key. Good, he thought. She leaves the door unlocked. Whenever he needed to, he could just walk in. That was important to know.

Why the hell was he still making these rounds?

He drove past Enoch Emery's office. Then past Alfred's house, then past Nell's. And so around. In the center of his circuit was the Rotary Club fairgrounds. If he were a moth, that's where his flame would be. Shaw had said, don't get too close. But couldn't he just stop by *for a minute*? For the sake of his sanity? Just take a little break from these orbits and go check out the crowd at the fairgrounds, see the heart of things, the pulse? Just for a minute. What could be the harm in that?

Tara lay in bed in one of the camp cabins with Clio next to her.

Came a soft knock and the door opened. Tara didn't

look, but by the very breeziness of his approach, she knew.

"What do you want?" she said.

"Checking on Clio. How is she?"

"Asleep."

He brought a stool next to the bed and sat down. He spoke quietly so as not to wake Clio. He said, "Listen. Thank you for standing up to me today. For saving her life."

"Yeah? OK. Fuck you."

He said, "I don't ever want to hurt you. Ever. Or anyone close to you. You know that?"

She just looked out the window.

Said Shaw, "You know what I *do* want?"

She shrugged. "Yeah."

"What do I want?"

"Love."

He wanted everyone's love. Hers, Dad's, Mom's, Jase's, Nell's. And from everyone else he seemed to be getting it. One by one, they'd fallen; everyone submitting but her. And maybe soon, her too. Or maybe not. She half-wished he'd try to take her right now. Either she'd kill him, or he'd overpower her and she could surrender and call him Lord and turn into some kind of gray nothing like Dad, and after that no one's life would be in her care.

But he didn't touch her. He only sat there in the gathering dark, without saying another word.

Burris knew the cop who was stationed outside the fairgrounds. Name of Mims, county guy. Burris had worked with him in his days with the Coastal Area Drug Abuse Task Force.

"Hey, Mims."

"What's up, Burris?"

"Well. I'm investigating a theft."

"Oh. Here?"

"Yeah."

Mims waved him in. No further curiosity, no bother. Well, right, thought Burris. If I'd been parbroiling all day in that Crown Vic I probably wouldn't give a damn who came or went either.

He drove up past the big cabin to the grassy field that met woods on three sides and a pond on the other. The sky was still brimming with light, but dusk had started to pool in the trees. Shaw's followers crowded the picnic tables, and sprawled on the grass and on the porch of the big cabin. Mercy. So many of them. And they were all eyeing Burris warily and seemed to be deeply suspicious.

A man advanced. Baby-faced, dressed like a scarecrow, but nevertheless carrying himself like a big tuna. Burris lowered his window. "I'd like to talk to Shaw McBride?"

"He's busy."

"Would you tell him a police officer wants to see him?"

"About what?"

"Just tell him."

The man withdrew.

The rude starers stared. Burris stared right back. Y'all are getting the airs of a damn *cult*, you know that?

After a few minutes, Shaw McBride came sweeping toward him from across the field, with a half-dozen acolytes trailing behind.

"Officer? Can I help you?"

Burris said, "Got a minute?" He unlocked the passenger door, and McBride got in—then Burris raised the windows and relocked the doors. Asking solicitously: "It's not too cold for you, is it? Air's not blowing on you?"

"I'm fine," said McBride. His devotees were out there gawking unashamedly, as though the cruiser were some kind of aquarium.

Burris asked him, "You used to this?"

"To what?"

"People staring at you all the time."

"I think it's *you* they're staring at. They've seen enough of me." His grin seemed natural and unforced. "So tell me, Officer, what can I do for you?"

"Well, I was just wondering. You went into Chummy's convenience store the other day? The day after you won the lottery? You recall that?"

"Yes."

"Why did you do that?"

"Oh, well. Seems silly now, but I felt I just had to go back there. To see where it all came down? That make sense?"

"The counter girl says you didn't even know. Till she told you."

"Know what?"

"That you'd won the jackpot."

"Well, right. We were keeping it a secret."

That easy smile again. He was good. Anyone else getting grilled in a patrol car might be squirming and sweating, but not McBride.

Burris got down to business: "Sir, you know a man by the name of Romeo Zderko?"

"Why do you ask?"

"Because I'd like to know the answer, sir."

But be my guest, Burris thought, and deny it. I'd love to hear you deny it.

McBride didn't deny it. He offered, in a surprisingly calm and flat voice, "Romeo used to be my best friend. Is he in some kind of trouble?"

"Used to be? No more?"

"Uh-uh."

"What happened?"

"Well. We came down here together, on vacation? We've been friends since we were kids. And we worked together up in Ohio. So we were coming down 95, and I saw the sign for Brunswick, and I remembered this was where Mitch Boatwright was from. So I said to Romeo, hey, I want to look up this guy I know, OK? This guy who helped me when I was so nuts? And he was fine with that. So I called Mitch, hung out for a while. And then, you know, I go back to the motel, and then I get that call from Mitch, he says, 'Shaw, I think we won the jackpot.'

"So I told Romeo about this, and he says, 'We won the jackpot?' And I say, 'Well, *I* won it.' He goes, 'Oh, no. We got a *deal* for this trip. We go half on *everything*.' I say, 'What? I'm not giving you half my jackpot 'cause of some deal about splitting expenses.' And he goes, 'Not *giving* me. What I'm *due*.' I say, 'You're my best buddy, and you *will* get something good out of this. A Porsche at least.' But he says, 'I want my *half*.' He starts, like, swearing at me. I mean he went completely apeshit. You know what I'm saying?"

It was hard for Burris to think straight. The radio kept buzzing in with news of trivial misdemeanors around the city. And all those silent spectators were staring at him, and fireflies were flashing their secret messages and this interview might have been the strangest thing he'd ever done in his life. But the story McBride was feeding him did have a sort of lit-from-within plausibility.

Could it all be moonshine? *All* of it?

Just then he noticed that one of the devotees had a video camera and was taping this encounter. "Wait a minute," he said. "Is that from a news station?"

"Uh-uh," said McBride. "One of our own. I could tell them to cut it out, if it's making you uncomfortable."

Burris murmured, "Too late now."

Though he had a strong sense he'd wind up on the eleven o'clock news, and by morning be nothing but ashes. His job gone, his pension gone, and Nell would get wind of this visit and think he was harassing her family and never speak to him again. So that'll be it then. So strike the tents.

McBride was going on: "Officer, you know the thing

that's setting Romeo off? What *I* think? This might sound odd, but I think it's not the money. It's just that he's alone now. I mean we've been good friends for a long time, and then we come down here, and me, I'm welcomed into this family. This world. But Romeo . . . well, he's just *out there,* you know? He's just all alone and drifting. You know? You understand?"

It did seem to cohere. Burris mumbled, "Yes I do."

"So if you do have to pick him up," said McBride, "Try to be kind to him, OK?"

"OK."

"Oh, and I think there's still some barbecue shrimp. The ladies made it. It's kind of amazing. Can I fix you a plate?"

"No sir," said Burris. "But thank you, sir. Been a long day. Feel kinda whupped."

Romeo had to jump a drainage ditch and negotiate a barbed-wire fence, then hike through swampy woods in the dark with only a rind of pale damp moon to guide him. It was the smell of the fairgrounds that he got first— bug repellent and lamp oil and roasting marshmallows.

Then he started to hear the shouts and laughter, and finally he came to the edge of the trees and beheld a field full of running kids. They were pursuing some peculiar game. A few of them, wearing red bandanas, were chasing the others around the field. It took Romeo a moment before it came to him: this was the old game from Piqua, the game that he and Shaw had made up when they were kids: Hawks and Sparrows.

Shaw himself was 'base'. He called, "Come out, little Sparrows!" and the kids came running toward him, except the ones with red bandanas—those were the Hawks. Their job was to catch the Sparrows. As Romeo remembered, if a Hawk caught you then you had to go to the Hawks Nest. But you were safe so long as you were touching Shaw, or touching someone else who was touching him. But since Shaw was always moving, the Sparrows had to scramble wildly to keep their holds, shrieking and climbing Shaw's back, and the Hawks hovered close to them and taunted.

When Shaw shouted, "Hide, little birds!" all the Sparrows had to leave him and run for their lives.

Romeo could see that everyone was in bliss. Because of the wild cycles of the game, of course, but also on account of the dusk, the fireflies, the colliding fragrances.

A small flock of Sparrows came running into the

shelter of the trees. They saw Romeo, and cried, "Hawk! Hawk!" and ran off again. He felt abysmally banished and unreal, and wished he hadn't come. Yet he didn't leave. He stayed there, watching. Even when the game faded, after the kids were called to their cabins and tents and campers and RVs, he stayed.

In the dark, his alarm buzzed. Time to call Shaw. He pressed 7 on his keypad—and across the field, Shaw opened his phone.

"How you doing, Romeo?"

"OK."

"I've got news. That old cop came by to see me. But I think I *broke* him. I mean really, I think he's shattered. You know what's amazing? It's amazing how much these people want to protect me. Jesus. Romeo, you wouldn't believe these people."

Even as he spoke, Romeo was watching him stroll along near the line of tents, like a general inspecting a bivouac. While Trevor, his aide-de-camp, lagged fifteen steps behind, to give him privacy for the call.

Shaw murmured, "Of course we have tricky moments ahead. Have to find some way to take our winnings and move on, and keep the Boatwrights scared from a distance. But we'll do it. I have a plan for that. Oh listen, you have to dump the Tercel."

"I do?"

"That old cop will be watching for it now. Get a new ride."

"But I like the Tercel."

"Jesus," said Shaw. "You should see these fireflies!"

"Yeah. I see them too."

"Where are you?"

"Patrolling. Shaw, I got a question."

"OK."

"Who should I kill first? I mean suppose you don't answer my call? I was thinking Nell but that seems too obvious. That's the first place the cops would cover, right? So how about Vanessa and Henry? Tara said how much she likes Cousin Vanessa's art and all. Right?"

Shaw had stopped in the field. "Romeo. You won't need to kill anyone. We're good now."

"Or I could do Shelby," Romeo went on, as though Shaw hadn't said a word. "But he's got those kids and could I really kill them? Maybe I could. Though if it's daytime the kids'll be in school and then I'm pretty sure I'd want to do Shelby first."

"Hey!" said Shaw. Sudden flash of impatience. "Stop talking about killing! This isn't about killing! This is about love!"

Romeo fell silent.

"Stop worrying," said Shaw, and he was soft again. "The whole world is on our side now."

Burris, checked off by doom, unsalvageable, sat in the cruiser in front of Nell's house, and watched Nell working in her kitchen. Nell was facing away from him, but by her slight hunch and the small rhythmic movement of her shoulders he figured she was washing dishes. He knew he should get away from there before he was tempted to do something stupid. Like going in and trying to talk to her. No. Drive away *now*. What are you doing here?

I have business, he told himself.

No you don't. Move along.

I have to warn her.

Go home.

Nell turned and hung a washcloth on a little hook. And Burris got out of the Taurus and marched toward the porch.

Losing steam quickly though. By the time he reached the top step of the portico he was thinking, this is *suicide*.

This will be added to the long list of memories that make me cringe and weep, and will stay with me forever. He was at the point of retreating—but then the automatic porchlight flicked on, and Nell came to the door to see who it was.

Through the open screen door she said, "Burris?"

He felt deeply the chill in her tone.

"How are you, Nell?"

"I'm fine." But she spoke it briskly, and pointedly she wasn't asking him in.

Behind her, two cats were on the kitchen table, one was on the floor, one was in the rocking chair. All were eyeballing him. The one in the rocker looked like a living electric shock. Burris knew he was an imbecile to have come, but now he had to play it through. He said, "Sorry to be visiting so late. I saw your light."

"I was just about to turn in."

"OK. Could I have one minute though?"

"Why?"

"Just something I need to talk to you about."

"What is it?"

What an indignity having to stand out here. What a rude stony-hearted woman. Which she's always been, come to think of it, and I was a sap to have ever chased her. She's always been a diva, and her looks which were never much are now completely shot. Also, this house reeks of too many cats.

Still, it gave him vertigo to be so close to her.

Finally she threw him a crumb: "Burris, you want to come in?"

"Thank you."

The screen door creaked. She gently purged the kitchen table of its cats, and he took a seat. Noticing the trophy head he said, "That's not a real buck, is it?"

"No. It sings."

Not deigning though to make it sing for *him*. She just sat across from him and folded her arms and waited.

At last he began. "Well, what I've come about? I've come about Shaw McBride."

"Yeah?"

"You notice any, anything suspicious about him?"

He'd wanted to avoid using the word *suspicious*—it sounded like phony cop-talk. But right away it had slipped out.

She said, "Suspicious? Burris, what's this about?"

"Well . . . well, maybe I got a tip that maybe, um, Shaw isn't really *in* on this jackpot deal."

"Huh?"

"Maybe he didn't really give Mitch that twenty dollars to buy lottery tickets with. Maybe he made that part up."

"Made it up?" she said. "I'm lost."

"I guess there's no way to ease into this. Nell, there's a chance this could be an extortion scheme. A terror scheme."

She gaped at him.

He said, "I think Shaw is threatening Mitch."

"What?"

"I got a tip. So think. You haven't sensed anything odd? Mitch hasn't shown any fear of Shaw McBride?"

"No."

"Or has Patsy, or the kids?"

"Uh-uh. They like him. Particularly Tara does. And I know her pretty well. If she were living in terror, it wouldn't escape me. Come on, where'd you *get* this tip?"

"I can't tell you."

"I mean, is somebody making up stories?"

Just at that moment, one of the cats leaped up onto the table. The electric-shock cat. Christ, he hated that one. Nell said sharply: "Buddy Bailey, get down!" She dipped her fingers into her tea and flicked them, and the cat shrank away.

Meanwhile the other two million cats were skulking around. Mercy. He hated all of them, and hated that she'd given them surnames. It was just too damn cute. Suddenly he was *glad* she'd treated him so cruelly these forty years. Jesus. What if she'd fallen in love with him? Then he'd have married her. Then all this cat-stink would be *his?*

He rose. "Nell, I better go. Sorry to have bothered you so late."

"That's OK."

"I mean, I was just trying to protect your family. You know?"

Though as soon as he'd said it, he wished he hadn't. Defensive-sounding. Like, see what a good Deppity Dawg I am? Nice and dumb. And how automatically and dismissively she came back with, "I appreciate it, Burris."

OK. That's enough. Just get out of here.

But still. He couldn't go. "If you have any more thoughts, or any more questions, you know where to call me, right?"

"Yes."

"Call me at home, though, OK? I'd like to keep this completely under wraps."

What a boneheaded remark! The lady's not calling you anywhere, *any time*, you fool. Just get out of here!

He went to the door. "See you later, Nell."

"All right, Burris. Don't let John Murphy out."

As he opened the door he used his toe to push John

Murphy out of the way. There was something tender and pitying in the way the cat let Burris forklift it away from the door. This house of Nell's! How much life there was here! And to think he'd never entered it once in these forty years, and probably never would again. He turned back to Nell one more time. Her eyes told him she was as lonely as he was. He was certain of it! He ventured, "Hey you know, there's a Turkey Shoot at the American Legion on Saturday. You ever do that? It's not real turkeys, it's just targets. It's fun. You want to come?"

A nervous smile appeared on her face. She walked right up to him, scaring him to death—but then she reached down, took the cat off his foot, stood up straight and said, "Burris. You gotta understand something. I don't want to be your girlfriend."

How uncalled-for! "Nell, I was just asking if you'd like to come to the Turkey Shoot. I wasn't—"

"The answer is no. I don't want to go to the Turkey Shoot with you; I don't want to go to the church picnic with you; I don't want to donate blood with you. OK? You keep asking me do I want to do things with you, and you always know the answer. You asked me, did I want to go to your niece's baptism? I didn't. I like your niece—"

"Nell, that was *years* ago—"

"I like her a lot, and I like you too, but will you please get it through your head that I don't want to be your damn girlfriend!"

A minute ago he'd thought he'd reached the bottom of his life. But not at all. Now came a level of mortification and despair that he'd never guessed *existed*. Like when a sinkhole opens up and swallows people alive. "OK," he said. He went and stood by the door. "I get it now. I'm going. So there's really no need—"

"But you *don't* get it. You told me once that you loved me, and you asked me if I could love you back, and I said no I couldn't. And ever since then, you keep suggesting that maybe the reason is because you lack something. Like you're not ambitious enough. Or you're not the county sheriff. Or you're not clever enough, or you're too bald for me, or you've got jowls or something, none of which is true! Do you understand? Do you understand what I'm telling you?"

He said, "Yeah. I guess."

But then he thought, so long as we're going down this road, I might as well take it the whole way. "So why *don't* you love me?"

She stared at him. "You're kidding, right?"

"No, I really want to know."

"You're asking me that? Why I don't love you?"

"Yes, ma'am."

"Well that's the silliest goddamn question I ever heard. *In my life*. How should *I* know? I don't know why I love or don't love anything! Why do I love my singing trophy head? Why do I love the three little fishies in my gold-fish pond? And my six cats and two parakeets, when one of 'em's always sick and every time one dies I gotta spend half a year mourning, which means mourning is how I spend most of my life? I don't know why I don't love you, Burris—I have no idea!"

He said, "You might shout a little louder, so that everyone in Brunswick will know your opinion of me."

"I'm sorry."

"Just to make my humiliation complete."

"I'm *sorry*."

They stood there a moment, squaring off. Then she sighed. "But I gotta go now, OK? Gotta get these animals to bed."

"All right. That's perfectly, that's a reasonable thing."

"So good night now." Then she was shutting the door again.

"Wait," he said.

Her utter exasperation. "Oh come on. What?"

"One more thing."

"Burris go home."

"I mean, something I would've said a long time ago, except you broke up with me over the damn *phone*."

She glowered at him. "Are you talking about *high school*? For God's sake. I've *gotta* go!"

"Twenty seconds! That's all I need."

"OK, what?"

"You won't give me twenty seconds? For the love of God, twenty seconds out of a lifetime—"

"I'm *giving* you your damn twenty seconds."

"You are?"

"Yes."

"Well then. Then it's very simple. I just wanted to tell you, I mean I never really told you before because—"

"Twenty seconds are up."

"Oh Jesus Christ! For the love of God, I just want to tell you! What I would have told you forty years ago but you hung up on me. But, the thing is, I mean forty years, or two hundred years, or forty *thousand* years, I *see* you, Nell. I see you in a way nobody else in this world can. That's all. You can try to hide from that, but it's still true and I wish you'd just open your damn heart!"

But she was hardly listening. She'd been increasingly distracted by the cat in her arms, who wanted to go outside and who kept struggling to get free. She was trying to hold it tightly so as to allow Burris to finish. But she was clearly relieved when he was done. She nodded and said, "OK, then."

"Just wanted to say that."

"OK." The cat took a swipe at her neck. She cried, "Ow! You little bastard!" and threw it down and it ran under the table. She turned back to Burris. "I gotta go."

"All right," he said.

He turned and walked away, went back to his Taurus. And he must have gotten in and started it up and driven off, because a few minutes later he found himself on Rt. 17 heading home.

Well.

There it was.

The moment he'd been waiting for. The moment he'd been climbing toward for forty years. Climb up, your whole damn life, make an asinine speech which gets interrupted by a squirming cat, then go tumbling down into hell forever and goodnight.

Shaw was ecstatic. Dancing with the young pilgrims around the campfire, amid the flying sparks, inexhaustible. When he finally took a breather, a girl approached him and said she'd been here all day, and that she thought he was wonderful. She said her name was Cheryl. She was blushing. She reminded him, "The clerk? From Chummy's?"

"Yes!" He looked into her eyes. "Didn't I hear you were calling me a liar?"

"I was," she said. "Before."

"And now?"

"Now I know who you are."

Her cheek was glistening in the dark. She was crying; she was shivering. He supposed he could have fucked her right then if he'd wanted, but he didn't want—he didn't want anyone but Tara. And he'd soon have her. She was holed up in her room but Shaw knew that her walls were crumbling and it was only a matter of time. And meanwhile he had his flock to watch over, and the sick to heal, and a fortune to give away, and the sparks were rising up amid the fireflies and the stars, and the pilgrims were dancing, and the universe from one end to the other was his.

Nell went to bed but of course she couldn't sleep. Wondering what had gotten into her? Burris Jones wasn't a bad man, wasn't a stalker, wasn't even much of a pest: whatever had possessed her to launch into him with such vicious cruelty?

Trying to be merciful? That's what I call *mercy*? Holy crap, what a selfish bitch I am.

And the other thing: why had his news upset her so? Maybe because it was true?

Because there *have* been some fishy things about this deal.

Like why hadn't Mitch told them all right away he was splitting the jackpot with Shaw? And how come he seemed so glum at the press conference? And also, come to think of it, why hadn't he come into the water the other day? He loved to seine. So what the hell was that all about?

How could he win all those millions of dollars and seem so damn *morose*?

Maybe Tara *was* lying. She couldn't lie at poker but maybe that was because poker meant nothing to her. She just came here, really, to spend time with her granny. They could have been playing Parcheesi for all Tara cared.

But if she was trying to protect me, Nell thought, that was something altogether different.

But, Lord. That flirty look she'd given Shaw while

teasing him about that bobtail straight: could that have been a *lie*?

No! She was Nell's baby; Nell knew her through and through. And Burris had always been an excitable fool, and this was just another proof of it. And for scaring her like this she would never speak to him again. Everything was fine with Mitch and Tara. Although just to be on the safe side, first thing in the morning she would call Chief Andrews, get his opinion. The Chief was young and always charming to her and seemed to know a lot: she'd let him put her mind at ease.

Burris loitered a while at Chummy's—not the jack-pot-ticket Chummy's by I-95, but the one on Gloucester. He went there because that was the only place still open except the Huddle House, and at the Huddle House someone would have tried to talk to him. He could have gone home, of course. But home was just a swamp of stagnant time.

He got coffee. He sipped it slowly, while staring at the headlines on the newspapers. He didn't read them—just stared. The clerk started to get nervous with this

deranged cop just standing around staring at the newspapers. Finally Burris gave the man a break and left him
alone. He went driving. He drove around and around as
if on patrol. He saw two colleagues, Buzz and Lou,
parked in the Rt. 17 median near G Street, and he
paused and said hello to them.

Said Buzz, "What up, homey?"

"Hey, not much," said Burris, his voice carrying in the
night air.

He drove on knowing they'd be talking about him till
daybreak, but so what? Leave me alone. He went down
Riverside Road because he knew he could park at the
end of it without anyone bothering him.

On the way, he passed the place where he'd seen
Zderko burying the animal. He recalled the odor of
putrefaction that had jumped out from that bag—and
how, according to Zderko, the creature had been dead
for less than forty-eight hours.

Forty-eight hours, thought Burris. Man or beast, in heat
like this, you'll start to stink. In forty-eight hours you'll
give it up to your essential stench. Think you're good-
looking? Or sweet-smelling? Watch what forty-eight
hours will do.

Thoughts like this suited his mood, and he'd have
gone on thinking them—but there was a little memory

that kept tugging at his attention. Something else that Zderko had said. Burris kept ignoring it, but it kept tugging. Finally he attended to it.

Hadn't Zderko said something about *Wednesday*? About running the animal over on Wednesday?

Burris parked in the little sandy place at the end of the road. He looked out at the marsh. Wednesday? He couldn't have said Wednesday. Wednesday didn't work. Burris took his Olympus voice recorder out of his shirt pocket, and switched it on, and worked back through the recordings till he came to Friday afternoon, to that first encounter with Zderko.

He heard himself asking, "*How long's it been dead?*"

And Zderko saying, "*About forty-eight hours. What's today, Friday? Well, Wednesday night, I was coming down through North Carolina? And I hit this thing and it must have been thrown up into the wheel well somehow, but I didn't even know it till a little while ago.*"

Now he thought about this.

Wednesday night was the night of the jackpot drawing. Shaw McBride claimed that on Wednesday afternoon he was here in Brunswick, giving Mitch the money to buy a jackpot ticket. But how could he have been, if he was still up in the mountains with his buddy Zderko, running down that unfortunate animal?

Which meant either McBride or Zderko was lying. And Burris had a feeling which one.

He checked his watch. 5:15.

Was he making some mistake? Was he leaping into boneheadedness again?

He replayed the exchange.

His only mistake was in taking so long to see this.

Because now he had just a few hours left till the Chief heard about his meeting with McBride and fired him.

Though if he was lucky and evasive, maybe he could keep his job till noon.

And now here was something to take his mind off Nell. Could he take this bastard down before noon?

TUESDAY

Burris hit the seediest motels first. At the Blue Pelican there was no one in the office, but he stepped up to a little rat-colored door behind it, and hammered with the side of his fist. Kept hammering till a voice shouted, "WHAT THE *FUCK* DO YOU WANT?"

Burris said, "Come out here."

"Who's that? Dawg? It's the fucking middle of the night!"

"Roque. Come out here."

Finally Roque appeared. Bloodshot eyes. Squashed apricot of a nose. "What'd they do this time?"

Burris showed Roque the license photo of Romeo Zderko. "You know this guy?"

"Uh-uh."

"Look closely. If I find out you're lying to me, I'll knock both of your teeth out."

"Wow, what is *with* you today, Dawg?"

"Last day on the job."

389

"You retiring?"

"I didn't say that."

"We'll miss you, Dawg."

"Call me that one more time."

"Whoo. I'm impressed, motherfucker." Roque studied the photo. "Still, I never seen him."

Burris judged that he was telling the truth. He moved on.

At the rathouse called Golden Isles Villas, it took the drunk behind the desk a while to focus on Zderko's mugshot. But just by the way he shook his head, clearly not giving any kind of a shit, Burris concluded he wasn't lying either.

Blackbeard's Motel had a camera above the reception desk, so Burris made the clerk step outside before warning her, "Becky, you lie to me about this one, I'll confiscate your whole drugstore—you understand me?"

"Oh, stop it, Burris. Just show me your mugshot."

He did. She said, "Oh yeah, I seen this character. Last week."

"When last week?"

They went back in and she checked her registration book. Found it right away: "Romeo . . . Zydeco? Is that how you say that?" She turned the book so he could look at it. It was for Thursday night.

"You remember him?" Burris asked.

"Sort of. Kind of a nothing little fucker. With some other guy. They checked in kinda early."

"On Thursday?"

"That's what it says. Can you read?"

"Seen him since?"

"Once. Like the next day or so. He came in asking about the missionaries."

"Who are the missionaries?"

"These two girls. They was staying here. But they left."

"Why do you call them missionaries?"

"That's what they was. From Missouri."

"Where'd they go?"

"Dunno. They still around though. I heard they ain't missionaries no more. I heard one of 'em's stripping."

"Where?"

Becky shrugged. "That I didn't hear. But you know, it's not endless fucking choices either."

Romeo, first thing in the morning, called Pirate Pete's Swap Show and described the Tercel, and said he would sell it for six hundred dollars.

Soon he got a call from a cracker with a mouth full of stones. It sounded like the guy was saying, "Beat me in the gutter, tie your shoe?"

"What?"

"Meet me at the Goodyear Tire store?"

Romeo drove there. The guy was goateed and had a puffy white head of hair, and wore a Monster Truck Showdown T-shirt. He also wore heavy shades so you couldn't tell where you stood as far as bargaining. Not that it mattered to Romeo—he didn't want to sell the Tercel anyway. He was just doing this because Shaw had told him to.

They drove around the block a few times and the guy seemed to like the car OK. But he asked, "Does it got any problems?"

"Pulls to the left, I guess."

"What do you mean, I guess?"

"It won't pull if you don't go fast. I don't go fast."

"Why does it pull?"

"Alignment. I guess. I ran something over and maybe that screwed up the alignment."

"I gotta pay for a fucking realignment?"

"No, not really," said Romeo. "You don't have to pay for anything. You don't have to do shit."

"I'll give you three hundred."

"OK."

"You caught the turtle?"

"What?

"You got the title?"

Of course Romeo didn't have the title, but they went over to the DMV where they were told that the Tercel was old enough that Romeo could just sign over the registration. So he did that, and took the money, and the guy gave him a lift to Tung's Auto on Norwich Street. When the Tercel drove away, Romeo was heart-stricken. In his life, he'd never owned another car. The Tercel was not a glamour car. It was about as exciting as doing your taxes. But he'd owned it for years and it had never given him any trouble; it had served him faithfully and in return he'd changed the oil and cleaned the points and plugs regularly, and he'd always been, quietly, proud of it. He was still feeling mournful when one of Tung's salesmen came out to see what he was doing standing there in their lot. Somehow he let the guy talk him into buying, for only seven hundred dollars, an old Chevy Bel Air, baby's-breath blue. A huge car, an aircraft carrier. The kind of car his grandfather used to drive (Romeo remembered him tooling around Dayton, whistling at the girls, looking like a maniacal leprechaun in his fedora and Ban-lon shirt). It was an impulse buy, this Bel

Air, and Romeo regretted it the moment he pulled out of the lot.

Shaw sat at one of the wooden picnic tables, disposing of business details with Trevor and a guy named Charlie Cope. Cope was a librarian from Texas whom Shaw had appointed church quartermaster. Cope was running through their options regarding portable toilets. It was already impossibly hot, and Shaw was hardly able to keep his eyes open.

Said Cope, "Danny's Flushes out of Savannah will rent us a full twelve-unit suite for sixty a week per unit. That's eight toilets, which we'll split two male, four female, two disability; plus four wash stations, plus cartage, which I've been quoted at about two hundred, but if we go with Clean Machine there's no cartage but the unit cost is somewhat higher . . ."

Shaw nudged Mitch and murmured, "The mighty work of the Lord." Mitch grinned.

No sooner were they finished with Cope than they had to deal with Mrs. Riley. She said, "Patsy says we're cooking barbecue today, and she says we gotta have pork. But it's in Leviticus, Shaw. Pork is swine and swine is unclean and you shouldn't even *touch* the carcass . . ."

And on and on. But Shaw had ceased to listen; he was following the progress of a sleek car that was coming up the long drive to the big cabin. Something European— a Lamborghini? A true Lamborghini in all its splendor? As he watched this car, he cut Mrs. Riley short. "Do what Patsy says. Patsy is a humble servant of the Lord and we should heed her counsel . . ."

The car stopped and Henry Lonsdale, the financial guy, got out. He gave a quick sidelong look to the crowd of pilgrims. If it was a disapproving look you wouldn't have known it: he was too elegant to give himself away like that. He strolled up to the picnic table and smiled just a little. He wasn't so crude as to announce that sixty-two million dollars had just landed in Shaw's bank account. He just said softly, "Mr. McBride. You ready to go fishing?"

Burris went to check out the "VIP" Lounge just after noon. The sun was in high broiling ascendancy, but inside it was midnight dark and cool. A handful of "VIPs" sat there. Pale, doughy, their waists blown, their earhairs corkscrewing out, each a private huddle unto himself. Burris took a seat at the bar, as far from the little stage as he could get. Making his own huddle, and averting his eyes from the dancing.

The bartender, Holly Ann, a stone dyke who'd worked there for twenty years, said, "Sup, Burris?"

"Not much, Holly Ann. Club soda?"

They knew each other from his unfortunate stint at the Coastal Area Drug Abuse Task Force. Burris had organized a big raid, and she was among those arrested. As usual his reach had exceeded his grasp: the club had a smart lawyer and she'd walked. In fact everybody had walked. The whole thing was a fiasco. And since then, whenever he'd been summoned to the "VIP" Lounge for one disturbance or another, she'd treated him with a kind of mocking disdain. She did bring him his soda. But wordlessly, and then she started to move away. He stopped her: "Holly Ann."

"What?"

"You got any new girls working for you?"

"Depends what *new* means."

"I mean like this week. Like she was a missionary before?"

"Missionary? Here?"

"There's a guy we're looking for. She might know him."

"Burris, what you up to? Give some girl a hard time?"

"Uh-uh. Just talk, I swear. It's not about her."

She sniffed. She left him there.

So as not to be watching the show, he studied the stains in the carpet.

After a minute Holly Ann returned with one of the girls. "Frankie this is Burris. Burris is a cop. Don't touch him, don't dance for him, don't do *anything* for him except answer his questions. Then make him go away."

The girl nodded. Holly Ann left them alone.

Burris said, "Frankie's your real name?"

"Yeah."

"You have any other real names?"

"Tess."

He instantly liked her. Her brow, big and bony, gave her a kind of petting-zoo vulnerability. He wished he could save her from this life. He said, "Were you really a missionary?"

"Yeah."

"What happened?"

"Church kinda folded."

"So you came here?"

She shrugged.

"Seems to me, between spreading the gospel and exotic dancing, there's a lot of room. Can't you work somewhere else?"

"Like where?"

"I don't know. Wal-Mart?"

"*Wal-Mart*? Jesus. This sucks but not that bad."

He felt stupid for having brought it up.

He produced the photo of Romeo. "You know this guy?"

She didn't say yes or no.

"Tess. Please. I know he's a nice guy. But right now he's in over his head on something. I just want to help him."

Tess kneaded her big brow with her fingertips, and Burris sipped his soda, and waited.

Finally she said, "OK. He was at Blackbeard's Motel. I was staying there."

"How long was he there?"

"Just a few hours. They didn't even stay the night."

"They?"

"Him and his friend."

"You talk to them?"

"Yeah. Mostly Romeo. I liked him."

"Did he seem dangerous to you?"

She smiled. "No."

"You see him again?"

"Once. Like Saturday night. He came in here."

"What'd he say?"

"Nothing. A friend of his had died. Some guy lived in a trailer. Out on that road with the Bible name. Palm of something?"

"Balm-of-Gilead?"

"Yeah."

He thanked Tess for her help and left a big tip for Holly Ann, and went out into the blazing day.

Back in the cruiser, he got the call he'd been waiting for. Rose Whittle on the radio, saying, "Burris? Come on in. Chief needs to talk to you. In his office."

Hell with that, he thought. *Hell* with that preening rooster. Come in when I'm damn well ready to.

Jase thought it was awesome when he caught his first redfish. Shaw had set him up with a quarter-ounce jig-head tipped with a minnow, and he got a strike in less than ten minutes. First on the boat to score. Way sooner than Tara. It wasn't big enough to keep, but right away there came another tug, and this one was a fighter. Shaw showed him how to handle it. Jase let out some line and the fish swam off the oyster bar and out toward the ocean. He let out some more and the fish jumped. Red with silver pouring off it.

Jase could feel the presence of Shaw next to him. And the whole family watching and envying him. Today he wasn't the kid who melted into the woodwork; today he was the *star*.

"What do I do?" he cried. "Shaw, what do I do?"

"You're OK," said Shaw. "Reel him in a little."

"I can't!"

"Yeah you can. Come on, get his nose up. He wants you to. He wants you to show him your power."

Jase pulled as hard as could. The rod bowed and quivered. He pulled till his arms were about finished—and then he felt the line slacken a bit.

"You got him," said Shaw. "Take him."

The fish kept fighting. But it gave and then gave some more, and pretty soon Jase was cranking him in. Finally it was close enough for them to net. Mr. Lonsdale said it was one of the biggest redfish he'd ever seen. Dad clapped Jase on the back and Tara applauded. Mom took photos while he held the fish. For one shot he puckered up his lips as though about to kiss it, and everyone laughed. Nobody told him his humor was gross, or stupid or childish; they just laughed with him. They were all with him, and he was with Shaw. Everything was awesome.

Then Shaw's phone started to buzz.

Jase knew who it was. It was Romeo.

Not *now,* he thought. Not in the middle of my perfect day! You jerk, stay out of our lives, we're sick of you!

Shaw took the phone from his pocket.

"Wait!" Jase cried. "Don't even answer."

Shaw said, "I got to, buddy."

"No, it's that buttwipe! Just let him go! We don't need him!"

Shaw turned away and opened the phone and brought it to his ear. Jase grabbed his arm and cried, "No, don't!"

Shaw yanked free, but the phone slipped from his grasp and went sailing. It bounced against the gunwale and flew out over the river and plunged in, vanished.

One long moment of quiet when they all stared after it.

Then Shaw turned and glared at Jase. With dark menacing rage. Jase burst into tears. "I'm sorry! Shaw, I'm *sorry.* I didn't mean to do that."

All of Shaw's fury was in his eyes. Otherwise he made no sign.

He drew a slow breath, and then asked Mr. Lonsdale, "How deep is this, Henry?"

"Nine, ten feet. Mud bottom. I'm afraid you won't find it again."

Shaw said hoarsely, "It's gone?"

"Afraid so."

More silence. Then Shaw said, "Well. No big deal, I guess. It was an old phone. I'm just concerned because my mother's supposed to be calling me from the hospital."

Said Henry Lonsdale, "Nothing serious, I hope?"

"Oh. My father had a stroke."

"My God, I'm sorry to hear that."

"So I've really got to get to a phone in a hurry."

"You can use mine."

"That's kind of you. But I don't have my mother's number. It was in that phone. I guess I better get back to shore."

"Sure. Of course."

"Hate to spoil the fishing."

"No problem," said Lonsdale, and he went to the wheel and cranked up the engine. "The fish'll be here tomorrow."

Shaw asked, "How long will it take to get back to your dock?"

"Well, this gal is pretty fast. Fifteen minutes?"

"Can we make it any quicker?"

"Do the best I can."

Jase sat in the bottom of the boat and curled his knees against his chest, and held his feet in his hands, and stared at his toes. He knew what he'd done. He'd unloosed Romeo into the world. He was the one who had brought Romeo into their lives in the first place, when he'd bragged to his friends about winning the jackpot. Now this. His fault again. Always his fault. Like he'd been sent here to destroy everyone's life. Like he was secretly working for the devil. He wished he were dead. He wanted to throw himself in the water and drown—although mixed with that was a deep shiver of pride that he knew he couldn't tell anybody about ever.

Burris found plenty of trailers on Balm-of-Gilead Road. No trailer parks proper, but all along were singles, or clusters of three or four. At each he pulled in, knocked, displayed the mugshot.

Some of the trailers had boxes of geraniums and stone reindeer and stained-glass caterpillars, and nice old ladies who offered tea and wanted to talk; some were less friendly. Set back in the pines, with Firebirds on blocks and chewed-up screen doors and the gaping tombs of freezers. At one stop, a brace of pit bulls charged him. The sound of galloping, the earth trembling, and there they were, leaping at his throat—but midair they hit the ends of their chains and were hurled into the dust as though stricken down by lightning.

The dogs' owner said he didn't know Romeo, but maybe his brother did. His brother was in the state pen at Reidsville.

Burris kept canvassing, canvassing patiently until he'd used up about three-quarters of Balm-of-Gilead, and nobody knew anything, and it was near three o'clock in the afternoon. Rose called again. "43? Burris? Where *are* you, Burris? You better get the Sam Hill in here."

He ignored her. He kept working.

He came upon a unit with a convivial jigsaw skunk out front, and a gardenful of happy tulips and sweet pea. He pulled up. Old lady standing at the door, behind her walker. When he told her his business, she laughed out loud. "*Romeo?* My goodness. And he's *dangerous?*"

She had a great growly voice. Burris got a kick out of her, and thought Nell would too.

Stop thinking of Nell. Nell is not the measure of

everything. What Nell will get a kick out of, or won't get a kick out of, is not your concern.

"We're just looking for this guy, ma'am. Have you seen him?"

"Well, he looks like that fella I saw going into Claude's."

"Who's Claude?"

"Used to live right there. He died though. I think his daughter's there now."

The trailer she pointed to was away from the road, almost hidden. Burris walked up and knocked. He heard a grunt, which he took to mean *Come in*. He opened the door.

A large woman lay in bed, smoking, drinking beer and watching TV. She wore a faded pink nightie. "Sorry I don't get up," she said. "I'm in mourning."

He said, "I'm sorry about that." He didn't ask her who'd died because he didn't care. He just showed her the mugshot and said, "You know this man?"

Her face darkened. "Oh, yeah. *Ro*-meo. What's his game this time?"

"Why do you say 'game'?"

"'Cause he's a bullshit artist. He tried to tell me he was like some kind of hit man. For some insurance scam or something. I never knew what the hell he was saying.

Officer, why don't you get yourself a beer out of the fridge there? Come have a chat."

"No thank you. He said he was a hit man?"

"He said he was the angel of darkness. Wait, you wanna see something? Let me show you something."

She reached into the drawer of the nightstand beside her. Fumbling around. "You'll like this. This is a hoot. Wait. Where is it?"

She reached down into the flop of tabloids on the floor beside the bed. Stirring them around. Burris took a step back, afraid she might roll off the bed.

Then she sat up and waddled in her nightgown to the TV.

On top of it she found a map. "OK, here. He left this. His little tourist map."

The map had been issued by the Brunswick Chamber of Commerce. Stars had been scrawled at various places. Near the top, someone had written, 'Points of Interest.' But Burris's eye was drawn immediately to the bottom, to the old part of town, where one of the stars had been drawn right on Egmont Street, near the corner of Albemarle.

Nell's.

Another star, encircled, was on Oriole Road: Mitch and Patsy's. There was a star on Poinsettia Circle, but

Burris couldn't place it. But the Belle Point star? That would be the house of Shelby Manford, Patsy's brother.

The stars assembled themselves into a pattern as he looked at them—the way the figure of Orion will jump out from the confusion of the night sky. The pattern was: Mitch Boatwright's family.

"Ma'am," said Burris, "do you mind if I borrow this?"

She shrugged. "*I* sure as hell don't want it. But wouldn't you like to join me for a beer, Officer? One PBR, come on. Don't be such an old lady."

Mitch went to the back of the boat, where Shaw was looking out at the water. Mitch said under his breath, "You know my child meant no harm."

Shaw gave him a tight-lipped smile.

Mitch asked him, "What does it mean? If he calls and you don't answer?"

Shaw shook his head.

Said Mitch, "You can stop him, can't you?"

"If we get to shore. Yes. I think I know where he'll go first."

They bounced along through the waves. Mitch

watched as Patsy opened the ice chest and carefully measured out a little cocktail for herself. Tara was gazing at the riverbank, at the solemn oaks. Jase sat in his heap of misery. Shaw said to Mitch, "It's my fault. I shouldn't have left Romeo out there."

Said Mitch, "There's lots of things you shouldn't have done. You shouldn't be here in the first place. But I know one thing. You're here because God wants you here."

They sat without speaking. Shaw began to softly weep. He said, "Is there a prayer for me? Is there anything that could save me?"

Mitch put an arm around him, and held him, and said, "There's the psalm. My God, my God, why hast thou forsaken me? Why art thou so far from helping me, and from the words of my roaring?"

Mitch turned his gaze to the boat's wake, as it opened into the river, and he went on: "I am poured out like water, and all my bones are out of joint: my heart is like wax; it is melted in the midst of my bowels. My strength is dried up like a potsherd; my tongue cleaveth to my jaws; and thou hast brought me into the dust of death."

Shaw wept into Mitch's chest. Mitch said, "Be not thou far from me, O Lord. O my strength! Haste thee to help me!"

Romeo had been braced for the world to collapse at any moment, but he'd supposed this fall would come violently, with lightning and thunder. Instead it was all happening in silence: the walls just quietly caving in.

Shaw wasn't answering his phone.

That was all.

Romeo kept up the rhythm with his thumb, calling again and again, but each time he got Shaw's message machine. *You know what to do.*

He kept driving. He took a left at the Sonic. Another left at Zachary Wiles's Funeral Home. He passed the Empire Title Pawn Shop. He thought about that cry he'd heard: *"No, don't!"* Whose voice could that have been? Someone younger than Patsy, shriller than Tara—maybe Jase? But Jase was too shy and timid to shout like that. Some girl at the fairgrounds? Just some girl Shaw was flirting with, and this was only a game?

But then he'd have called right back.

Maybe he's got no signal? He's out of range?

But then why doesn't he get back *into* range?

Well. He's thoughtless. Like a child sometimes.

Romeo was back at the Sonic. He turned left, and made another left at the funeral home. Passed Empire Title again. He was driving in circles. Why not admit it? he thought. *They've got Shaw.* It's so clear. Here's what happened: the porks came, Shaw pulled his gun, some-one yelled, "No, don't!" So that's it. It's over. He's either caught or dead—and I better hope dead, considering the torture that prison would be for Shaw.

Shit.

3:06. Time was running out. Fourteen minutes left.

Call me, goddamn it!

He stopped at a construction site on 17. He took half a dex; then he went back to the trunk but couldn't remember how it opened. He looked everywhere before he finally checked the glove compartment and found the release switch. He went back and opened the trunk and took out the Phoenix .22. Above him were black storm-clouds. The very air was stressed. He'd have to start killing any moment. He needed the whirling. Oh shit. Shaw, *call me*.

Burris called the Lieutenant as he drove toward town. He didn't want to be overheard so he used his cell phone. It took a while to get through. When he did, he said, "Lieutenant, I need a BOLO on this guy and I need it right now. His name is Romeo Zderko."

"Who?"

"Friend of Shaw McBride's."

"Burris, you can't work this case."

"This time I've got real evidence."

"Chief's gonna *fire* your ass."

"But this guy, this Zderko, he's stalking the Boatwrights. He's got a map of Brunswick with little stars where all the Boatwrights live."

Silence, while the Lieutenant tried to process this. It was painful for Burris to wait, but he did. After a long while the Lieutenant said, "What do you mean, stars?"

"It'd take too long to explain. The point is, he's targeting the Boatwrights."

"Where'd you find this map?"

"The trailer where he's been staying."

"You had your warrant and all?"

"Didn't need one. His girlfriend gave it to me."

A sigh. "OK."

OK was just two letters but the Lieutenant drawled them so slowly it was like he was reeling out the whole alphabet. Then he said, "Burris, this map, would you say it represents an imminent threat?"

"He's never met them! Yet he's got a map showing their houses!"

"Yeah. I guess that's a threat. You bringing this in?"

"Fast as I can. But we need a BOLO right now."

"Can it wait till the Chief gets back from lunch?"

"For God's sake. Jimmy! Gimme the fuckin BOLO!"

He hadn't called him Jimmy for years—not since his demotion. Soft crackle of static.

Finally: "All right, Burris. I'll put it out there."

"Thank you."

"But now it's my own nuts hangin over the coals."

Shaw leaped out of the boat the moment it touched Lonsdale's dock—then reached back and pulled Tara off, and the two of them left the others behind. They sprinted down Lonsdale's curving elegant driveway to where the Liberty was parked.

"Get in," he ordered her. "Drive."

She got behind the wheel. As they were turning onto Sea Island Road, she asked, "Where?"

"I'll tell you when we get back to Brunswick."

"How much time do we have?"

He checked his watch. 3:11. "Nine minutes."

"I can't get to Brunswick in nine minutes!"

"Try."

At the corner of Frederica Road, she ran a red light, leaning into the horn. She shouted, "Who does he kill first?"

"I'll tell you when we're closer."

"Can't you just call him on *my* phone?"

"I don't know his number," he said. "I just press 7."

She gave a sigh of disgust.

Shaw thought, was he supposed to have foreseen *this*? That her brother would be a psychopath, and throw his phone in the sea? Get out of my head! What we want is light, pure light, not all these questions. Who sent you to destroy my dream? This ugliness, I can't bear this right now.

She was doing eighty on the Sea Island Causeway, weaving through the lanes.

She tried to speak gently: "Shaw, please tell me where's he's going first."

"When we're closer."

"But I could call and warn them."

"Not without giving me away."

"But it's not Nell? Nell's not first?"

"You'll know soon."

"For God's sake, just tell me this one thing! Is it Nell?"

"Drive as fast as you can."

Romeo was coming down Indian Mound Road toward Shelby and Miriam's. There were still three more minutes left before he'd be obliged to kill anyone, but it was time for him to get into position. He should be ready. It wouldn't be too hard. The kids, MacKenzie and Benjamin, would still be at school. So he could just waltz in there. Then Shelby would be bound to say something nasty, and that would get the whirling going in Romeo's head.

He pulled up across from the house. The kids were not in school. They were out on the lawn, playing badminton. He was horrified to see them. But he said to himself, you're a soldier. Good soldiers say fuck the kids.

The girl MacKenzie stopped playing a moment. She looked straight at him. She even seemed to remember him. She gave him a little wave. He lowered his eyes.

Think about Shaw. They've got Shaw. Remember what Shaw said that night of the Perseids party, looking up at the stars. "This thing *we* have, between the two of us. This friendship? This will last. In some form. Because this is the only worthwhile fucking thing in history."

Go. Keep your head down and don't look at her, if that'll make it easier. But go. Now.

Tara and Shaw came off the causeway, and finally Shaw revealed their destination: "Shelby and Miriam's. He said that's where he'd go first."

Her first thought was, it's not Nell!

Not Nell! Thank God!

Then she thought about the kids. MacKenzie and Benjamin. Oh Lord the kids. I'm thanking God that Romeo's killing the kids? She took a right on 17 and went north—and floored it. Running a red light and then sliding across the traffic and running another, horns lighting up all around her, and she shot into the oncoming lane to pass a half-dozen cars, and found herself in the path of a truck. Panic rushed up from her chest and blinded her. She jerked the wheel back, and somehow found her own lane again, and held on, and the car steadied.

The whole time, Shaw sat silently. Keeping his eyes on the road, holding his gun in his lap, saying not a word.

The clock on the dashboard said 3:24. So time was up, she thought. Time was up already! They were already four minutes late!

But still Shaw was quiet. Maybe none of this was real? Maybe it had all been staged, just to scare her?

But if it was real, and they were too late—if they found that Shelby and Miriam and the kids were already dead—then what would Shaw do? He'd kill her, wouldn't he? He'd have to. Instantly. What other choice would he have?

She skidded right onto Belle Point, then left on Indian Mound Road.

The house. Badminton net out front, on the pristine carpet of grass. There were two rackets and a white birdie, lying there. Would the kids have done that? Shelby's kids, ever? Just left their stuff out on the lawn like that? She burst her car door open and ran into the garage, and Shaw followed her.

The door to the kitchen was ajar.

She gave it a little push. As it swung open, she called, "Hello?"

The fieldstone walls returned an echo. No one called back. Lucky didn't bark. She stepped inside. Shaw was right behind her.

They walked through the kitchen and the only sound was the murmur of the refrigerator. She was too scared to call again. She felt Shaw's presence at her back. I'm dead, she thought, the moment we find the bodies. Where are they? Where are they? She stepped into the great room, where everything was immaculately arranged: the tall vase full of lilies, the candlesticks, the *Architectural Digest*s. A broad view of the marsh. No movement anywhere. She thought, I should run now. Why am I looking for them? They're dead—I can't help them. Make a dash for the front door and start screaming.

Then she heard a small voice. One word: "Marco."

Again. "Marco."

It was a boy's voice.

Then a girl: "Polo."

Followed by a frenzy of splashing. Tara went up to the sliding glass doors till she could see the pool in the back-yard, where Benjamin and MacKenzie were playing happily.

Lucky the dog spotted her and starting barking. MacKenzie cried, "Tara!"

Tara went outside, followed by Shaw. MacKenzie ran up to her still soaking wet, but Tara gave her a huge hug anyway.

Miriam, sitting by the pool, said, "Hey darlin. Hello, Shaw."

MacKenzie cried, "Come into the pool!"

Tara said, "We can't. We're looking for Shaw's friend. Has he been here? Kind of a small guy? With big eyes?"

Miriam said, "That's *your* friend? The religious guy? He was just here. He scares the heck out of me."

"Did he speak to you?"

MacKenzie said, "He spoke to *me*! He asked me who was winning. We were playing badminton. I was winning. Now Mom won't let us play."

Miriam said, "What's he doing talking to my children? He doesn't know my children. I don't like it. I was about to call the police. What does he want here?"

"I wish I could say," Shaw murmured. "I'm afraid he's kind of gone off the deep end."

Romeo turned off Altama onto Poinsettia Circle, and parked in front of Vanessa and Henry's little house. If I go quick I can do this. The secret is going quick.

He stepped out of the car, the Phoenix .22 at his side, and crossed the street. He went to the side door, the kitchen door. Vanessa was standing there, at the island, turning a crank. Grinding something. Was she making fresh pasta? Yes she was. There were sliced tomatoes, eggs and onions and cloves of garlic on her cutting board. And of course Romeo thought of his mother, and felt that somebody or something was trying to make his job as difficult as possible.

Strike. Go. Can't kill children, OK. But this sour banal

bitch? You'll be done in twenty seconds and you'll feel a million times better.

His hand was on the knob, the old-fashioned mother-of-pearl knob. He couldn't turn it.

For shit's sake. This bitch is one of them! She's one of the soulless bastards who suffocated the life out of Shaw, with their fear and their dullness, and she's complicit in his death, so *kill her.*

But this line of thinking didn't work.

After half a minute, he gave up. He went back to the car and sat there, and had a memory of Shaw telling him, *But it all comes down to you. To you suffering in that darkness. To my knowing that you won't let me down.* Romeo put the muzzle of the gun into his mouth. That cutting blood-metal taste. OK, *this* you can do. For God's sake. Get out of this world now, while you still can.

But he couldn't. He tossed the gun on the seat beside him and turned the key and drove away.

Soon Shaw would know. How Romeo had driven around Brunswick killing no one, not even himself. Effecting no revenge. Wreaking nothing. Making a mockery of Shaw's vision. How Romeo had stained with his cowardice all of Shaw's dreams.

Back at Altama Avenue he turned south. He clenched

the steering wheel and threw his head forward, slamming his brow as hard as he could into the windshield. But the windshield didn't break, and he was dizzy but still conscious, and his shame was not assuaged. He saw a convenience store and pulled in. He drove up to the pumps. He got out of the car and took the fuel nozzle and aimed it at himself, and squeezed the trigger. Since he hadn't paid, though, nothing happened.

He hit the HELP button.

"Yes?"

"I need gas," he said. "Turn the gas on."

"Sir, if you're not using a credit card, you'll have to prepay."

He fished his wallet out, found his credit card, and shoved it into the slot. RECEIPT? YES/NO. He pressed NO, and then START. He held the nozzle over his head and this time gouts of golden gasoline came pouring out, and for one instant this was refreshing. But then he started breathing in the fumes and they made him so sick that he had to fling the hose down. Also he got some in his eyes which stung like a bitch.

He wiped his face with a T-shirt from the backseat. Then he ran up to the store.

But the clerk had locked the door.

Romeo pounded on it. "I need your help, man! I'm

not gonna hurt you or anything. I just need you to light me up!"

But the clerk didn't respond. He was probably cowering behind his counter.

"Come on man! You just have to toss a match! I'll give you five hundred dollars for one fucking match! I'll take out five hundred dollars from the ATM, right now, and it'll be yours! *Please!*"

No reply.

Romeo kicked at the door. "I'LL GIVE YOU EVERYTHING I HAVE! I'LL GIVE YOU LIKE THIRTY MILLION DOLLARS! JUST LIGHT ME UP, MOTHERFUCKER!"

But the clerk didn't come out.

Romeo limped back to the car and got in.

He had no idea where he was going but it didn't matter. He only needed to find someone who would do him this favor. He drove down Altama heading south, and saw some black kids on bikes. Ask them? No, I doubt they've got matches and anyway they'll take off the moment they get a whiff of the gas. He passed the Cypress Mill intersection. Suddenly there were sirens, sirens everywhere. Wailing-ghost sirens, machine-gun-electronica sirens, barking air horns. Everything became unstable. Even the daylight flickered. He looked in the rearview mirror and saw the pork blasting toward him. Three cruisers. And they weren't coming to put him out of his misery; they were coming to *get* him. They'd have a big show trial of all his failures. If Shaw was still alive he'd hear of Romeo's every fuckup and cowardice in vivid detail. They'd put Shaw in a cell no bigger than a crypt, and for sixty or eighty years he could stew over Romeo's failure, over the courage that Romeo hadn't shown when the barnyard-fuckjuice came raining down. Romeo himself would be in the next cell, and every night Shaw would shout out COWARD and TRAITOR all over the cellblock, and tell them all how Romeo had fucked up the whole world.

For the next sixty years.

He jammed his foot into the accelerator. The Bel Air coughed and stalled out, and sat in the middle of the road with the three squad cars bearing down.

They sailed right past.

Howling, lit up like shooting stars, one, two, three they blew past him and left him sitting there. They had some other mission in mind.

A stillness settled around the car. A dragonfly came buzzing up to his window. He thought, OK. There *is* something I can do about this suffering. Give it to her.

Burris was on Newcastle Street, just a few blocks from the station, when the call came that the Tercel had been pulled over outside Spanky's restaurant off Altama Avenue.

He hit the siren and spun around, and came roaring up MLK Boulevard, making Spanky's inside of three minutes. And there, in the parking lot, it was: that boxy, zero-colored, '91 Toyota Tercel. Police lights flying all around it. Already there were five or six units, and more sirens homing in from all compass points.

The Lieutenant had gone all out for him.

Burris emerged from his cruiser. A moment later, the Lieutenant himself arrived, and then the Chief. Though the Chief seemed appalled by all the hubbub. He said, "This is not the way I like to see my city run." He also declared, "I was eatin my damn lunch. Three o'clock, I can't eat my lunch? Would you tell me what is so important I can't eat my lunch?"

A sergeant barked into a megaphone: "STEP OUT OF THE VEHICLE! COME OUT WITH YOUR HANDS ABOVE YOUR HEAD."

The door of the Tercel opened. A lanky man with a goatee and a pompadour of white hair emerged.

The megaphone told him: "LIE DOWN! LIE DOWN! LIE DOWN ON THE GROUND RIGHT NOW!"

423

As Goatee was splaying his limbs on the pavement, Burris decided to come right out with it. Don't try to preamble or anything, because it won't do any good. Just say it.

"That's not him."

"What?" said the Chief.

"That's not Zderko."

"That's not the car you wanted?"

"No, that *is* the car. It's not the guy though. It's some other guy. Maybe it's a friend of his, or something."

The Chief fixed him in his gaze.

"Corporal. Didn't I tell you to get off this case?"

"Yes sir."

"Did I slur my words?"

"No sir."

"I spoke clearly?"

"Yes sir."

"Then you're fired. Now can I eat my damn lunch?"

Patsy and Mitch and Jase got a ride back to the fairgrounds from Henry Lonsdale's driver, who let them off in the big field.

Twice as many pilgrims as there had been in the morning.

Trevor said, "Where's Shaw?"

Mitch shrugged. "Off with Tara somewhere."

"There's a cop here to see him," said Trevor.

"You know what he wants?" Trevor asked. "Is everything OK?"

Mitch said, "Everything's fine. But pray for us." He walked over to the cop, and Patsy stood there thinking, Please God, protect my daughter. Please God that she's safe and she comes back to me. And Lord, *please* take care of Shaw. Don't let anything happen to Shaw.

She was vaguely aware that cameras were clacking away at her.

Someone in the crowd yelled, "We love you, Patsy!"

Others echoing: "We love you!" "Praise the Lord!" "Praise God!"

She looked out and smiled at them, these simple folks. It was Shaw who had taught her to love them back. She felt as though she were looking back at this scene from some future vantage, and she thought, "That was the moment, Diane. That's when first I truly felt the power of Shaw's love." Diane listening with all her quiet intensity, and perhaps grasping her hands. It brought tears to Patsy's eyes to foresee this moment.

And the pilgrims' cameras saw her tears, and feasted on them.

Shaw and Tara slowed beside Vanessa and Henry's house.

There was Vanessa, working obliviously and happily in her kitchen.

So where was Romeo? Oh, gone, Shaw knew. He'd flown. He'd be hiding somewhere, in some dark corner, trembling, getting drunk.

Shaw had always known this would happen.

Now he was alone. And Tara must have seen this. She must have been thinking of how she'd destroy him now. No matter what feelings she might have for him, she'd murder him the moment he let his guard down.

I've got to get her to Nell's. In the presence of Nell I can still control her.

And after that?

He didn't know after that. Somehow he had to make her think he had others working for him. Trevor, for a start. And maybe he should call in his friends from Ohio:

Chris and Pissboy. Fly them down here. Tell Tara this was his gang; she'd be terrified.

That's the key. The key is to keep her scared. Fear, discipline.

He told her, "All right, let's go to Nell's now. We better go fast though."

She cast him a look of deep alarm. She crushed down on the gas and went whipping down MLK Boulevard.

He smiled. "You still need my mercy, don't you?"

"Yes."

"You can't kill this dream. It's too powerful. So make your choice. You want to see realms of great love, they'll be shown to you. You want pain, I'll show you that. What do you want, Tara?"

Romeo turned off of Egmont Street well before he got to Nell's house. He eased down the alleyway and parked, and limped up to Nell's wooden fence. A TV game show clanged somewhere in the neighborhood. He studied the bungalow. Nothing stirring. He leaped the fence into her garden. Fat gourds, tomatoes, chili peppers. Two gray sparrows on the rim of the clawfoot tub.

And right beside the house was an ancient potting shed. He opened the door and looked in. It was so hot that it hurt to breathe. The closeness, the smell of loam, the pitch dark: it all put him in mind of a coffin, and this seemed inviting. Wasps were tap-tapping in a loose rhythm, and there was an old canopy-green lawn chair, and he hadn't slept in days.

I could just steal five minutes.

But he knew if he shut his eyes he'd wake up on the way to prison.

Work first. Then sleep.

As he was stepping from the shed to the house, he heard the sound of a car on Egmont Street.

Tara and Shaw pulled up in front of Nell's. She had to wait for him to put his jacket on over his gun; then they got out of the Liberty and ran to the portico.

They found Nell at the kitchen table. She was safe and sound, and buttering raisin toast. She cried, "Well, hello, *ba*-by!"

Tara said, "Nell, are you OK?"

"I'm fine, honey. What's the matter?"

Said Shaw, "Has anyone been here?"

"Like who? Y'all ready for seven stud?"

"Nell, we have a problem. Could we sit down?"

They did, arranging themselves at the kitchen table.

Then Shaw said, "Listen, this is going to seem strange to you. There's a guy, a friend of mine, he wants to hurt me. Well, he *was* my friend. Since the jackpot, he's gone, well, kind of nuts. He thinks he should get a share of the money. He says he's going to hurt Tara, as a way to get to me. He's going around spreading lies about me. But the lies aren't working! They're not working, are they, Tara? It's just, he's dangerous now. You know? He's like a *cyclone*. He's out of his mind."

Nell said, "You told the police?"

"I don't want the police! You don't understand! This man is my best friend. I love this man! I just need to talk to him."

Nell said, "But if he's that insane—"

"I know! I'm packing a gun, Nell. I know I may have to kill him. But I want to try to save him if I can."

Then there was a movement at the edge of Tara's vision. She felt it before she saw it—she cried out. Romeo. Stepping out of the hallway. He stank of gasoline. He had a gun, and his gaze was fixed on Shaw.

Shaw spoke with his most lulling voice. "Romeo, oh

my God, what happened? What happened to you? We've got to talk. Things you might not understand. Things I was saying to other people, but you've got to see them in another light. Oh, God. If you knew! If you knew how good we are now, buddy, how *set* we are—"

Romeo murmured, "I do know. We're good." Then he turned to Tara. He said, "Tara. Come here."

"Leave her alone," said Shaw. "We're all right."

But Romeo summoned her again: "Come here."

Shaw said, "What the hell are you doing? Stop it. We don't have to hurt anyone."

Romeo aimed the gun at Nell.

"No!" said Shaw. "You don't have to do this!"

But Romeo held his aim. "I said, come *here*, Tara. Or I'll kill her."

Tara rose. In such terror that her legs hardly worked. But she went to stand before him with her eyes lowered.

"Now turn around. Face your grandmother."

I should fight this, she thought. Not submit to my own execution. I should resist this *now*.

But how? Do what? She couldn't think.

"Turn around," said Romeo. And then in a sudden rage: "NOW! NO TIME! TURN AROUND *NOW*!"

She obeyed. Her eyes were shut so she saw nothing,

but she heard Shaw pleading, "Romeo, listen, we don't have to do this. We don't have to punish them. They're OK; they love us, they believe in us. Please trust me. Show me some trust here, for God's sake, *listen*."

Silence.

Tara's breath came via little seizures in her throat.

She thought, Why does Nell have to watch this? It's not fair. Why should Nell have to watch? Why this price? Why this high? Could my sins have been so great? *Lord? Please! Whatever I have done, please forgive me for the sake of my innocent Nell. Please forgive me!*

She felt Romeo right behind her. His breath on her neck.

She wanted to say, "Nell don't look," but her voice wouldn't surface.

And then she felt Romeo taking hold of her right wrist, and lifting it—and her fingers touched cool metal.

He said, "I'm giving you this."

She opened her eyes and looked down: he was handing her his gun.

He said, "I can't do it; I'm not strong enough. But you are."

Shaw was looking up at him. Revelation began to gather in his eyes. Romeo wrapped Tara's fingers around the gun, while keeping his own finger in the trigger guard.

"I know you can do this," he said. "You were born for this. But you have to promise you'll kill us *both*."

"I don't . . ."

"He can't live in prison. Be torture. For me too. Promise me."

Just get the gun, Tara thought. He's insane. Do whatever he asks *but get the gun*.

She said softly, "All right."

Romeo said, "You'll kill us now? Both of us? You promise?"

"I promise."

Shaw said nothing. But Tara could see the trace of a smile begin to work at his lips: he was proud of her.

Romeo said, "Feel for the trigger guard. You feel it?"

"Yes."

"When I tell you, put your finger in. Then kill him right away. You know the way he talks. He'll talk you out of it. And then he'll destroy us. Don't let him talk to you!"

"All right."

Romeo took his hand away. He stepped back.

Then Shaw exhaled, and said, "Jesus. Tara. You were beautiful."

She didn't move. She kept the gun trained on him.

Shaw turned to Romeo, and said softly, "My old

432

friend. I wish I'd never seen you like this. But whatever's happened to your mind, I swear I'll take care of you. For the rest of your life—"

Romeo whispered to her ear, "Kill him now. While you can."

Shaw shook his head. "There's not going to be any killing, Romeo. Jesus. If she did what you wanted, she'd never heal. Never. *She'd never heal*."

Romeo whispered to her, "Now."

Shaw's boyish smile. "Listen. I know that everything we're going through takes strength. There's a lot of danger; there's a lot of pain. But there's also so much love here! It feels like half the love in the universe is in this town, right now. What we've done! We've made ourselves into some kind of magnet, and all the stars, and all the power of the universe, and all the love—"

She shot him in the face.

The concussion, the blowback of blood. Nell shrieking.

Shaw was still on his feet. Trying to speak. But his mouth was filled with a slurry of blood and teeth, and what he said sounded like hissing.

He lunged toward Tara but she stepped back, and he lost his balance and fell to his knees.

Shaking his head. Trying to shake it clear of confusion. He reached back to draw his gun from its holster, and she stepped forward and shot him again. Crumbs of his skull and brain flew everywhere. His gun skittered across the linoleum.

Tara stood over him, and drank in the sight of him. The cratered jaw, the eye of horror, the spasms of his dying. Trying to burn this in her memory, to fix it forever—that all other memories of him would be erased.

Romeo was begging her, "Now me, Tara. You promised."

She *had* promised. She turned toward him and raised her gun again.

Nell screamed, "TARA, NO! WHAT ARE YOU DOING! STOP! NO!"

Romeo looked up at her. There was no fear in his eyes, only urgency. "I'm sorry to ask you. But you gotta help me. I think he was wrong, what he said about healing. You *will* heal. But I won't. Please."

Nell shouted, "DON'T KILL HIM!"

Reaching for her arm, but Tara evaded her. Moved around the kitchen table to get a clear shot. Thinking, finish this quick. Pay this debt. Then behind her, she heard the screen door scrape open, and a deep male voice bellowed: "GET DOWN ON THE FLOOR!"

The old cop. Officer Burris. With his gun aimed at Romeo. "I SAID GET YOUR FACE ON THE FLOOR!"

Then he demanded of Nell and Tara, "Who shot him?"

"I did," Tara said.

But he wasn't really taking this in. He was barking into his police radio, "49, homicide at 1412 Egmont near Albemarle! Suspect in custody, need backup! Backup!"

While Romeo begged her, "*Please*. Tara. You made a promise."

"GET ON THE FUCKIN FLOOR!" Burris bellowed.

Romeo had a look of exasperation. Casting his eyes around frantically—till suddenly he made a lurch for the windowsill and grabbed a book of matches.

"Do I have to do this? *Do I have to burn myself alive?*"

Holding a single match over the book, ready to strike.

"Tara," he said, "why don't you *help* me? Finish this!"

A moment of silence. The whine of distant sirens.

Then Burris said, "Son, you know what you could do?"

Speaking quietly but with such grave solemnity that it drew Romeo's attention. "Go for that," said Burris, gesturing toward Shaw's gun on the floor, "and I'll take care of you."

Romeo just gazed at him, uncomprehending.

Then he understood.

He mumbled something, maybe thanks—and made his move. Scrambling, half-crawling, half-diving, across the floor, and reaching for the gun. Just before his fingers touched it, Burris fired four shots.

Then Tara wanted to go to him, to take Romeo into her arms—but Nell wouldn't let her. Nell held her tightly, and lifted the gun from her fingers, and walked her through the carnage toward the hallway. Pausing for a moment to pass the gun into Burris's care, and to lay the back of her old bony hand against his cheek. Then she led Tara down the hall to the back porch.

All the cats in the house had retreated there. Several were on the sill; one was perched on the antediluvian TV. A long tortoiseshell tail emerged from under the swinging bed. Nell said, "Lie down now, child."

Tara did as she was told. Nell stretched out beside her, and Tara put her head on her grandmother's breast, and breathed in that faint smell of popcorn. With one ear she could hear the sirens and the shouts outside, but the other heard nothing but Nell's heart. She shut her eyes. My God, she thought, I'm on this porch again.

She knew it wasn't quite the same as before. Everything

in sight—cats, pillows, garden, clawfoot tub—had taken a certain distance from her. A formality, a reserve.

Still. She was here.

It felt almost like good fortune.

She knew she owed this to Romeo: to that sad man, and a rush of gratitude filled her. She prayed that his soul might find its way to a well-lighted place. Just then a cat jumped onto the bed, and made it swing. The cat was Horace Jackal: she knew him by the way he went padding around her legs. He would take his time making up his mind, but in a minute or two, with any luck, he'd come and curl up against the back of her neck, sandwiching her between himself and Nell. Tara lay there quietly, hardly breathing, so as not to scare him off.

Romeo had gone back home. Back to Piqua, Ohio. He found himself in Hollow Park just as dusk was falling, crouching behind a stout walnut tree, hiding from Hawks. But one caught sight of him and shouted, and flushed him out to the open field. Then more Hawks came swooping in from all sides. In a second they'd have him. He was about to be changed, but he wasn't afraid. In truth, this particular moment in Hollow Park, hovering between one thing and another—he thought this was about the best moment of his life. He liked everything about it. He liked the new rules that Shaw had added to the game. He liked the red bandanas, the summer evening, the surprising warmth; he liked even the poison-ivy itchiness around his ankles. He thought everything was perfect except that the dark was coming down too fast.

Acknowledgments

Thanks to the folks at the Brunswick Police: Betty McGregor, Captain Larry Bruce. Particular gratitude to the wise and patient Detective Roy Blackstock, Jr., who took me along on endless counterclockwise rounds of the city.

Thanks to Wanda and Larry, my poker instructors at the Magnolia Sports Palace. Thanks to Pat Vinton, Theresa Martin, Bob, Om, Margot, Mimi. Courtney Dyche and Vanessa Cunningham.

Thanks to radiant Ashley, her mother Rhonda, her grandmother Mary.

Thanks to my line editor Inez Green, who taught me how to write.

Thanks to my co-author Molly Friedrich. To Lucy Carson and Sheri Holman. To Jamie Raab who is as beautiful as Ozma.